RED
DEATH

The Works of Alan Jacobson

Novels
False Accusations
The Lost Girl

KAREN VAIL SERIES
The 7th Victim
Crush
Velocity
Inmate 1577
No Way Out
Spectrum
The Darkness of Evil
Red Death

OPSIG TEAM BLACK SERIES
The Hunted
Hard Target
The Lost Codex
Dark Side of the Moon

Essays
"The Seductress"
(*Hollywood vs. The Author,* Rare Bird Books)

Short Stories
"Fatal Twist" (*featuring Karen Vail*)
"Double Take" (*featuring Carmine Russo & Ben Dryer*)
"12:01 AM" (*featuring Karen Vail*)

RED DEATH

A KAREN VAIL NOVEL

ALAN JACOBSON

OPEN ROAD
INTEGRATED MEDIA
NEW YORK

Cover design by Ian Koviak

Author photograph: Corey Jacobson

ISBN: 978-1-5040-6357-9

Published in 2020 by Open Road Integrated Media, Inc.
180 Maiden Lane
New York, NY 10038
www.openroadmedia.com

For Wayne Rudnick

. . . my cousin, one of the most honest, kind, and accommodating individuals you will ever meet, the kind of person who makes you believe there's hope for humanity. A skilled chiropractor, Wayne has brought life-changing pain relief and functional improvement to countless men, women, and children, laborers, physicians, and athletes for over two decades . . . the antithesis of those who spend their lives bringing destruction and loss into the world (such as the antagonist featured in *Red Death*).

RED
DEATH

"The first requirement in catching a murderer is to recognize that a murder has been committed."

—ROBERT CHRISTISON,
professor of forensics,
the University of Edinburgh, 1836

"Almost 700,000 children in the United States are abused every year and close to 2,000 children died from abuse in 2015."

—RAFAEL J. LÓPEZ, commissioner,
Administration on Children, Youth, and Families,
Department of Health & Human Services,
Child Maltreatment 2015

"`A`ohe lokomaika`i i nele i ke pâna`i" (English translation: No kind deed has ever lacked its reward.)

—Hawaiian proverb

1

The man looked at his customer and asked for her name. She was in her sixties, he could tell that much. Her skin was sagging around the chin and her eyelids were losing their battle with gravity. The way she applied her makeup—thick and overdone to mask the lines and wrinkles—reminded him of his mother.

"Joanna," she said.

"Joanna." He tried not to let the disappointment register. He had considerable practice over the years, but even so, he knew that the human face gave away a lot more than age. He forced a smile. "Very nice."

She grinned and thanked him. They made small talk about the time spent in Iraq, then she wished him well and went on her way.

A half hour and four customers later, another woman approached him about the same age as Joanna, a few inches taller and a bit more skilled with the makeup. They chatted for a moment, but it wasn't until he asked her name—Mary—that he felt his spirits lift.

"Nice to meet you, Mary. Have you lived on the island a long time?"

Mary laughed . . . an easygoing chuckle. "You could definitely say that." Her eyes canted up to the ceiling and her fingers moved, as if she were counting something. "Sixty-three years. Born in Los

Angeles, but my parents moved to the island when I was two. Been here ever since."

"Lucky you," he said. "I'm thinking I might just stay here in Oahu. Live out the rest of my days in peace."

Mary scrunched her brow. "But you're so young. Why on earth would you even be thinking about living out the rest of your days when you've got so much *life* ahead of you?"

"Well . . ." He took a deep breath. "Darn, Mary. Nobody's ever quite put it that way. I don't have too many deep discussions with people, let alone people who remind me of my mother." He looked away.

"Didn't mean to make you feel uncomfortable, son."

He waved her off. "Ah, no worries. And please, call me John. I'm fine, honest. But I'm really glad I met you, Mary. You made my day." John smiled—and it was genuine this time.

"Me too," Mary said. "And thank you again for your service. Oh—have you had a chance to visit the national cemetery?"

"Punchbowl? Of course. Quite the setting, isn't it? Incredible views. So serene. Truth is, that's the kinda place I wanna be buried, when all is said and done." John held up a hand. "I know, you don't think I should be talkin' like that, but I'd be lying if I didn't tell you it *is* something I've thought about."

"Well, my mama used to tell me to make the most of life. Live each day like it's your last. Enjoy every sunrise, every sunset. Because life is precious."

John nodded thoughtfully. "That's awful nice. My mother never said anything like that to me. Maybe that's why you have such a great outlook on life."

"The present is a gift. It's a pun, but it's so true."

John chuckled.

"You just keep your chin up. And you keep working hard. Every day will bring new surprises, new challenges. Things to live for." She gently touched his hand. "And stop thinking about death. It'll become all consuming."

"And you're a wise woman, Mary. *You* have given me that challenge today. And you know what? I've got something special for you." He pulled the cap off his red sharpie. "What's your last name?"

"Burkhead." She spelled it.

John wrote "Mary Burkhead" in flawless calligraphy and handed her a small package. "Made it myself. When you get home and open it, I want you to think of me."

"How sweet. But I can't accept this."

"Yes you can," John said. "Please. You brightened my day." He held the gift out and she looked at it, then took it from him. "Try to use it soon, in the next few days. It's got an organic floral scent that might not last."

"Thank you."

"No—thank *you*." He looked deep into her eyes, his pinpoint pupils holding her gaze. "This means more to me than you could know."

Mary gave him another easygoing smile, wished him aloha, and left.

John watched her walk away and knew that his work was done. For today.

2

The brisk cool breeze zipped around the buildings in downtown Honolulu, blocks from where the Kamehameha statue and Iolani Palace stood, known as the only royal palace in Hawaii. More colloquially, it was the fictional Honolulu police headquarters, the location of the iconic but equally imaginary—Hawaii Five-0 task force.

Freshman detective Adam Russell stepped into the rear yard of his small house and pulled out a stick of gum. Earlier this year, it would have been a cigarette—but he figured he should do his part to help maintain Hawaii's famed air quality. Actually, he quit tobacco for health reasons—and had been off it for six months.

As he felt the burst of mint hit his tongue, his phone buzzed. He knew the number and cursed under his breath as he answered the call.

"Russell."

"Dead body at the Iolani Palace."

"My day off."

"I know. Sorry."

Russell tossed the gum in the garbage and headed into his bedroom to change his clothes. Nine minutes later he arrived at the crime scene.

The extravagant nineteenth-century Victorian-influenced palace was a fusion between Hawaiian and Western architecture: while exhibiting the sense of a medieval castle, its planners softened the look with large windows and doors.

Russell pulled into a spot and walked through the expansive parking lot to the area where the yellow tape was strung. Several humongous banyan trees were on a grassy knoll to his left. Thick vertical pole-like striations extended from the lower branches to the ground, joining and twisting around one another or enjoying a lonely solo drop straight down to the grass. Russell always marveled at the weight and density of the hanging wood posts—as immovable and as solid as the trunk itself, which sat somewhere behind the nature-constructed wall.

Russell joined a knot of crime scene personnel to the left of the banyans. A Gothic building—part of the palace complex—stood twenty feet away.

That was where he found the medical examiner, Keiki Kuoko. "Aloha, brah."

"Aloha." Russell blinked away a speck of dirt the wind had deposited in his left eye. "What's the deal here?"

"Sixty-one-year-old female. Worked for the state archives, that building to your left. Superficial examination shows a fit middle-aged woman, no overt signs of disease. Or trauma."

"Cause of death?"

"It's a toss-up. Cardiac arrest or asphyxiation. But until I get her under the knife, I'd have to go with the latter."

"Okay, so asphyxiation. But no signs of trauma?"

"Nope."

"Why are we thinking this is a murder?"

"Because there's no reason for her to choke. Airway looks clear. I'll confirm all this when we get her back to the morgue. But kind of looks like last week's vic."

"Hmm. So that's two."

"Yeah," Kuoko said. "We can go years without seeing one and now we get two a week apart?"

"What do you make of that?" Russell asked.

"Nothing good, I'll tell you that."

"I don't like it." Russell pulled out his phone.

"Who you calling?"

"Buddy of mine I used to work with in San Francisco. Mentored me, kicked my ass about pushing to make detective when I moved here."

"He know about asphyxiation deaths?"

"Nope." Russell pressed SEND. "But he had a big serial killer case a few years back."

"Whoa." Kuoko removed his reading glasses. "Serial killer? You think that's what this is? You're assuming the vics are related."

"Don't know *what* we're dealing with. That's why I'm calling him."

Russell waited as the number began to ring. The wind ruffled his blond hair and he brushed it out of his eyes. "Yeah, this is Detective Adam Russell with Honolulu PD. Lance Burden reachable by mobile?"

"I'll put you through."

A couple of minutes later, Burden answered. "Adam. Long time no hear. You haven't been on Facebook."

"I'm avoiding my ex."

"Just un-friend her."

"Already did. I divorced her."

"No, I mean remove your Faceb—your social media connection to her. Or use the privacy settings to lock her out. All you have to do is—"

"Wait, wait, wait. This sounds like you're trying to teach me some kind of technology thing. Must be, because my eyes are starting to glaze over."

"You're such a fucking Luddite."

"Just TC. Technologically challenged."

"Listen, Adam, I'd love to catch up but I'm in Colorado. Pulling into the convention center parking lot. I'm speaking at a conference on violent crime."

"Can you spare a minute? Just wanna run a case by you."

"A minute. Need be, I can call you back tonight."

"Two murders. Both asphyxiations. Only a week apart."

"How old are the vics?"

"First was sixty-five, second was sixty-one."

"They look the same? Physically?"

Russell turned and studied the body. "Both were brunette, five-five to five-seven. Stout. Glasses." He crouched closer and examined the head. "Maybe some similar facial structure."

"Hmm."

Russell heard a door open and then close.

"You could have a serial on your hands."

"That's what I was worried about," Russell said. "Can you help me with this one?"

"Really not my forte. Blind leading the blind kinda thing."

"C'mon, man, don't sell yourself short."

"Got a better idea. I'll text you the name and number of Karen Vail. Call her."

"Who?"

"Profiler at the Bureau."

"Shit no, Lance. No FBI."

"Trust me. She'll do right by you. Worked with her on that Alcatraz case. Couldn't have broken it without her."

"Wait, the redhead."

"Yep."

"I remember her. I was in the room when Friedberg went missing. Never got to meet her though. You know, face-to-face."

"She's worth the call. Trust me."

He sighed audibly. "You better be right."

"She's a handful but all you gotta remember is that if she jabs you, jab her back."

"Don't I always hit back?"

"This is different. You'll see what I mean."

Russell grinned. "Miss you, brah."

"Sweet Jesus. Please stop with that island lingo."

"I'll call you next time I'm in town to visit my parents. We can grab lunch at your favorite place, the one by the Ferry Building. Slanted Door."

"You buying?"

Russell laughed. "Don't I always?"

"You *always* forget your wallet."

"Yeah, yeah, yeah." Russell grabbed hold of one of the banyan tree's vertical branches. "Hey, don't forget to text me that fibbie's number."

"Soon as I get inside."

"Break a leg. And Mahalo."

3

Karen Vail was in an Uber on her way to McCarren International, an uneasy feeling settling in her stomach. Vail and airports did not get along well. It had nothing to do with air travel. If the place had been a person, she would have to admit, "It's not you, it's me."

Her fiancé, Robby Hernandez, would say that she was *always* the problem. And she could not argue with him. Well, she could, and often did. But much of the time he had a point.

And sometimes I even admit he's right.

Vail glanced back for one final look at the casinos. The last time she had been in Vegas she was working a wide-ranging case that exposed a criminal ring with roots in Northern California. It was one of those cases that stayed with you for your entire life. The only positive to come from it was the realization of how she felt about Robby.

It was now time for them to get married.

As she examined her calendar and pondered potential dates, her phone rang. It was a number she did not recognize. She had been getting spammed by stupid robocalls so she recorded a new outgoing voice mail message: "I'm screening my calls, so leave a message and I'll call you back. If you're a robocaller, may whoever programmed you be struck with pestilence and cyber plague."

Okay, so the announcement was not quite that harsh—but it was close. Robby suggested she make the outgoing message more, well, *outgoing*. More friendly, less angry.

She countered that suggestion by pointing out that her tactic had worked. People stopped phoning her. Even her friends.

Of course, that was her personal line. Her Bureau voice mail was another matter. That had to be professional. And she could not screen her calls because she never knew who might need to reach her.

She caught it before it clicked over the voice mail. "Karen Vail."

"This is Adam Russell, Honolulu PD. San Francisco Inspector Lance Burden gave me your name."

"You a hitman?"

"A what?"

"An assassin."

"I'm a detective. Why would you th—"

"Never know with Burden."

"Umm. Okay."

"So you're a detective. Let me do some detecting. You'd like my help on a case."

"A couple of cases, actually."

"Two? Did not see that coming."

"What would it take for you to sit down with me and look things over? On these cases."

"I'm in Vegas on my way to the airport right now. Headed home. Virginia. Wrong direction—for you."

"Can I convince you to change your flight? You're already half-way here. Be a shame, you know? You're so close."

Yeah, a shame. "Not sure a five-hour flight is what I'd call *close*. There's paperwork you have to fill out. And my unit chief has to approve it."

"You think it'd be a problem?"

With my unit chief? You better believe it.

"Shouldn't be. If it's legitimately something the Behavioral Analysis Unit should be consulting on, we're at your service. Tell me what you've got."

Vail listened to the quick summary and absorbed it all. She did not offer anything of value because, well, she did not have enough information to reach any kind of conclusions. "Okay. Let me see what I can do. I'll email you the forms, check with my boss, and call you back."

Personally, diverting to Oahu was not a big deal. Robby was working long hours on a case for the Drug Enforcement Administration, so it was not like he would miss her much if she were gone another few days. Her son Jonathan, a student at George Washington University, could stop by the house and feed and walk Hershey, their brown—and gradually turning silver—standard poodle.

Professionally, Vail had no court appearances for the next ten days and she was current on all of her cases. But Oahu was not her decision.

She thought of calling her unit's assistant special agent in charge, Thomas Gifford, and asking him, but she knew that would be overstepping. Now that she had a unit chief again, the request had to go through her. It's not that Vail didn't *like* Stacey DiCarlo. It's just that she didn't respect her. And DiCarlo could be a bitch at times, spiteful and jealous. She also overcompensated for being a woman and treated Vail with a double standard.

Hmm. So maybe it is that I don't like her.

Vail's call with DiCarlo went as she suspected.

"Agent Vail, this isn't how we do things. It's not how *I* do things. Have the forms submitted and I'll review them. If it makes sense for the unit to take the case, I'll put it into the system."

"I understand that. But—"

"This detective needs to know we have procedures for a reason. Otherwise he'll expect an immediate response from us going forward. And then other departments will find out that we pushed his case to the top of the pile and they'll want us to drop everything too. *You* need to understand that as well."

"I get it," Vail said. "Wasn't my idea, ma'am. He called me. And I *am* already out here on the west coast, so flying to Hawaii to get the lay of the land, see a fresh crime scene, and get a head start on this case is a big help. And a hell of a lot more efficient than flying ten hours again next week. Better use of my time. But believe me—I'd be very happy to come home."

"Did you hear anything I just said?"

"Yep, I sure did. If you give me the go-ahead, I'll make it clear to him that this isn't the way we normally do things."

And I'll tell him you're an anal administrator who doesn't know a thing about profiling, let alone policing.

"And I'll let him know you're making a special exception and that he owes you. Big-time."

Silence.

"It does make sense," Vail said. "And it'll ultimately be a lot more efficient for us."

After a long moment, DiCarlo groaned. "Fine. Do it. Just don't ask me for any more favors this month."

"I'm not asking for a favor here. I'll do whatever you prefer. If you want me to come right home, I'm very happy doing that."

"Do you want to go Oahu or not?"

Didn't I just answer that? "Whether or not I want to go is irrelevant. It's your call. Obviously."

"That's not an answer."

I think I'd rather have a root canal than continue this conversation.

"Okay, I'll just keep my scheduled flight and come home."

"No. Divert to Oahu. Lenka will email you your new itinerary."

"Yes ma'am." *Bitch.*

Vail dialed Russell and told him he was in luck. "I got approval to take the case. I'm obviously not packed for a longer trip, so as long as you can point me to a Victoria's Secret to get some clean underwear, I can be on the next flight."

"We just had sensitivity training, Agent Vail. I don't think I should touch that comment with a six-inch pole."

Sensitivity training, eh?

"Sounds like you need another course. Forget Victoria's Secret. Macy's is fine. Or even a local laundromat where I can do a wash."

"Boss wants you to get right to work. Tell me what size you need and I'll pick up some underwear for you."

"And tampons."

"Maxi or mini?"

Wise guy.

"You're married."

Russell laughed. "Let's just say I *have* gone on shopping runs for the wife. You'd be surprised at some of the stuff I've bought. Tampons ain't nothing. What about you?"

"Married? Was. Divorced. Or actually widowed. Doesn't really matter, I guess, because I would've killed him anyway."

Russell laughed.

I wasn't joking.

"But I figured I can't make the same mistake twice, so I decided to go for a sequel. Get it right this time. If my fiancé and I ever get our acts together." Vail felt her Samsung vibrate: Lenka's email. "Pulling into the airport. I'll text you the flight info. Have someone pick me up?"

"Already got it covered."

4

The air in their apartment was hot, humid, still, and stale. A cockroach scrambled by Scott's feet. He watched it disappear under the beaten-up wood of the kitchen cabinet.

A growling rumble of disappointment emerged from his mother's throat. She was a stout woman built like a wrestler, with a constitution to match. "Whaddya want, an invitation? Eat your cereal."

Scott squirmed in his seat. "I don't like it. It tastes bad."

Mary took a step forward, right up to Scott's back, and leaned over his head. He hated when she stood behind him and issued orders. It made him uncomfortable. "Eat the oatmeal."

"I want Cocoa Puffs."

"Don't got no Cocoa Puffs. Wasn't on sale this week. Eat what you got. Or go hungry. Ain't tellin' you 'gain."

Scott craned his young neck back and looked up at his mother. "Okayyy," he said, drawing out the word. He dug his spoon into the thick, congealed mass and dug up a well-formed crescent of muck. As he pondered it, wishing he had a dog to feed it to under the table, he saw another cockroach crawling on the windowsill. A train rattled by outside, the glass shaking and vibrating for a long moment as the subway passed on the elevated platform.

"All right, gimme that."

She reached forward for the bowl—just a gesture, Scott knew— she was not really going to take it away. Not yet.

He looked down at the red-tinged oatmeal in front of him. He stuck the oatmeal in his mouth and a syrupy sweetness smothered his tongue. "I don't like it."

"You're talkin' back. Don't talk back. Now eat."

"It's too sweet."

"You knucklehead. What kid don't like his sugar?"

Scott shrugged. He liked candy. And chocolate. And Pop Tarts. But this wasn't like any of those. "Why's it red?"

"I put some Hawaiian Punch in it. You like Hawaiian Punch."

He closed his mouth and made a face as he worked the mush to the back of his throat. Another spoonful and again he forced it down.

His mother harrumphed and turned, walked over to the sink and started washing the dishes, her back to him. He looked at the garbage pail that stood six feet to her right, about three steps away from him. He knew there were roaches in there, likely some ants too, but he did not want any more of this disgusting cereal. It never tasted so sweet like this before. Whatever it was, he was not going to swallow another bite.

"You eatin'?" Mary asked, not bothering to turn around.

"Yes, ma'am."

She did not respond, just kept scrubbing the pot with a Brillo pad.

Scott quietly rose from his wood chair—it was the one that squeaked, so he had to be careful—and tiptoed over to the trash bin. He lifted the top—and dammit, there were about a dozen reddish-brown cockroaches inside crawling about the trash.

He tipped the bowl over and the lump of hard, red gelatinous oatmeal fell inside atop the bugs. Scott smiled at his ingenuity and stealth, then turned and walked up to his mother.

Her right arm stopped and she turned slowly, her brow hard and eyebrows downcast. "Whatchoo want."

"I'm done."

"Bullshit. You eat any?"

"Yes."

"Yes what?"

"Yes ma'am."

"Don't believe you. How much?"

"Half."

Mary stared at Scott. He had become good at disguising his emotions, at lying and not letting it show on his face.

"Open your mouth. Stick your tongue out."

He did as instructed. She looked—perhaps inspecting it for the deep red shading of Hawaiian Punch as proof. "Fine. Go get ready for school."

"I have to go today?"

"Well I don't want you around under my feet all day."

"First grade sucks."

She slapped him across the cheek. "Watch your mouth. You ain't allowed to curse in front of me."

Scott did not cry. He just stood there staring at his mother. "Yes ma'am."

"Now go get your backpack from your room. And wait by the door for the bus."

Scott did as he was told, feeling the urge to vomit but keeping it down long enough to gather his things.

5

An hour later, Scott was in class when he began experiencing pain in his stomach, low down, deep in his belly. It felt like something was grabbing him, pinching him from inside.

He went to the front of the room and asked the teacher if he could have a hall pass to go to the bathroom.

"Are you feeling okay, honey? You look a little pale."

"Stomach hurts."

She gave him the laminated card and Scott waddled down the hall, trying to get there before he made in his pants. That would be very embarrassing, so much so he did not want to think about it. He was focused on the bathroom, now about twenty steps ahead.

As he pushed through the door, he felt something coming up his throat—and he couldn't stop it. He grabbed onto the sink and vomited, heaving contractions that felt like his insides were exploding up and out of him.

It came out his behind, too, and stunk like dog poop. He finally stopped throwing up and stood there in front of the sink catching his breath.

He turned on the water and let it run, trying to flush the sink clean. It didn't really work and he just stood there with his head over the faucet.

The door opened and a kid walked in—then yelled "Oh, gross!"—and ran out.

The pain was now more intense, gripping his belly and

pinching—in multiple places at the same time. He dropped to his knees, then lay on his side on the cold white tile.

Scott drew his knees to his chest, holding his breath with each stab, when a moment later a teacher walked in.

"Oh my Lord," the woman said. "Are you okay?"

Scott could not answer. He shook his head no, and she said something about being right back—then ran out of the room. Scott did not care as long as the pain stopped.

Time passed. He was not sure how much, but the teacher returned with another woman, the school nurse. Scott recognized her from once before when she sent him home with a fever.

"I'm Doris. What's your name, son?"

"Scott. Scott Meece."

"Who's your teacher?"

"Mrs. Ortega."

"And where's the pain?"

"Stomach. Real bad."

Doris glanced around, appeared to be sniffing the air. She looked in the sink. "Did you throw up also?"

He nodded.

"I'll call your mom and see if she wants to pick you up."

Scott knew she would not want to. What then? Could they force her to come?

"Can you get up?"

"Hurts too much in my tummy."

"Okay." Doris removed her pink sweater, balled it up, and gently lifted Scott's head. "Not as comfy as a pillow, but better than lying on the tile."

He nodded. Why was she being so nice to him?

The door opened and the first woman who had come into the bathroom reappeared. "Office is calling his mother right now."

"Thanks, Catherine," Doris said. She touched Scott's hair, stroked it. "Still hurting?"

Scott nodded again.

"Your mom will be here soon, okay?"

He wanted to tell Doris his mother would not be coming, but she would find out soon enough.

"When did this start, Scott?"

"Right after I ate."

"What did you eat?"

"Oatmeal."

"With milk?"

Scott nodded. "And Hawaiian Punch."

Doris drew her chin back and crumpled her brow. "In your *oatmeal?*"

Scott nodded. "Didn't taste good. Way sweet."

"Sweet." Doris chuckled and shook her head in disapproval. "I can see why."

A few minutes later, Catherine appeared again. "His, um, his mother said she can't come, that we should take him to the doctor."

"We don't do that."

"I told her that."

Scott crumpled tighter as a wave of pain grabbed him.

"And?"

"She wouldn't budge. Said she was busy, that he can wait till he gets home."

Doris mumbled something under her breath, then said, "What about the father?"

"At work. Can't be reached."

Doris growled. "We can take him to my room, but—"

Scott moaned. More pain.

"Call an ambulance," Doris said. "This isn't normal. I don't know what's going on, but it's more than we can deal with and if the mother isn't willing to come get him, we've got no choice."

"Okay," Catherine said with a sigh. "I'll call the ambulance."

6

QUEENSBOROUGH COMMUNITY HOSPITAL
THIRTIETH AVENUE, LONG ISLAND CITY

The ride to the hospital was painful, the rocking of the van intensifying both his headache and the cramping in his belly.

But at least someone was going to do something to make him feel better.

The doctor examined him, nurses came and went . . . but no sign of his parents.

Finally, another white-coated man entered and pulled the curtain around behind him. "I'm Dr. Bratt. How are you feeling?"

"A little better."

Bratt nodded. "We gave you something to ease the pain. And we tried reaching your mom, but she didn't answer and we left a message for her. Same for your father."

"I guess they're busy," Scott said.

"Right." Bratt shared a look with his nurse, who was standing nearby, on the other side of the gurney. She was blonde and had red lipstick on. Scott wanted to look at her, not the doctor.

"So, we're gonna have to wait until we hear from your parents. In the meantime, this is Annette from Child Protective Services."

Scott swung his gaze back to Bratt, where another woman had walked in.

"Hi Scott." She smiled.

Scott just stared at her.

"Annette," Bratt said, "a moment. Scott, excuse us please."

Bratt took a few steps away and huddled with Annette while the pretty nurse with red lips came closer to his bedside. "You ate some bad oatmeal, I hear."

"I dunno. Guess so." But Scott heard the doctor say the words "arsenic poisoning." Obviously Scott was not supposed to hear this—they were having an adult conversation—and he did not know what arsenic was. But he was pretty sure poisoning was not good. "All I did was eat my cereal," he said to the nurse.

"I know."

"But my mom put Hawaiian Punch in it."

The nurse made the same face of disbelief Doris had made in the bathroom.

"Didn't taste good."

She placed a warm hand on his forearm and squeezed. "Dr. Bratt's going to give you something that'll make you better, okay?"

Scott nodded.

Someone parted the curtains and her eyes found Bratt. "Dr. Bratt. Father's just arrived. Wants to see his son."

"Send him through."

Scott tried to sit up but his arms wobbled like rubber and he fell back into the pillow.

A man in his late thirties with jet black hair and pock marks punctuating his face walked in.

"Scotty!" He glanced at the doctor and nurse but went straight to his boy and gave him a hug—then pulled back and planted a kiss on his forehead. The man swung his head around toward Bratt and said, "I'm Waverly Meece. Is Scotty gonna be okay?"

"Yes. We need your approval to administer some medication for treating him."

"Anything you say. Is he okay?"

Bratt motioned him aside.

"Will this medication fix him?"

"It should, yes. He's lucky."

"What—what happened? No one would tell me anything over the phone."

Bratt drew back the edge of the curtain. "Follow me. I'll explain what I know."

Waverly turned back to Scott. "You're in great hands here. They're gonna make you good as new. Okay?"

Scott nodded weakly, his eyes at half-mast.

Waverly followed Bratt out of the ER treatment area and into the hallway.

"What happened to Scott?"

Bratt contorted his lips, studied Waverly a moment, then said, "Do you keep any kind of unusual chemicals around the house?"

"We live in a small apartment. Not much room for us and the kids. We don't have anything that ain't necessary. What kind of chemicals? You mean like bleach? Or nail polish remover?"

"Well, those are good guesses. But no, more like pesticides."

"In an apartment?"

"Insecticides, then. You have roaches or ants?"

Bratt snorted. "Who doesn't in Queens?"

"Any chance Scott was exposed to it?"

"Wife hates the smell. She works graveyard in a factory so by the time she gets home she doesn't want anything that reminds her of the job. She breathes bad chemical smells all day. So we don't have any of those sprays in the apartment."

"You sure?"

"Yeah I'm sure. You learn which fights to fight and which to let go. Killing roaches ain't one of them." He laughed, but Bratt did not share the humor. "Listen, Doc, why are you asking me these questions?"

Bratt contorted his lips and nodded, then looked down. "Your son was poisoned, Mr. Meece. Arsenic."

"Arsenic. You serious?"

"Dead serious. Arsenic is a naturally occurring chemical, but it's not a substance usually found in high enough concentrations to do damage. Obviously, a child is more vulnerable. Water can contain arsenic, but the city's water is exceptionally good. Absent chemical exposure, this looks to be a highly suspect toxicity."

Waverly looked at Bratt a long moment. "Come again, Doc?"

"It looks like he was deliberately poisoned."

Waverly's bottom jaw dropped and hung open. He swallowed hard. "By who?"

"Good question."

Waverly searched his thoughts. He knew Mary could be mean at times, and she had a problem with Scott, but she also had her moments with their other son, Phillip. Poison? Kill her son? No.

"I don't know what to say, Doc. I can't believe anyone'd wanna poison my son. Maybe it happened at school. They have more of them chemicals than we would."

Bratt studied his face a moment. "There's a lady from Child Protective Services. You'll need to talk with her before we can release Scott to you."

Waverly bit the inside of his bottom lip. "What does that mean?"

"I'm not the one to answer that question." Bratt placed a hand on his shoulder. "I'm sure she'll go through everything with you."

Waverly nodded, but a million thoughts were rushing through his mind, starting with, *Had Mary tried to kill his son?*

7

The following morning Waverly led Scott into their apartment. Dr. Bratt had administered chelation therapy, in which a chemical compound is used to bind with the offending toxin to help the body excrete it.

Scott was feeling well enough to be brought home. The doctor explained that arsenic, consumed in large amounts, can kill a person rapidly. In smaller amounts over a longer period, it would cause serious illness or a slow, prolonged death.

The working theory was that Scott had inadvertently consumed something that contained an unusually high amount of the toxin: not a continued exposure but a single dosing.

Child Protective Services could not find any evidence of wrongdoing, especially with a naturally occurring substance that could be present in a number of household products, despite Waverly's insistence that they did not have any of the chemicals at home.

Mary had not come to the hospital. She called once to find out how Scott was feeling but said that she could not get a sitter for Phillip, so she would wait until Waverly called with updates.

Waverly tried to find a solution and offered to call a few of his friends at work to see if they could watch Phillip for a couple of hours. "I think it's important for you to come. For Scotty."

"He knows I love him. Why should I waste two hours to walk to the subway, stand in a hot station, and wait for the goddam train to come? And then repeat all that just to get back? I'll see him when he gets home."

Waverly let it go—as usual.

As he walked into the apartment with Scott, Phillip was on his way out the door to catch the school bus. Waverly gave his older son a hug and a quick explanation—"Your little brother accidentally ate something that was bad for him and the doctors had to make him feel better"—then sent him on his way.

He put Scott to bed, turned on his room fan, and shut the door. He trudged into the kitchen and sat down heavily on the chair. Mary was sweeping the floor.

"Take the garbage out. It's next to the table."

"I just need to sit for a few minutes," Waverly said. "Was up all night and I've gotta shower and get to work. They know I'm gonna be late."

"Then take the bag out on the way to work."

A moment later, with Waverly waiting for some kind of inquisition on his wife's part about Scott's condition—and getting nothing—finally said, "A woman from Child Protective Services is s'posed to come by today."

"What for?"

"She said they need to talk with you."

Mary, back to Waverly, stopped sweeping. "About?"

"The poison. They also want to take a look at the apartment, make sure we don't have any unsafe chemicals around."

"What kinda unsafe chemicals?"

"Anything that has arsenic, I guess."

"Arsenic?" She gave a couple of swats in a corner with the broom, then stopped. "They have a search warrant?"

"A warr—I don't know. They need one?"

"To search our home, yeah."

"I don't think it's a legal search. Just a—a—I dunno, to make sure Scotty's safe."

"Whatever." She resumed sweeping. "Ain't gonna find nothing."

A moment later, Waverly shook his head. Sometimes he did not understand his wife. "Don't you wanna know how Scotty's doin'?"

"I assume he's fine."

Waverly snorted. "I don't know about 'fine.' But he's gonna be okay. Feeling better. It was kinda dangerous."

She kept sweeping. "Yeah?"

"Yeah. He ate *poison*, Mary. I mean, you never asked me why he was in the hospital. Every time I called, you listened to what I had to say but you never asked what happened."

"You told me. He was vomiting and had diarrhea at school."

"And you couldn't even get there to take him to the doctor?"

"I had errands to run."

"Weren't you worried about your son?"

Mary stopped sweeping. She turned her body, both hands on the wood handle. "What kinda question's that? You're asking a *mother* if she's worried about her son?"

Waverly swallowed. "Well, I was—you didn't—you weren't real upset about what happened. You weren't there for him. Didn't sound like you . . . cared."

Mary walked toward Waverly. She shifted the broom to her left hand and slugged him, a roundhouse punch that knocked Waverly back in the chair and tipped it onto the floor. She was on top of him almost immediately, the handle shoved up against his throat.

"Can't . . . breathe. Mar—ry."

"What happened? Heard something fall."

Mary's head snapped back. Scott was standing in the hallway looking at her. She rolled off Waverly's hips and pushed herself up. "Your father fell. He's fine." Mary swatted at Waverly's side with the broom.

He craned his head back to see his son, exposing his now apple-red neck. "I'm fine, Scotty."

"Go back to bed." Mary shooed him off. "You need your rest."

"Yes ma'am," he said under his breath, then turned and headed back to his room.

Mary got down on her knee, digging it into Waverly's abdomen. "Don't you ever say I don't care about my son. You hear?"

Waverly nodded, rubbing his throat.

She pointed an index finger at his nose. "Don't make me do this to you again. Now get up and get showered. You gotta get your ass to work."

Scott sat on the edge of his bed listening to his mother admonish his dad. He did not know why she was so mean to him. And he did not know why his father let her do it.

But it was nothing new. He had seen this kind of thing happen before. It seemed to be more frequent during the past few months, which bothered him a lot. Why was his mother like this? Was it something he had done wrong? Was he a bad boy? Was his dad bad too?

There was a banging on his door. The thick, scary shadows at the threshold told him it was his mother. "Get your butt in bed."

"Yes ma'am."

Scott crawled back and drew the sheet up to his chin. He did not know if he would be able to fall asleep, but moments after closing his eyes he felt the weight of the medication pull him into a foggy, dark dream.

8

When Vail arrived, the someone who met her at the airport was Adam Russell.

He seemed to like the Karen Vail package, as he smiled broadly when she walked out into the bright sunshine of Honolulu.

"You're still a redhead."

Vail rolled her suitcase over the rough pavement. "Not sure how to take that."

"I like redheads. Don't find many female cops with red hair. Well, naturally red. You're a natural."

"I am. In many things."

Russell shot a glance at Vail. "And I'm not sure how to take *that*."

Vail held up her left hand, where a two-karat emerald cut diamond occupied her ring finger.

"Flirt only," he said with a nod. "Don't touch. I get it."

"Good," Vail said. "And don't forget *you're* married."

He grunted. "My wife and I are getting a divorce. Besides, you're too old for me."

Vail's eyes widened.

Russell held up a hand. "Just kidding." He gave her a double take. "You weren't going to slug me, were you?"

"I was thinking about it. But I just realized my anger management classes worked."

Russell jutted his chin back. "Oh yeah?"

"Yeah. You're still conscious."

Russell's squint suggested he did not know whether or not to believe her.

Vail gave her rolling bag's handle a tug as she started walking.

"You know," Russell said, "we kind of met once before. A few years ago."

"How do people 'kind of meet'? You mean we were in the same room?"

Russell pursed his lips. "Exactly. Good guess. I'm impressed."

"If *that* impresses you, I might end up knocking your socks off on this case."

"I wasn't really *that* impressed. I was just being nice."

"Like when I didn't slug you?"

"Yeah, kinda like that."

He directed her across the road.

"I assume we're going right to your morgue?"

"Actually, I got us tickets to tonight's Jack Johnson concert at Aloha Stadium. Figured we'd go straight there, catch the warmup band." He gauged her response. She did not bite. "Yes, directly to the morgue."

"So we've got two dead middle-aged women. And no signs of trauma?"

Russell nodded. "Weird, I know."

"Unusual—as far as asphyxiations go. But not weird. What did the tox report show?"

He pointed the way to the parked car. "Nothing. All we got was a heart rhythm issue. Arrhythmic heart dysfunction. Something like that. Apparently it causes suffocation pretty quickly. Best we can tell, the second victim—Dawn Mahelona—was in her office and started coughing and choking. Ran outside to get some fresh air. But she didn't make it very far. Twenty or thirty feet and she dropped dead."

"Same thing with the first vic?"

"More or less. Daughter found her after the fact, but that's what the ME thinks happened."

Vail processed that. "Highly likely this UNSUB is going to kill again." Vail did not want to insult Russell by defining UNSUB as unknown subject. Although originally a Bureau term, detectives had been adopting it for a while now.

Russell stopped behind an unmarked Ford Interceptor police vehicle. "You sure of that?"

"Unfortunately. Yeah. These offenders enjoy killing too much. That much I know. But I don't know who, when, or where. Although I *can* tell you how."

Russell pulled open the driver's door. "How?"

"Pretty much the same way. These UNSUBs have a certain way of doing things. We used to call it a signature, but that term's outdated. We now refer to it as *ritual*. Ritual behavior. No matter what you call it, concept's the same."

"So this ritual is something they deliberately do. For effect?"

"Actually, no. They're not aware that they're doing things a particular way for a particular reason. It feels right to them, comforting in a way. The fact that they do these specific things with their victims helps us link different murders together because their ritual doesn't change over time, which is extremely important. If we can also use their MO to link the cases, so much the better. But because MO changes, it's less reliable.

"Ritual also tells us a great deal about that UNSUB. His level of education, his probable age range, upbringing, occupation, things like that."

"Now I know why Lance recommended you."

"Criminal investigative analysis is a handy tool to have in your forensics kit."

They arrived twenty minutes later. Russell led Vail into the building, then stopped when he saw a balding man in his fifties. "Chief!"

The man turned, saw Vail, and his face brightened—for a split second, and then creased into a squint.

"Karen, this is Deputy Chief Brad Ferraro. Chief, Karen Vail, FBI. Behavioral Analysis Unit."

Vail held out her right hand and it hung orphaned in the air for a moment before Ferraro took it and shook—and quickly broke the bond.

Something's up with this guy. Did I once meet him and piss him off? There are so many, I've lost count.

"Why are you here?"

"Nice to meet you, too," Vail said with a toothy smile.

"I asked her here for a case."

Ferraro cleared his throat. "Uh-huh."

Russell looked from Ferraro to Vail, who shot a glance at Russell.

"I'm sorry," Vail said. "Have we met?"

"No."

Oh, but there's something.

"Okay then," Russell said, clapping his hands together. "We've gotta run. Meeting up with Dr. Kuoko. Good to see you, Chief."

"Yeah," Ferraro said, giving Vail a sideways look as he moved off to his left.

As they continued down the hall, Vail nudged Russell's right arm. "What the hell was that?"

"Weird. That's what it was. Never seen him behave like that. He's a good dude. Laid back, friendly."

"Sometimes I bring out the worst in people."

"So I'm told."

Vail stopped abruptly. "Say again?"

Russell turned and slowed. "Burden. He warned me."

They began walking again, Vail processing that. "Did he really—"

"He was joking. I got the impression Burden likes you a lot. You want, I'll touch base with Ferraro later, see what the deal is."

"Let it go. I wanna keep a low profile here. Do my job, avoid conflict, help you put this bastard behind bars, and go home."

Who the hell am I kidding? When have I ever been able to do that?

"Consider it forgotten."

They entered the morgue, where they found Keiki Kuoko, who looked official yet scholarly in his blue scrubs and black rimmed glasses and charcoal-and-gray hair. Russell made introductions—which went more smoothly than their encounter with Ferraro.

"Where do we stand with Dawn Mahelona's autopsy?" Russell asked.

"Just completed the postmortem. I assume you want to see the body."

"Let's start there," Vail said.

Kuoko led them down a hallway, his black wide-soled Clarks carrying his thick mass as the others' shoes clippity-clapped down the corridor. He pushed through a locked door and walked over to a table, then tapped the edge of a spotlight. It brightly illuminated the corpse.

He gave his report to Vail and she absorbed all the details without comment. She already had a sense of what they were dealing with but did not want to interrupt. It was something she had promised Robby she would work on.

He bet her that she was wasting her time.

"So," Russell said, glancing across the table at Vail. "What are we looking at here?"

"Keep in mind we've only got two bodies. But I think there are some conclusions I can draw based on the behavior I'm seeing."

"I'm not seeing much 'behavior,'" Russell said.

Vail grinned. "Which is why Burden told you to call me."

"Good point."

"Think of what I do as having someone who can speak a language that you can't. So there could be writing all over the crime scene walls—symbols that contain all sorts of clues as to who the killer is. But it looks like gibberish to you because you don't speak that language. Then I walk in and tell you what it says because I can read it."

Russell pursed his lips and nodded. "That's pretty cool."

"It usually is. But then you get an offender like this who doesn't interact with the body and it kind of makes it tough to read, even for me."

"What do you mean, he doesn't interact with the victim?"

"Interaction with a victim's body is a hallmark for a number of offender types. Until we know more, based on witness reports, there was no direct confrontation between the victim and offender. He didn't physically choke them."

And that doesn't really add up. But first things first.

Vail fixed her gaze on Dawn Mahelona's face. "Your offender is selecting specific women. Again, we've only got a small sample size, but it's probably not a coincidence the killer chose two older brunette females. And that they were killed in largely the same way: asphyxiated."

"And there was no trauma," Russell said.

"Careful," Vail said. "The absence of something doesn't necessarily mean you can assume the presence of something."

"Come again?" Kuoko said.

"Could be there's no trauma because trauma wasn't necessary, not because it says anything about the killer." Vail looked over Dawn Mahelona's body. "Tox screen was unremarkable?"

"Yep."

Vail thought a moment, then pursed her lips and nodded slowly. "Give me a couple of minutes." She walked away, removed her phone, and dialed Tim Meadows, her crime scene colleague at the FBI lab in Quantico.

"And to what do I owe the reason for your call?" Meadows asked.

"I have a case—"

"Of course you do, Karen. Do you ever call me for any other reason? Like to go on a picnic?"

"That'd be weird, Tim."

"Why?"

"Because I don't like picnics. Too much work just so you can sit outside with ants crawling all over your feet, flies landing on your food, having to swat away yellow jackets and bees. All while sneezing because your allergy meds can't keep up with pollen's assault on your system."

"You're such a killjoy, Karen."

"So I've been told. Listen, I called because I've got a question. On a case. Sorry, no picnic invite this time."

"Truth be told," Meadows said, "I'm not sure I want to go on a picnic ever again."

"Right. Well, we've got an offender here who might be a poisoner. Vic asphyxiated, no signs of trauma, clean tox report, some kind of heart arrhythmia, and I'm thinking—"

"Aconite."

"Yeah."

"So then what's the question?"

"I really just called to see if you want to catch a movie some time."

"Seriously?"

"Tim, I love you. You know that. Yes, we'll grab a movie. Some emotional rom-com. Sound good?"

"Hell yeah. Name the time and place."

"You have no idea what a rom-com is, do you?"

"Not a clue. But I'm up for it."

"Romantic comedy. And thanks for the confirmation on the aconite."

"Just a guess. You know that, right? You didn't give me much to go on."

"Don't worry. It's not like I'm going to put your name in my report. If you're wrong, that'd be . . . embarrassing. No one'll know. I'll keep it to myself. My idea. My deduction."

"But what if I'm right?"

"Then you can take solace in knowing you were right."

"Thanks. I think."

"I'll make sure you get credit."

"Just so we're on the same page here, tell the ME that aconite won't show up on a tox screen. He'll want to look for the alkaloids aconite and aconitine. Aconitine is thought to be the key toxin. Ingestion of even a small amount will damage the heart and cause severe slowing—and stopping—of the heart. That's what causes death. Heck, even touching it can kill you."

"How fast?"

"Too many factors. Aconitum napellus isn't that well studied. There aren't many documented cases. The root's the most toxic part of the plant, but some literature suggests that the leaves can also cause significant health problems. There are some anecdotal stories of a physician dying from chewing on a couple of leaves to demonstrate that it's not deadly."

"Joke was on him, I guess."

"Uh . . . yeah. The *joke* was on him. You know, sometimes I wonder about your mental fitness, Karen."

"Go on, Tim."

"You've also got the usual variables of how potent the strain is of that particular plant specimen, how concentrated the toxin is, how it's administered, the victim's mass, her rate of metabolism—all that technical stuff you're not interested in. Are you asleep yet?"

"What?" Vail said. "You still talking?"

"Exactly. Take care, Karen."

Vail worked through that information as she walked back to the huddle with Kuoko and Russell. "I've got some ideas. I'm going out on a little bit of a limb here, but I believe our UNSUB is a poisoner. Poisons have been used as an efficient method for killing for about two thousand years."

Russell and Kuoko shared a confused glance.

"I just told you," Kuoko said. "Tox screen was unremarkable. No evidence of a toxin of any sort in either victim."

"I know. But there are some extremely effective, deadly poisons that would present in ways that mimic what our victims experienced. Belladonna will cause a dry throat and can cause coughing. But the most obvious is aconite. It's very deadly—and *won't* show up on a tox report. You need to look for the alkaloids aconite and aconitine."

Kuoko's mouth dropped open. "Yes." He pointed at her. "Yes."

"No," Russell said. "Explain."

"Aconite isn't that hard to come by," Kuoko said slowly, still processing the revelation. "It's derived from a plant. Monkshood or wolfsbane, I believe it's called."

"Leaves behind no blood toxicity," Vail said. "And I think this is the most likely one used by our UNSUB because the only postmortem sign of aconite poisoning is—wait for it—asphyxia. The toxin causes—"

"Malignant ventricular tachyarrhythmia," Kuoko said with a nod. "Fancy medical term which means that the electrical signals that normally make your heart beat in a specific rhythm get interrupted. The heart's lower chambers, the ventricles, quiver, or fibrillate, instead of contracting rhythmically and beating normally."

Russell folded his arms across his chest. "Well that doesn't sound good."

Kuoko snorted. "The heart beats to pump oxygen-rich blood to the brain, liver, kidneys—all your organs. If your heart doesn't beat in rhythm, it doesn't pump the blood. And when it stops, you're in cardiac arrest."

"The person stops breathing," Vail said.

Kuoko nodded. "And dies, yeah."

Russell shook his head in disbelief. "So how'd our killer get the poison into their bodies?"

Vail held up a hand. "That's the second question. To narrow our field of suspects in a poisoning case, first question I ask deals with access. How'd the killer acquire the toxin?"

"Why is that more important than how the killer gets the poison into the vics' bodies?"

"Because if we're dealing with an unusual substance or chemical, who has access to it could tell us a lot about who the offender is and where he works. What his knowledge level is. How resourceful he is. And a lot more depending on the toxin used."

"Unfortunately, that's not the case here." Kuoko spread his hands apart. "Remember? Aconite is a plant. Its roots are sold in lots of places. They're used in herbal medicine for treating neck and back pain. But if you don't handle it properly—or God forbid take too much, which is very easy to do, you're a dead duck."

"So back to my question," Russell said. "How'd our killer poison his victims?"

Kuoko shrugged. "Doesn't take much. The toxin's very rapidly absorbed, even through the skin. Touching the plant's leaves is all it takes."

Russell dropped his gaze to Dawn Mahelona's face. "Jesus."

"The root is the most potent part of the plant," Vail said. "At least that's what I was told by my forensic guy."

Kuoko nodded. "Pacific Islanders used to put it on the ends of their harpoons. They would shoot whales and wait till they washed ashore a couple of days later."

"If I'm remembering correctly, the most famous case of murder by aconite was the Roman emperor Claudius," Vail said. "His wife mixed aconite in with his mushrooms. Don't ever cross a pissed off woman."

Kuoko chuckled. "I knew there was a reason why I don't like mushrooms."

"And why you have to keep your wife happy."

He laughed again. "You got that right."

"Let's get some tissue samples over to the lab for testing. Maybe they can test for the metabolites of aconite. I'm assuming that's what we're dealing with here, but let's confirm it."

"Done," Kuoko said.

"So how do we catch this guy?" Russell asked. "Not like we have something to trace, and even if we could, it's just a plant. Not like it's a drug with restricted access or processed in any unique or monitored way."

Vail nodded slowly. "Makes it harder, for sure. I'll see what I can do to narrow the field, point us in the right direction. For one, historically, poisoners have often been women. Male poisoners are doctors and nurses and their murders take place in nursing homes and hospitals. Female poisoners take a less direct, less violent approach. Since it's generally speaking harder for a woman to overpower a man, a toxin puts them on equal footing."

"I'm sensing a *but*," Russell said.

"You're sensing correctly. And here it is: *But* I'm not ready to commit one way or another just yet. I'm processing everything. And it's still a very small sample size."

"You *will* share your thoughts when you reach a conclusion, right?"

"Of course. There's no fun in keeping it to myself. Misery loves company."

9

Vail walked outside and realized it had been almost thirty years since she visited Oahu. Some new office buildings had been built in the intervening decades, but there were still a lot of older structures. She was just a kid back then, so even if she passed a few longstanding landmarks, she would probably not remember them.

Vail pulled out her phone and called her sometime partner and all-the-time pain in the ass, Frank Del Monaco.

"Stacey said you were stopping off in Hawaii?"

I hate when he calls the unit chief by her first name. Best buddies.

"Landed this morning."

"Lucky you. Beaches and warm weather."

"I'm working, Frank."

"Of course you are."

Vail rolled her eyes. She was not going to let Del Monaco bait her. "I need you to have an analyst run a search on ViCAP. Can you do that for me?"

"I can. But as my mom used to say, 'You really meant to ask if I *will* do that for you.'"

Vail forced a smile. Del Monaco could not see it, but it allowed her to shed her anger. *Well, that's the theory.* "Your mother was a wise woman, Frank." *Can't say the same for her son.* "*Will* you have an analyst run the search for me?"

There was a long hesitation, followed by an exaggerated sigh. "Yes."

Vail gave him the parameters, then asked him to expedite it.

Del Monaco snorted. "And what if I'm in the middle of a case, too?"

"Look at it this way, Frank. The longer it takes me to make headway with this, the more time I get to spend lying on the beaches in paradise."

He groaned—just loud enough for her to hear.

That made her smile again, only this time it was real.

"I'll get right on it."

As Vail hung up, the young detective cleared his throat. "What kind of search is he doing?"

Vail spun around. "Sneaking up on me?"

"If I was, I wouldn't have cleared my throat."

"True that." She held up her phone. "I asked my colleague to search ViCAP."

ViCAP, or the Violent Criminal Apprehension Program, was a nationwide database of serial violent and sexual crime cases that enabled law enforcement agencies to link victims in different jurisdictions. The program was voluntary, but if a detective took the time to complete the forms, a cop in one state could search for distinguishing factors about a victim or offender and find crimes in other states committed by the same individual.

"Problem is," Vail said, "if the medical examiners classify the deaths as natural heart attacks, there won't be any 'cases' to find. They have to search MSRs," she said, referring to miscellaneous service reports.

"Talk about a needle in a haystack."

"And how many haystacks have you searched?"

"As a detective? Too many. And I'm just getting started."

Vail realized she was perspiring and tugged on her blouse to get some air movement. "What is it, eighty degrees?"

"Eighty-three. Good thing you came from Vegas or you'd have to buy a new wardrobe."

Thirty minutes later, her Samsung rang and she dug it out of her pocket. "Frank. Anything?"

"You can thank me later. Got hits in Chicago, Los Angeles, Dallas, and Atlanta. Linkage isn't ironclad because you didn't give me a whole lot to go on, and the ViCAP database had nothing because if they were classified as natural deaths, there aren't actually any homicide cases—"

"Yeah, I just realized that."

"Fortunately, Jeri McMaster, that ViCAP analyst? She always goes the extra mile. She reached out to her contacts at a few major cities. They plugged it into their systems, did some manual searches, checked with the MEs, looked for matches regarding the asphyxiation signature of the killer, victim age range, hair color—and got some."

"And there could be more that went unreported as homicide," Vail said, "because it can look like a simple heart attack. This obviously wasn't an exhaustive or definitive search."

"My thinking, too."

That's scary.

"Oops," she said, cupping her mouth. "Did I say that out loud?"

"Say what?"

Vail shook her head. "Nothing."

"Another sarcastic remark, I'm sure."

"You're right, Frank. I apologize."

"You apologize?"

"Doesn't happen often, so enjoy the moment."

"This is how you thank me?"

"No. Absolutely not. Who said anything about thanking you for doing your job? Please thank Jeri for her terrific work. And email me those MSRs." Before Del Monaco could get the last word, she hung up.

"You two don't play well together," Russell said.

"How could you tell?"

Russell chuckled. "It'd be a trip to work with you every day."

"I'm not always this pleasant. I can be a real pain in the ass."

Russell pouted his lips as if he were considering her comment. "Never would've guessed."

Vail stuck out her tongue in mock insult, then gave him a friendly wink.

"While we're waiting for those files, you wanna go take a look at the two crime scenes?"

"Matter of fact, I do."

10

Only the Lonely" by The Motels was playing on the radio. Scott ran into the living room, his arms spread out at his sides and making a vroom! noise as he swooped high and low over the couches.

"What are you?" Phillip asked.

"A fighter jet!"

"Oh yeah? How do you know about fighter jets?"

"Dad was telling me about 'em. He said they're super-fast and can drop bombs and stuff. We got the best in the world."

"F-16s are cool. Wanna see a picture?"

"Yeah!"

Phillip disappeared for a moment as Scott resumed dashing about the periphery of the small room. A moment later, Phillip walked back in with a forest green and cream-colored *World Book* "update" volume. He splayed the pages open and dropped the encyclopedia on the sofa. "See?"

"That's bad!" Scott revved up like a car engine and sped away, zooming left and right.

"What the hell's all this noise?"

Phillip hid the *World Book* from his mother's sight. "Scott's playing air force. He's an F-16 fighter jet."

Mary rolled her eyes and muttered something under her breath.

"Scott, why can't you be more like your brother?" She glanced over. "Scott Meece, are you listening to me?"

Scott swooped to a landing on the couch, sound effects and all: a momentous crash, complete with explosions.

Mary stepped over and smacked Scott on the back of the head. He stopped and looked up at her, in his own world, unclear as to why she had struck him.

"You hear me?"

"No, ma'am."

"I said be more like your brother. Stop doing stupid stuff and— be smarter."

Scott stood up, unsure how to do that. "Yes, ma'am."

"Go get your backpack. Time for school."

"But—but I didn't eat yet."

"Tough shit. Next time don't be in dream land. You get up in the morning, you brush your teeth and eat breakfast. No fuckin' around."

Scott pouted his lips. "I'm hungry."

"You'll get lunch at school."

"But I'm hungry now."

She drew back her right hand, threatening a smack across the face. Scott winced, waiting for the blow.

"Get your backpack. Now. Don't make me tell you a third time."

He ran out and into his room, walking by the mirror on his wall. He stood on his toes to take a look at his face. Tears had pooled in the bottoms of his lids. Drawing a sleeve across his eyes, he mopped up the moisture, then grabbed his book bag and headed out. Phillip was waiting by the door. He pulled it open and they walked into the corridor.

"Here," Phillip said, removing something from his pocket. "Piece of toast. All I could get without her seeing."

Scott's face brightened as his lips spread. "Thanks."

"Couldn't let you go hungry."

They walked to the front of the apartment. As they stood in the brisk morning air, Scott turned to Phillip. "Why does Mom hate me?"

Phillip put his left arm around his brother's shoulders.

Scott realized that Phillip had not answered him, but he felt comforted and strangely satisfied.

11

Waverly sat down in the kitchen and rubbed his eyes.

"Elbows off the table," Mary said as she watered the plant by the window.

Waverly dropped his arms to his sides and looked at her with a bloodshot weary expression. "Sorry. I'm beat."

"Don't gimme that. You just woke up."

"Didn't sleep well."

"You were tossing and turning all night."

He took a deep breath and sat back as Mary placed a plate of scrambled eggs and bacon with a side of home fries in front of him. "Wow. You made breakfast. What is this, a special occasion?"

"Can't I make a nice breakfast for my husband?"

"Hell yeah," Waverly said, grabbing his fork and digging in. "What's this?" he asked as he chewed.

"A flower."

"For what?"

"Decoration. I think it's called a garnish. Saw it in a magazine. I also ground up a little bit of it and put it in the eggs. For extra flavoring."

"No shit?"

"Whaddya think?"

Waverly cleared his throat. Again. Turned his neck to the side and coughed. Grabbed his water glass and tried to gulp it—but ended up spilling it on the table. He jumped up from his chair and looked at Mary, clasped his throat with his right hand, his eyes wide and his face shading red.

"You okay?" She advanced on the table, leaning in closer to get a look at his face. "Waverly."

He shook his head vigorously from side to side. He could not get air into his lungs. Choking—felt like he had something jammed down his throat.

Waverly dropped to his knees and began crawling toward the door but only got about ten feet.

He felt a sharp pain in his chest, sending lightning bolts into his left shoulder and arm.

Pressure.

Squeezing.

Hard to breathe.

He fell to his stomach, then his face hit the hard floor. Blood seeped across his tongue, a piece of tooth wedged in his throat . . .

And then nothing.

Phillip and Scott were waiting by the front entrance to PS 122. The school, also named for Mamie Fay—the first female principal in Queens and the administrator who guided the institution starting in 1925—was a large rectangular red-brick building bounded by black wrought iron fencing.

But its most distinctive feature was its four two-story-plus marble columns flanking the front entrance, with a grand light fixture suspended from the center of its atrium, similar in design to that of the White House, of all places.

Mary was late and the boys were standing at the rightmost light post, by the tall gates. Now in junior high, Phillip walked over every day to wait with Scott so that their mother would not have to make two stops—which she said was "a waste of my time."

She pulled up to the curb at a spot a few car lengths away. She slammed her door and trudged toward them, pulling her winter coat around her torso.

"Sorry I'm late, boys. Your father kicked the bucket."

"What bucket?" Scott asked.

"*Died*, you dimwit. Your father dropped dead."

Scott's backpack hit the cement.

Phillip's face blanched. A weak, "What?" managed to scrape from his throat.

"Called the ambulance but they couldn't do nothin' for him. Had to wait at home until they loaded him up. That's why I was late. So blame him, not me."

Scott's knees buckled and he fell to the pavement.

"How?" Phillip asked. "Why?"

"They sayin' heart attack, but don't know for sure. I came home this afternoon and found him there. Paramedics said he'd been dead a while, maybe three or four hours. Body was cold. Peed himself, pants were wet. Broke a tooth when he hit the floor."

Phillip swallowed deeply. "I—but how?"

"I'm not a doctor, Phillip. All I know, heart stops beatin'. Mighta just been his time to go. He stood to lose some weight."

Phillip knelt down and huddled with Scott, who was mute, staring straight ahead at the street.

"Everything okay here?" a woman asked as she passed by with her dog in tow.

"We're fine," Mary said. "Thanks."

"We need to get up." Scott felt a tug at his arm. "Scotty. C'mon, we gotta get up. People are staring at us."

Scott licked his lips and turned to face Phillip. "Daddy's dead?"

Phillip nodded silently.

"I'm scared."

"Nothin' to be scared of," Mary barked. "Now get your ass up and get in the goddam car."

Phillip bit his lip and nodded, telling Scott it would be okay.

But Scott knew it would not be okay. How could it be?

12

Vail and Russell were pulling into the Iolani Palace parking lot when she felt a rumble in her pocket. It was an encrypted PDF with the files Del Monaco sent. She opened the document and gave a cursory look while Russell parked.

"Hmm. All the vics' names were Mary."

Russell swung his gaze over to Vail. "That's bizarre."

"Not really. The UNSUB apparently chooses his victims based on their first names."

"And that's not bizarre?"

"These types of killers have certain psychological characteristics—characteristics that govern their behavior."

"Meaning?"

"Meaning that the things they do, there's a reason behind them. They're not random. He's not killing women in their sixties named Mary by accident. He's chosen them for a specific reason. And if I can make an educated guess here, an older woman wronged him at some point, likely when he was young. An older woman in her early sixties, named Mary."

"Mother?"

"Probably. Or a mother figure. Teacher. A woman in a position of authority. Some kind of abuse."

"Sexual?"

"Can't really say because we don't have enough info yet, but I doubt it. If he was sexually abused we'd see signs of sexual assault on his vics. He'd have sodomized them. Or done something with the genitalia. Sliced a breast, cut it off."

Russell cringed. "I get it."

"Point is, there's lots of things he could've done. He did none of 'em."

"So you really *can* say."

"Huh?"

"You said you can't really say. But then you *said*."

"What's your first name again?"

"Adam."

Vail nodded. "Shut up. Adam."

He fought back a smile. "Yes ma'am."

"And don't 'ma'am' me. I'm not *that* much older than you."

"Right."

"There's something else that bothers me."

Russell lifted his right arm and sniffed. "Do I have body odor?"

"What?" Vail squinted confusion. "No. I mean about the case."

"Wait. You just referred to the killer as a male. Did you decide on his gender and forget to tell me? What happened to 'misery loves company'?"

Vail pursed her lips. "Consider yourself miserable."

"Partnering with you—that's miserable."

"Now *I'm* impressed," Vail said with a nod. "You can take it *and* dish it out. But to answer your question, males are generally less, rather than more, likely to be poisoners—but when they *do* poison it's in a medical setting. That said, the dynamic of victimology and the fact the killer is not witnessing the deaths makes me think this is more likely a male."

"And beyond the gender of the killer, does that help us in any other way?"

"Not sure yet. Based on my experience—and what we're seeing in terms of victimology—my sense is that he's killing his mother."

"Then how do you explain the poisoning MO?"

"Could just be a means to an end—doing it this way allows him to be somewhere else when the vic dies. Increases his chances of success—much harder to catch a killer who's nowhere nearby when the cops show up." Vail unbuckled her belt. "But—keep in mind that at this point we don't know what's ritual and what's MO. I'm making educated guesses. I'll refine them as we get more information."

Russell pushed open his door and got out, led the way down a path. "Not to burst your profiling bubble, Karen, but your theory doesn't work here."

"Did I give you permission to call me Karen?"

"No, I, uh—you didn't want me to call you ma'am, and you called me Adam, so I—"

"*Agent Vail* works for me. Respect your elders."

"I see," Russell said. "So this is one of those times where you can be a bit of an asshole."

"Excuse me?" Vail stopped walking and looked at him. "I said I can be a *pain in the ass*, not an asshole. There's a difference."

Russell laughed.

Vail resumed strolling along the path. "So you were saying. What doesn't work here?"

"Vic's name is Dawn Mahelona. Not Mary."

Vail twisted her lips. "What about the first vic?"

"Mary. So that fits."

"Yeah."

But why would he break with his ritual? Doesn't make sense.

"For now we'll pretend you didn't bother me with that bit of trivia. Okay?"

Russell shrugged. "Yeah. Sure."

"What do we know about Dawn?"

"Single. Never married. No siblings. Lived here all her life."

"And the first vic?"

"Widowed. A son who lives in Texas. He's alibied, but I've got a Texas Ranger following up on that to confirm."

Vail gestured at the vegetation ahead of them. "Weird trees. I remember them, though. When I was a kid. What're they called?"

"Banyans."

"Yes! Coolest trees I've ever seen."

"You want a picture in front of one?"

"What I want is to catch this killer. Take me to the crime scene."

"There are two."

They walked another thirty feet and just around the bend Vail saw the yellow tape swaying to and fro in the breeze, marking off the boundaries.

"What do you know?" Russell said. "Here's one."

Vail glanced around. With the body removed, there was not much to see.

"Other crime scene is inside."

They ascended the steps and walked in the back entrance of the ornate building.

"Pretty cool history," Russell said. "The palace was built in the 1880s by King Kalakaua, Hawaii's last reigning monarch. It was the official royal residence until the monarchy was overthrown about a dozen years later. The only official royal residence in the United States."

"Well that's . . . worthy of note," Vail said with a hint of sarcasm. "I spent some time in England and I don't get the whole royalty thing. But I'm just an American, what the hell do I know about kings and queens?"

Actually, I was born in Queens. So there's that.

Russell led the way along the crime scene tape into an office space with a few empty desks. Phones rang in the distance as workers had been moved to a different area.

"Employees aren't too happy that we roped off half their office space. Can't say I blame them, being displaced like that."

"Yeah, well, at least they're still alive. Dawn Mahelona would trade a little inconvenience for another two decades of life."

"Sorry," Russell said. "Stupid thing to say."

"Not stupid. Just trying to put things in perspective." Vail stood in the center of the room and pivoted in a circle, following the yellow ribbon. "The crime scene includes the bathroom?"

"Yep. Dawn had just gone to the restroom when she was headed back to her desk. Started coughing nonstop, then had difficulty breathing. She ran outside and a coworker followed about a minute or so later. He's the one who found her. Sprawled face down."

Vail harrumphed and made her way into the bathroom, Russell a few steps behind her. She glanced around. Nothing unusual—well-appointed but spartan. It had been updated to include electric hand dryers, but otherwise it had the original, well-maintained fixtures. Fingerprint powder dusted the surfaces.

Vail knelt and looked under the vanity, then stood up and checked each of the stalls. "We now think she was killed with a toxin. Did Crime Scene check out the toilet paper and . . . well, there are no paper towels . . . but what about the soap?"

"Don't know, but I can find out." Russell pulled out his phone and made a call while Vail continued to poke around—being careful not to touch anything. She could not be sure the technicians had taken samples of the types of items capable of carrying a toxin.

She crouched back down, pulled out a pen, and used it to pick through the garbage pail—which was relatively empty because of the lack of paper towels.

Russell held the phone down by his thigh. "They dusted for latents, vacuumed, took photographs. And swabbed for DNA."

"Get them back here. We need them to go through this garbage." Vail stood up. "And there's toilet paper in the stalls. A bar of soap. Toilet seat covers. We need all those things run through the lab looking for aconite. Any one of them making contact with the skin could've killed her."

Russell lifted the handset back to his mouth and asked them to send a unit there as soon as possible.

"Half an hour," he said.

Vail nodded. "Then let's make use of that time." She led the way out of the crime scene and into the temporary quarters where the workers were setting up card tables and laptops. "Sorry to bother you," Vail said, standing at the front of the room. "I'm Special Agent Karen Vail, FBI. I need to talk with anyone who saw Dawn Mahelona yesterday."

"We all saw her," one of the women said.

"Anyone notice anything unusual in her behavior? Anyone see a stranger hanging around that shouldn't have been? Was Dawn upset or concerned about anything?"

Vail looked around the room, making eye contact with each of the dozen individuals—both women and men. Some shrugged. A few shook their heads.

Russell nodded in the direction of a male in his thirties. "Jim there was the last one to see her alive."

Vail gestured for Jim to join them over on the side.

"Anyone else think of anything, contact Detective Russell."

The employee, well-groomed in a long sleeve dress shirt and slacks, started talking before he got close to Vail.

"Not gonna be much help. I didn't see anything. I've got no idea who killed her."

"Where's your desk in relation to hers?"

"Right next to it. I work in the adjacent cubicle. She went to the restroom, asked me to cover her phone for a couple of minutes. When she came back, she started coughing."

"Just coughing?" Vail asked.

"Yeah."

"Not short of breath?"

"Maybe. The coughing seemed to get worse. I didn't think of it at the time, but yeah, maybe she was short of breath."

"Did she say anything? Like, 'Help—I can't breathe'?"

He glanced up at the ceiling. "No. She just kind of touched her chest."

"So she went outside," Vail said. "Why? To get some fresh air?"

"You'd have to ask her." Jim winced. "Sorry. Didn't mean that. I—I just don't know what she was thinking."

"And that's when you went to check on her?"

"Well I heard her still coughing. Outside the window. And then she just suddenly stopped. I ran over and saw her on the ground, face down."

He's right. Not much help.

"You really think she was murdered?"

Vail glanced around the office. "Where's her desk?"

Jim gestured past her left shoulder. "Second one on the left."

Vail and Russell made their way down the hall. "I assume you already looked at it."

Russell ducked under the crime scene tape. "No threatening emails. Nothing in her purse or on her phone that'd indicate she was in trouble or that she had a dispute with anyone."

They stopped in front of Dawn Mahelona's cubicle. As Vail

slipped on a pair of gloves, she scanned the top surface. It was fairly orderly. She pulled open a drawer and noticed a sealed letter. "Paycheck." Vail set it aside and continued rummaging through the paperwork—all work related—and stopped. She went back to the envelope, lifted it up, and stared at the name. "*Mary* Mahelona?" Vail looked up and yelled down the hallway. "Hey. Jim!"

He came jogging down the hall seconds later and stopped at the taped boundary.

Vail held up the envelope. "Why does her paycheck say Mary?"

"Mary's her first name. Dawn's her middle name. Back when she first started working here, we had two Marys and it got real confusing, so she started going by her middle name. It stuck. No one here called her Mary."

Vail and Russell shared a look.

"It fits," Russell said.

Vail nodded at Jim, dismissing him. "Thanks."

As he headed back down the corridor, his dress shoes clacking against the tile, Russell elbowed Vail. "It does explain what we thought was a deviation away from women named Mary."

"Detective?"

Russell turned and saw a Honolulu Police Department criminalist standing there.

"Sorry to make you come back here, but we need you to check out the restroom."

Vail told her what they were looking for and the technician went to work.

"Meantime," Vail said, "let's do some old-fashioned police work."

"I thought that's what we were doing."

Vail ignored him. "Let's see if we can find a male in his forties who has a mother named Mary."

Russell squinted. "You're kidding, right?"

"Yes. And no. That's a bit ridiculous, so we'll narrow the search. Our offender's mother likely has a criminal record that includes child abuse. Or she was arrested for abuse, even if no charges were filed or she wasn't convicted."

"I thought you said earlier there wasn't any abuse."

"No *sexual* abuse. But physical, emotional abuse? Different story."

"So you think that because his mother abused him, he's angry at her and killing women who remind him of her?"

"Exactly. He's killing his mother each time he kills one of these women. He's killing her over and over. And getting pleasure from it."

Russell harrumphed. "I didn't particularly like my mother, especially when she drank too much. But I never wanted to kill her. Or anyone else who reminded me of her."

"That's a good thing, Adam. Means you're normal. Or—well, at least not a psychopath."

He looked at her. "I'm not sure, but I think that was an insult."

"Excuse me. Detective?"

They turned to see the forensics technician holding up her kit. "Good to go. I'll run these tests as soon as I get back."

"Ping me the minute you've got something," Russell said.

"As soon as you're done, I want the materials sent to Tim Meadows at the FBI lab in Quantico." Vail pulled out a card and jotted down his information. "Tomorrow if possible."

"For what?" Russell asked.

"Analysis." Vail shrugged. "Best lab in the country. Let them do their thing. Might find something, might not." After the tech left, Vail glanced around. "I'm done here. Let's go visit the first crime scene."

13

Vail and Russell arrived at the home of Mary Burkhead in Kaneohe thirty-three minutes later, a well-maintained residential area that featured homes with terraced, dense-foliage yards that sprouted papaya and mango trees. Others sported stellar views of Kaneohe Bay.

They parked outside the crime scene boundary and ducked under the tape. They slipped on booties and gloves and walked in the front entrance.

"Vic was found on the deck," Russell said as he led the way out the back slider.

"I take it no one saw it happen."

"Nope. No witnesses. Like I said, daughter found her. About a couple of hours after she died."

Vail walked the one-story house and rejoined Russell in the kitchen a few minutes later. "You were wrong about there not being any witnesses."

"What do you mean?"

Vail held out her right fist, then slowly opened it. Five microSD cards sat nestled in her palm. "Security cameras, the kind that record directly to an internal memory device." She held up a hand. "And that's the extent of my technobabble. I have a friend who used to work for Intel, so I've learned a thing or two over the years. Enough to make me dangerous but not enough to make me smart."

"Dangerous but not smart." Russell chuckled. "That's how Lance Burden described you."

"Funny."

"Be right back." He returned a few moments later carrying a thin Surface tablet. "Do those thingama-cards go in here?"

Vail took the Surface and rotated it around a couple of times, then popped the kickstand out and found what she was looking for. She pressed the first microSD chip into a slot on the back and navigated its contents.

Russell huddled with her over the computer. "Looks like three files."

"Yep," Vail said, studying the File Explorer window. "Videos if I'm not mistaken." She reached out and double-tapped the screen. The program launched and played the surveillance footage.

Mary Burkhead walked out of the bathroom and headed down the hall to another room. Two minutes later, she came back into view, bent over slightly, coughing.

"Switch to a different camera, see if we can pick her up."

Russell did as Vail suggested, finding nothing of interest on the next two SD cards, before locating Burkhead stumbling into the kitchen and then the nook. She struggled to pull open the slider to her deck, then after moving about two feet, dropped to her knees and collapsed to the ground, half in and half out of the house.

Vail straightened up. "Yep, about what I expected."

"Me, too."

"Let's get CSU back here, have them check out that bathroom."

Russell laughed. "Already done. I texted them when we were on our way to the car. Probably be here soon."

And they were. It was a different technician, so Vail again explained what they were looking for. The man went to work while Vail took another look at the information Del Monaco had sent her.

"You wanna see anything else while we're here?"

Vail lifted her gaze from the phone. "Huh?"

"Ready to go?"

"I'm ready to go *eat*. Stomach's growling."

Russell chuckled. "I know a great place about a mile away. View will blow your mind. Their Polynesian and Hawaiian food's second to none on the island."

She checked her watch. "We probably have time before we hear from the lab, right?"

"At least an hour, maybe two. Depends on what they've got in queue."

"Then let's go. I've had a long day of travel and I'm running out of gas."

While en route, Vail pulled out her phone and googled Brad Ferraro's name. She engaged in a little law enforcement officer geography but did not stumble on anything obvious. They overlapped in a few places, particularly DC, but they didn't work any of the same cases.

Did he just dislike profilers? That was an attitude she encountered early in her career—buttressed by long defunct television shows that portrayed her profession as seers who could touch a victim's clothing and get a vision of the killer. Hell, if she did not know any better and had come across a behavioral analyst, maybe she would have drawn the same ignorant conclusion.

But it was more than that with Ferraro.

Why is it bothering me so much?

"What's on your mind? Something with Mary Burkhead?"

"Huh?" Russell's voice jarred her back to the case. "Um, no, just . . . my head was somewhere else. Sorry."

She texted Robby and asked him to poke around online:

dont know what it is about the guy
has to be some reason why
he wants to rip my heart out and eat it

Seconds later, Robby replied:

thats a bit extreme honey
sure ur not reading into this

She almost grunted aloud.

very sure
poke around
got a feeling
has to be something

Vail put her phone down but her mind kept working, shifting to the case. A couple of minutes later, they arrived at Haleiwa Joe's.

They parked and walked up to the rustic restaurant, then entered and passed the largest pair of sandals Vail had ever seen—a wood wall hanging behind the hostess stand on a rough stone facing. Ceiling fans whirred above. But what lay across the room is what caught her attention: a garden setting that was pristine. Perfectly manicured. Idyllic.

They walked over to the far wall—which was not a wall at all but an open area with a railing that looked out over a small lake with a pier that ended in a covered gazebo. Lush foliage bordered the periphery—full trees and meticulously pruned bushes, with a picturesque mountain peak just beyond.

"This is . . ." Vail paused, searching for the correct adjectives.

"Exquisite. Outstanding. Charming."

"Paradise."

"That works, too." Russell gestured to the greenery below. "Haiku Gardens down there. And of course the Ko'olau Mountains."

"Of course."

"Would you like a table?"

Vail turned to see a young woman holding two menus. "Yeah. How about a window seat?"

The hostess grinned broadly. "I think I can arrange that."

She gestured at a table to their left. They sat and took the menus, but Vail was still staring at the scenery. "I could retire here."

"Didn't realize that was on the horizon," Russell said. "You look . . . well, a little too young to retire."

A little too young?

"Nice of you to notice."

"I didn't mean—" He blushed. "Put my foot in my mouth, didn't I?"

"You can pull it out now. I forgive you. This time."

"Right." Russell dropped his gaze to the menu.

Vail perused the dishes and ultimately decided on ordering one of everything. But she thought better of it and settled on the Black & Blue Ahi—blackened ahi sashimi.

"Good choice," Russell said as the server turned and headed toward another table.

"Thank you."

"For what?"

"I'm in an island paradise and I won't get a chance to enjoy it. But this scenery . . . well, it makes me feel like I was really here." She took out her Samsung and snapped some photos—including a selfie.

"Who you sending that to?"

"My fiancé. We haven't settled on a wedding venue. Maybe Oahu? Destination wedding."

"Joe's does do weddings," Russell said. "Down there in the gardens."

Russell's phone vibrated. He extracted it and said, "Yeah." He listened a moment, then his brow rose and he nodded. "Okay then. No, no—this helps a lot." He pocketed the handset and looked at her with a frown.

"Lemme guess. We've gotta go."

"Yep. Wanna take the food with us? You can eat while I drive."

Vail glanced back at the mountains. "Not quite the same. But yeah. I need to eat. And we need to go."

Within ten minutes they were in the car and Vail was devouring her ahi, the requisite oohs and ahhs making Russell smile.

When she was finished, they changed places so he could eat his Kalbi ribs, not nearly as easy a task in a moving vehicle as Vail's fish.

They arrived at the Scientific Investigation Section at HPD's Alapai Station. Vail and Russell were led back to the trace evidence examination unit, where a technician was bent over a gas chromatograph.

"Nice digs," Vail said.

He looked up, his eyes flicking over to Russell, and then back to Vail. "You're the profiler." He held out a hand and Vail shook it.

"And you're the criminalist."

He laughed. "I've been accused of worse."

Hopefully not in a court of law.

"This is Harry Bachler," Russell said. "Best we've got. We could use all the help we can get on this case."

Bachler removed his reading glasses. "We're the twentieth largest police department in the country out of eighteen thousand. And we're the only crime lab for Hawaii. Actually, not just the state of Hawaii, but for the entire Pacific Rim. So we're busy. And because we're busy—"

"We'll get right to the point," Vail said. "You found something for us. The Burkhead asphyxiation case."

"Ah, yes. Right." He shook his head. "Sorry, too many cases. Someone called you, Adam?"

"Yep. We put a rush on this one."

"Of course you did," Bachler said. "Because why not? We're the ones buried here, not you. Give me a minute to pull it up." He sat on a stool and rolled over to a double-monitored computer. "Yeah. So first let me get the easy stuff out of the way. No clear latents on the packaging, other than the victim's prints. Next . . . the soap wrappers have the vic's name written in calligraphy. And judging by the microscopic bleeding off the strokes, it's in permanent marker, not pre-printed. Red marker."

Vail absorbed that.

"Same writer. Handwriting matches," Bachler said. "Bigger deal is that we found *Aconitum napellus*. Also known as—"

"Aconite," Vail said.

"Familiar with it?"

"We are. Question is, where'd you find it? We need to know where the offender is putting it, how he's poisoning the women."

"Already decided it's a 'he,' eh?"

"Yes."

"Based on what?"

Vail shrugged. "It's what I do. I can give you a long explanation, but . . ." She grinned. "You're super busy. Buried, I think you said."

"Buried." He mumbled something under his breath as he scrolled through the document. "We found your toxin in the same place at both crime scenes. Bathroom."

Russell nodded. "That's what we figured."

Bachler looked at Russell over the tops of his glasses. "Did you know it was in the soap?"

"Nope," Vail said. "That we didn't know. Milled into the bar?"

"Trace on the soap, but that's because there was a thin, oil-infused liner wrapped around the bar."

Vail canted her head. "Oil-infused?"

"My guess is that the oil facilitated the absorption of the toxin into the skin. The external wrapper had a waxy coating that prevented the oil from bleeding through."

"Sophisticated," Russell said.

Vail turned to Bachler. "This soap. Are we talking about a commercial product that was tampered with? With a lot number?"

"Definitely not commercial. And definitely no lot number. Looked like generic packaging. We're not done running our analysis on the ingredients in the soap itself, but so far there don't appear to be any industrial chemicals, the kind you find in large batch products."

Russell groaned. "Which'll make them harder, if not impossible, to track down."

Bachler pulled the keyboard in front of him and tapped away. "Triacylglycerols, free fatty acids, glycerol—how about I just translate the chemicals into substances you're familiar with? Olive oil . . . uh . . . vegetable fat . . . medium chain fatty ac—that'd be coconut oil. Then water, sodium hydroxide—also known as caustic soda—and terpenes, which in this case looks to be an essential oil. To make it smell nice or relax you, that type of thing."

"Sounds like you can buy any of these materials in a supermarket," Russell said.

"Correct. Oh—and they noted something else. Not sure how significant it is, but the soap also had a trace of Disodium 6-hydroxy-5-[(2-methoxy-5-methyl-4-sulfonatophenyl)diazenyl] naphthalene-2-sulfonate."

Vail tossed a quick glance at Russell, who shrugged.

"Sorry, Harry, but did you just switch to a different language?"

"A mouthful of geek, I know." Bachler laughed. "Thought about shortening it since neither of you are chemists and you probably wouldn't mind."

"Or notice."

He chuckled again. "It's a red azo dye commonly known as Allura Red, FD&C Red 40, or Red Dye number 40."

"Correct me if I'm wrong," Vail said, "but there'd be no purpose of using that, right? I mean, in a trace concentration, it's not going to actually color the soap. So why add a dye, or colorant, if it's not gonna tint it in any way?"

"Good point," Bachler said with a nod of his head. "I don't have an answer for you. Unless it was contamination. Not with us. But with the manufacturer. Or the killer."

Vail nodded. "If he's mixing this stuff up in a kitchen, that could be a place you'd find red dye."

"Yeah," Russell said. "But it can also be a contaminant in the manufacturing process. Can we track *any* of those compounds to a chemical company or a known product or a manufacturer?"

"Maybe," Bachler said. "Not sure yet. That'll take time. If I find anything, I'll let you know."

"Text me as soon as you've got something," Russell said as they started to back away. "Anything."

"Oh—" Vail turned to Bachler. "There's a strong possibility this offender has killed in other states. So that might impact our search for the ingredients."

Bachler rotated on his stool to face Vail. "Do you think he's mobile? Not staying in one place very long?"

"Hard to say." Vail folded her arms across her chest. "We don't have enough victims to determine how long he's staying in one town, or state. There may be a lot more vics than we know about because most—if not all—probably went unreported as murder. The mechanism of death looks like natural causes, especially in someone sixty or older. The death probably isn't questioned very often. So our sample size is likely much smaller than his true victim count."

Bachler scratched his forehead. "If he's spent less than a month on Oahu, he didn't buy these materials on the island."

"Really." Vail rested her palms on the countertop, bringing her face-to-face with Bachler. "That could be important. Why do you say that?"

"Because it takes a month to make soap. I mean, you can make it in twenty or thirty minutes, but it has to cure for a month before it can be used. In this case, packaged and sold."

Vail lifted her brow. "Interesting."

"Harry." Bachler turned to face an approaching technician.

Vail elbowed Russell. "We should get going."

"Thanks Harry," Russell said, backing away. "That's helpful."

They returned to Russell's vehicle, chatting as they sank down into the seat.

"So would he hang around in one place more than a month? Take a chance the cops would realize these aren't natural deaths? Or would he move on and reduce the risk he'd be caught?"

Vail took a breath of warm, moist air. "Or he makes a large batch at home. Packs one or two suitcases or boxes full of 'em, brings his stock with him. Or ships it ahead so it's here when he arrives."

"Not much we can do if he's bringing them with him. Let's first focus on whether or not he can get the soap bars locally. We may get lucky—or at least be able to eliminate the local angle." Russell stopped in front of his car door. "Who sells soap that doesn't contain commercial chemicals?"

"Probably not a supermarket chain. A local shop. A health food store."

Russell inserted his keys into the ignition. "If he sells his wares out of a local store, it's probably a locally produced product, right?"

"Maybe. Not necessarily." Vail chewed on that. "But if that's the case, then he could be a local. And he committed the other murders when he was traveling."

"That would mean he's hanging around for a while in each place, regardless of the risk that poses. Or as you said, bringing his stuff with him."

"I feel like we're going in circles."

Russell turned the engine over. "Let's head back to my office, get in front of a couple of computers and do some research on local health food stores."

"What if he sells to a company that specializes in small batch product distribution to specialty stores?"

Russell pulled out of the parking lot. "Is that a thing?"

"Don't know about soap specifically, but yeah. Specialty chocolate bars are sometimes distributed in small batches."

"For our killer, it'd give him a big advantage. He could stay at home, in whatever state he lives in—Hawaii or somewhere in the Midwest, who knows—and kill elsewhere. Talk about lowering your risk of being caught. Hundreds or thousands of miles away from your crimes."

Vail thought that through. "No," she finally said. "I mean, yeah, that'd give him certain advantages. But he chooses his victims. He has to pick them. *Emotionally* he has to do that. He's missing the direct contact with the victim. He can't *feel* them dying. Poisoning like this is done from a distance. If he can't get satisfaction from killing this mother figure, Mary, there's no enjoyment for him. He has to at least personally select her."

Russell snorted. "No 'enjoyment' in killing?"

"Think about it logically. They're all named Mary. They're all around the same age, with the same hair color. That can't happen randomly if he's not there to choose his victims."

"Good point."

"But the fact that most male poisoners kill in a medical setting—which this obviously isn't—still bothers me."

"Because male serial killers kill up close."

"Yeah, violently. With their hands—usually. They like to feel the life leaving the vic's body. And slicing, cutting, interacting with it in some way."

Russell shuddered.

"Welcome to my world."

He was quiet for a moment. "Isn't that narrow thinking? Generalizing? Shoe horning people into categories? I mean, yeah, maybe there's a book on this stuff but not everyone fits neatly into arbitrary classifications."

"True, but we—"

"Look at prescription medication. There're always outliers, a very small percentage of people who have side effects that ninety-nine percent of the test subjects don't experience."

"Of course. Look, I've been doing this a long time. Just when we think we've got everything figured out, some killer does something that throws us a curve, doesn't fit our experience and research on serial offender behavior. We like to think we have all the answers, but fact is, these offenders don't read the book."

"So there *is* a book."

"Lots of books. For some reason we profilers feel we have to tell every goddam killer out there how to practice and perfect his craft."

Russell hung a right, then glanced at Vail. "So when are you going to write your book?"

Vail snorted. "Not till I retire. Obviously."

Russell examined her face. "I think you're a certified nut case."

"That's the nicest thing you've ever said to me. Now, as to our UNSUB, I believe he's right here, on Oahu. But he is somewhat mobile. How long he stays in one location, we have no way of knowing. Just means we've gotta move fast before he decides to pick up and leave."

"So you're sure he's male?"

"Hell no. The fact that men almost always kill up close and personal really bugs me. Poisoning is a female MO except in a medical setting, which this isn't. So I'm gonna assume he is a she. Until proven otherwise."

"Are you always this ditzy?"

"Definitely not." Vail thought a moment. "Must be the Hawaiian air."

"So are we referring to him as a she? Or she as a he?"

"Now you're confusing *me*. Until I figure this out, we'll go by the book. He's a she. Female offender."

"Maybe this will make sense in the morning. Because right now . . ."

"Right now let's not focus on gender. I know that flies in the face of reason, but—"

"And why would this be any different?" He shook his head. "Fine—we'll put gender aside for now. We're looking for a woman."

"We're looking for a serial poisoner. Does that help?"

Russell shrugged. "A serial poisoner who could be male or female, who could live anywhere. Maybe even on the Big Island and spend a couple weeks on Oahu. Does his—I mean *her*—killing, then returns." Russell's cell vibrated. He extracted it from his inside jacket pocket and shoved it against his left ear. He listened a moment, but his face betrayed him. "You're kidding me." He glanced at Vail, then said, "Okay. Be there in fifteen, give or take."

"Problem?"

"Another vic. I'd call that a problem. And that's not our only problem because apparently the media's figured out what's going on."

"How do you know?"

"Because they're already there."

"Shit."

Russell snorted. "Look on the bright side. Maybe the reporter's figured out if the killer's a man or woman."

14

Waverly Meece was a pillar of the community, a man who served his country, a man who volunteered at church, a man who would carry groceries for you if you needed the help."

The reverend cradled the Bible in both hands as he spoke. A dozen or so people had been standing in the cold on a gently sloping grass hill in one of the many Brooklyn cemeteries, a plot Waverly's company had paid for as part of its benefit package. The dreary, low-hanging clouds threatened rain as the ceremony droned on. Friends sniffled. A few coughed back tears.

Scott and Phillip Meece stood stoically, in shock if not fighting a sense of being overwhelmed, Phillip's arm around his younger brother's shoulder.

Moments later, as the service drew to a close, Scott stared at his father's coffin as it was cranked lower into the hole in the ground. He had said only a few words since his father's death a week and a half ago. Phillip was equally in shock but was able to attend school and complete his homework—barely.

Although only four years older, Phillip had taken the loss of Waverly with greater maturity—perhaps because he felt he had no choice. Perhaps because Scott needed him to be strong. Perhaps because he now saw himself as the man of the house. It was heady stuff for a young man who had turned ten not long ago, who no longer had a father figure to guide and mentor him.

Waverly had two siblings, but both had died young: his sister from an accident at work and his brother from prostate cancer. Mary was an only child.

They were alone, but they had each other, Phillip told Scott when they had gotten home from the cemetery. The boys sat in Phillip's room, a larger space than Scott's—which was wide enough to hold a twin mattress and little else. Their father had told Phillip it had been a walk-in closet that they had gotten permission from the landlord to convert into an extra bedroom. Waverly and two friends worked all weekend to put up a wall and break down another. But it kept them from having to move. It was a rent-controlled apartment, so it was valuable beyond considerations of comfort for a child. Mary wanted to stick a bunk bed in Phillip's room, but Waverly had grown up sharing a room, and he felt it was better to live in a room not much larger than a closet and retain more privacy, especially when the boys got older.

"You've gotta talk to me," Phillip said.

Scott kept his gaze on the grimy carpet, at his cemetery-dirt-crusted dress shoes. He shook his head.

"It's just us in here. Mom can't hear."

He lifted his chin slowly, his lips tightly shut. His eyes searched Phillip's face and then he dropped his gaze.

"I'm gonna look after you. I'll make sure nothing bad happens."

Scott did not speak.

"What do you want? Just tell me." But Scott did not answer him. Finally, Phillip turned on his radio and "Eye of the Tiger" by Survivor was playing. He got down on his knees and dug underneath his bed. Finding what he was looking for, he pulled out his Nintendo Game & Watch device, switched on the handheld monochrome screen, and played *Ball*. A few minutes later, he offered it to Scott, who merely shook his head.

Phillip frowned, then went back to his handset and was engrossed in the game when suddenly Scott spoke. His voice was raspy, perhaps because he had hardly spoken in so long.

"I want to kill her. That's what I want."

Phillip swung his gaze to Scott. His answer was as succinct as it was surprising: "Not unless I do it first."

15

They arrived at the home of a middle-aged woman in the small town of Wahiawa. There weren't a lot of streetlamps, and they were miles away from Honolulu, so there was not much in the way of light pollution. The sliver of a moon was muted by the deepening cloud cover.

Before they got out of their vehicle, a text came through from Robby:

your instincts were right as usual
asked around my old buddies at vienna pd
ferraro was a colleague of

wait for it

chase hancock
remember him 😜

Vail texted back:

can never forget him
or the dead eyes case
for obvious reasons
so what

Vail tapped her index finger on her thigh. Robby's response:

so like i said
ferraro was a colleague of hancocks
and

Vail thought about it some more. Was it enough to cause intense dislike of someone, even if she and Hancock had a contentious relationship? Probably not.

and what else

"You about ready?" Russell asked.
"Just a minute."
He sighed.
Robby's reply vibrated in her hand.

hancock is ferraros bro in law

Vail sighed. So this was personal.

crap
ok thanks honey
ill take it from here
talk soon love u

"All right," Vail said, shoving the phone in her pocket. "Let's go."

Vail got out of the Ford and saw a sedan parked just outside the cordoned off crime scene, a newspaper logo printed on a yellow placard in the windshield above the word PRESS. A man was leaning his buttocks against the fender of his vehicle, but upon seeing their car pull up, he pushed off and made his way to the taped-off boundary.

Vail made an end run around the reporter, using a couple of large officers as offensive linemen clearing a path for their running back.

As she and Russell approached the front door, Vail stifled a yawn and Russell badged Ty Palakiko, the first cop on scene.

"Aloha," Palakiko said.

"Aloha." Russell glanced around. "Where's our vic?"

"Inside. Living room, near the back door."

"Name?"

"Let me guess," Vail said. "Mary."

Palakiko looked up from his spiral pad. "Yeah. Mary Grant. You know her?"

"I know the ritual."

Palakiko narrowed his eyes. "The what?"

"Never mind," Russell said. "What else can you tell us?"

The young officer looked down at his notes. "Sixty-six. Works at Macy's."

"Which department?" Vail asked.

Palakiko glanced at Russell, then back at Vail. "Huh? I didn't ask. Is—is that important?"

Vail slipped on her left bootie. "Nope. Just yanking your chain."

Palakiko frowned.

"Go on," Vail said as she moved to her right foot. "What else do you have for us?"

Palakiko waited until she stood up, then said, "You know about 'aloha,' Agent Vail?"

She snorted. "Of course. Means hello and good-bye."

"No," the officer said with not a hint of respect. "In Hawaiian, the true meaning of 'aloha' is love, peace, compassion—a way of life where you try to influence others with your spirit."

"That's a helluva lot of meaning packed into one five-letter word."

"And yet you continue to be disrespectful."

Who the hell is this guy?

"Respect our customs," Palakiko said. "When in Rome, do as the Romans do."

"I thought I was in Hawaii." She grabbed Russell's arm and whispered in his right ear. "Did I say that out loud?"

Russell fought back a smile.

Palakiko shook his head. "Sarcasm has no place here."

"I'm a native New Yorker. Sarcasm is *our* 'aloha.' It's also in our spirit. It can mean 'I love you, man'—like 'aloha,' that'd be the peace and compassion part. It can also mean, 'Don't fuck with me, asshole.' That'd be—well . . . hmmph. There's no parallel to 'aloha' for that."

Russell cleared his throat. "Who discovered the body?"

Palakiko frowned at Vail—again—then tore his gaze away and faced Russell. "Co-worker. Ms. Grant went home for lunch but never returned. Co-worker called, got no answer, so she came by. Went around back and saw the vic on the floor through the living room window."

"Co-worker still here?" Vail asked.

"It's late. Sent her home. Got her cell." He jotted it down and tore the page off his pad, then handed it to Russell, ignoring Vail's outstretched palm.

Guess I hurt his feelings.

"Good work, officer," Vail said. "And I'm sorry for being sarcastic. Aloha."

Palakiko was not buying it. He frowned again.

Someone's spirit *needs an attitude adjustment.*

They proceeded down a narrow hallway to where Mary Grant was located. She was lying face down near a door. They knelt and took a closer look at her face. From what they could tell, she had sustained an abrasion from the fall, but no overt signs of trauma indicative of a violent altercation.

Of course there wasn't. The offender was miles away.

A moment later, Vail stood up. "Let's go check out her bathroom. But I think we know what we're going to find."

"CSU is on the way." Russell consulted his phone. "Two minutes out."

Vail did not want to risk contaminating the area, so she waited in the hallway as Russell visually inspected the bar of soap and trash can contents.

"Looks like the others. Let's leave it alone and let CSU bag it and do their thing. I doubt we're going to find anything unusual."

They walked outside to get some fresh air and stood on the porch, about thirty feet from the crime scene tape, which was stretched across the edges of the postage stamp lawn.

A moment later, the forensics technician was exiting her vehicle.

"Process the scene normally," Russell said, "but we're fairly confident there's a wrapper or two in the bathroom garbage that we need to be very careful with. And the bar of soap."

"Rush on this stuff," Vail said.

"Isn't there always?" the tech asked. "Do my best."

"Agent Vail?"

Vail turned and saw a man in his fifties looking directly at her—the journalist she had spotted earlier. He was holding a digital recorder and a lanyard with press identification bearing the same newspaper logo as the one emblazoned on the sedan.

"Agent Vail," he repeated. "Can you comment on the victim?"

"I can't, sorry."

"But—just a few questions."

Vail growled internally. "Sorry. I can't."

"But if you're here, does that mean there's a serial killer on the island?"

This guy knows me somehow. But he doesn't look familiar.

"Please," the reporter said. "Just give me a minute of your time."

If I pull my Glock, I've got a clear headshot. Problem solved.

Instead, she grinned and said, "Aloha."

The man was not prepared for this response. He closed his mouth and tucked his chin back.

Vail slipped back into the house with Russell and peered out the living room window through a gap in the camel-colored drapes. "We're losing our advantage. Once they go public with this, the UNSUB's gonna realize we know it's murder and not a natural death."

"Nothing we can do about it. But that guy seemed to know you. Wanna ask him if he'll bury the story? At least for a few days?"

"You ever know a journalist willing to delay a story he's broken? One that's potentially big, involving a serial killer on Oahu?"

"Not personally. Nope."

"Didn't think so. Let's make better use of our time. We have an army. Let's deploy them."

"Army? Oahu's got a huge military presence, but—"

"Not that kind of army. The Honolulu police force. We can draw up a list of stores and send cops to see which sell the kind of soap our UNSUB makes."

"I'll make a call."

As she waited for the phone to connect, Vail said, "I just had a disturbing thought. What if she doesn't make the soap at all?

What if she buys the soap and rewraps certain bars with the toxin?"

Russell's face went blank as the line was answered. He refocused and made the request, then hung up and faced Vail. "Yeah. What if?"

"Didn't mean to freak you out. It's a possibility, but we can't consider all possibilities. We have to determine by reasonable inference what's the most likely scenario and pursue that. If it doesn't bear fruit, we back up and start expanding our assumptions. Agreed?"

"Agreed."

"An offender like this, if he's a male, would not be getting as much satisfaction from the kill because it's more removed."

"Because he doesn't see the victim die."

"Right. He doesn't *feel* her die. He needs to get that connection to the kill in some other way. Again, this is extremely unusual—if not the first offender I've encountered like this. But if we accept this as an aberration, at least for now, his connection to the vic might come, at least in part, from him personally making the soap and wrapping specific bars with the toxin."

"I'll buy that. If it's a male."

"That's not all I'm selling." Vail's gaze drifted off into the dark streets of Wahiawa. "I overlooked something."

Russell waited a moment, then shifted his feet. "You gonna keep it to yourself?"

Vail groaned, then rubbed her temples. "Dammit. I need to figure out if the offender's male or female. This is too confusing."

"No shit."

She rocked her head back and stared at the sky. Closed her eyes. "The UNSUB needs to choose the right Mary, hand the bar to her personally. But Kuoko said that the victim's name is written in marker on the outer wrapper. Same person wrote the name in calligraphy on all the wrappers."

"So she pre-marks all the bars. Like it's the name of the soap."

"But the offender is writing their first *and* last names on the bars, so to do that you have to *personally* ask each woman her name at the time of sale, then write it on the wrapper. Right?"

"Good point."

Vail dropped her chin and yawned widely before answering. "Sorry. It's three hours later for me. Or actually six. My body's not sure what time zone it's in."

She sat down on the stoop and took a deep breath.

"You okay?"

"Thinking."

"That's good. I'll just stand here and look stupid while you . . . think."

"Yeah. Great . . . thanks."

A moment later, Vail got to her feet. "He's a guy."

"Who is?"

"The offender."

"Okay. You sure?"

"Don't start that again." She yawned, then shook her head, trying to wake up. "Here's my sleep deprived, confused, but entirely clear-headed thinking. The—"

"You realize that makes no sense."

"The UNSUB needs to interact with these women so he can choose which one he wants to kill. The interaction is extremely important to him, right? As we discussed, offenders feed off contact with their victims. Our UNSUB doesn't physically interact with his, so he needs to do it on some other level, another way of connecting with them. I shouldn't really say 'connecting,' because psychopaths—assuming he is one—don't really experience emotions like you and I do."

"Okay."

"So he *relates* to each woman on some level that has meaning to him. The victim being named Mary is extremely important to him. It's a big part of why he chooses that particular target. So he has to ask her name when she's in front of him. His excuse—so that it doesn't seem weird that this stranger is asking a woman her name— is that he personalizes the soap by writing her name in calligraphy on the wrapper. When he comes across a woman named Mary, if she fits his image of his mother, he gives her one of the bars that has the toxin."

"Mary's obviously an incredibly common name."

"Definitely helps in victim selection."

Russell nodded. "Okay. And what's convinced you he's a man and not a woman?"

"A woman wouldn't need to interact with the vic like our UNSUB does. She'd find some other way of poisoning her victims because the one-on-one contact is less important. And riskier. Plus, there's no connection with the vics."

Vail stopped and thought a moment. "This isn't set in stone. There are exceptions."

"Nothing is absolute."

"I just want you to realize that there were one or two female serial killers who *did* need the physical contact. Males have unfortunately given us a rather large database to study. But women, there've been so few of them that it's hard to craft an accurate profile. Like, one, Juana Barraza, in Mexico, she physically punished her victims, who were all women sixty and over. She brutalized them, strangled and bludgeoned them. They reminded her of her mother."

"Just like our killer."

"Yeah. Barraza was a professional wrestler, a large, strong woman who had no problem overpowering her victims. So she isn't the best example to study."

"Because someone like her can kill like a man. Overpower the vic."

"Right. So let's throw Barraza out."

"Happy to."

"If we follow the facts—the best facts we have—that leads me back to my belief that the UNSUB is a man."

"Great. Since that's settled," Russell said with an eye roll, "how long does he have to be in contact with people before he not only finds a woman named Mary but one that 'fits' his mother?"

Vail shrugged. "The answer might simply be 'long enough.' I have a feeling he's been doing this for a while. And he's apparently good at what he does because he's had success finding victims. If this method didn't work for him, he'd have to find them some other way."

He nodded. "You make a good point."

"It happens sometimes."

Russell laughed.

"And 'fitting the image' of his mother doesn't necessarily have to be physical. Could be a way she says a word, a look she gives him. A phrase she uses, perfume, food that she—"

"I get the point. Could be something we may not associate with the real object of his violence. Not that we know who that is, anyway."

"Not yet. But we may figure it out—and when that time comes, I don't want to be blind to the fact that there are other things that can set him off besides physical appearance."

"Got it."

"And I think red is important to him."

"Red. Representing blood?"

"I don't think so. I think it's got to do with the color. He writes their names in red marker on the wrappers. And there was a trace amount of red dye in the soap."

"Unless it was contamination."

"Can't say just yet, but I'm betting it wasn't an accident."

"Because?"

"Red has meaning to him. For some reason, he associates it with his mother. He's incorporated it into his ritual."

"Because it's got nothing to do with him being able to kill the women."

Vail nodded. "For whatever reason, adding the dye to the soap while he's making it is important to him."

"If your theory is correct."

"If it's correct. Yeah." Vail yawned again. "Sorry." She shook her head vigorously, trying to knock away the cobwebs. "He's missing out on the actual kill, the physical, personal violence that so many of these offenders crave. So interacting with the woman at the point of sale, and possibly even the hunt for the right victim, has to be what fuels him and feeds his anger."

"You realize you're repeating yourself."

She looked at him with glassy eyes. "Huh?"

"Sounds like you're trying to convince yourself of something."

"I'm thinking out loud. I'm out on a limb here, so yeah, maybe I'm having some trouble accepting it."

"I don't think I want to know what an argument sounds like inside your head."

"Worse thing is that because he doesn't interact with the body—which is key to understanding what makes him tick—there are fewer behaviors for me to evaluate."

"What you're saying is that you could be so wrong about this we could be wasting precious hours. Days."

"It's possible, but I don't think so. Thing is, I don't want to disregard what we've found at the crime scenes. I have to fight the urge to make my profile fit the evidence. The profile has to come from the offender's behaviors and my analysis of what's going on with the . . . uh . . . the UNSUB." She closed her eyes. "Okay, I think my brain is officially powering down."

"Let's get you to your hotel room."

"Not yet."

"You can hardly think straight."

"Nice try, but this is the way I usually am."

He laughed again.

"Take me to the journalist working on the story. The one we saw at Mary Grant's house."

Russell snorted. "It's late. They're long gone."

"Don't be so sure. They're going to be working on that story. Front page stuff."

"You mean home page?"

Vail chuckled. "Both."

"We don't even know which paper it was."

"*You* don't know what paper it was. Speak for yourself. He's with the *Waikiki Vacationer*."

"Are you clairvoyant too?"

"Just observant. Printed on a placard in his car. And on the lanyard around his neck."

He pursed his lips. "Impressive."

"Thanks."

"Don't let it go to your head."

"Too late," Vail said, closing her eyes. "But that's a good thing. Maybe it'll keep me awake."

16

They arrived at the offices of the *Waikiki Vacationer* in downtown Honolulu fifteen minutes later.

Russell pulled to a stop at the curb. At this time of night, parking was not an issue.

Vail popped open her door—as did Russell.

"Wait here," she said.

"Why?"

"Whatever connection I have with this guy, there's some kind of personal element to it. He knows me from somewhere. May be easier to establish a professional rapport if it's just him and me."

"Fine."

"Unless I pissed him off big-time on a case or gave him some sarcastic remark when he asked for a quote."

"In which case he may tell you to take a hike."

"He won't do that." Vail fought back a yawn. "He's gonna try to get me to talk about what's going on. He wants to confirm that it's a serial killer. I do that for him, he can confidently report his story. A serial killer/profiler headline will sell papers. And his name will be associated with breaking the news."

Russell pulled open the glovebox and extracted a protein bar. "Here. It's got some chocolate and quinoa, green tea ext—"

"All you had to say was chocolate." Vail grabbed it and tore it open, took a large bite.

"What if . . ." Russell stopped, thinking.

Vail chewed, waited. "What if *what*?"

He shrugged and pulled his door shut. Vail did the same. "Maybe this is splitting hairs, but why can't you tell this reporter it's *not* a serial killer?"

"You mean lie?"

Russell shrugged. "Maybe not. I mean, is there a real definition of serial killer? Why not just tell him it's not a serial case. If he presses you, you can call the guy a . . . a, I dunno, a spree killer? Then you wouldn't be lying."

Vail laughed. "That's a loaded question."

He lifted his brow. "I thought it was a *good* question."

"Nothing wrong with the question per se. But there's a story behind it. Back in 2005, the BAU held a serial murder symposium in San Antonio. Idea was to bring together experts in the field to definitively define serial murder."

"Isn't it obvious? I thought the definition of serial killer is common knowledge. A series of murders committed by the same individual."

"Yes and no. Bureau's had a definition—and Congress even legislated one to help determine which cases the BAU could legally get involved with in terms of jurisdiction. Not for taking over cases, but for assisting local law enforcement. But different definitions were used by detectives, clinicians, academics, and researchers. They differed in terms of the number of murders committed by the offender, his motivation, and the time periods between murders. Important details."

"And that created problems."

"For ViCAP alone, yeah. If we define these cases differently, they'll be reported differently and we may not link them properly— or we could miss out on linking them at all. Might skew the results and detectives could end up missing something important."

"I don't get why this makes my question complicated."

"During that symposium, the definition of serial murder was formalized as the killing of two or more victims by the same offender or offenders in separate events."

"So our killer definitely appears to fit the definition. But why can't he be a spree killer? Is there some fudge factor we can, I don't know, exploit? A white lie."

Vail pointed at Russell. "That's the dicey part. Before that symposium, spree murder was considered two or more murders committed by an offender or offenders, without a cooling-off period."

"Okay, so basically the lack of a cooling-off period was the difference between spree and serial. But how long is a cooling off period?"

"Yeah," Vail said with a chuckle. "Exactly. That was never defined. And because it was ambiguous, it was open to interpretation. The symposium's panel voted to get rid of spree as a separate category and to shift those cases into serial at one end of the spectrum and mass murder at the other."

"So spree doesn't exist? As a category?"

"Not in the Bureau's lexicon."

"How'd that work out?"

Vail bobbed her head. "Some may say okay, others, not too good. Problem is, there are hundreds of cases that don't really fit. A mentor of mine, Mark Safarik—who was at that symposium and voiced his objection to getting rid of spree—wrote a book with Katherine Ramsland, a well-known violent crime researcher. After studying all these cases, they proposed restoring the category and broke it up into lots of subcategories. It removed a lot of the ambiguity and confusion because there are lots of cases that don't really fit the serial or mass murder definitions—but do fit spree."

"What's the new definition?"

"Spree is three or more victims in two or more locations with the first murder acting as the inciting incident, continuing the spree. So different locations, but one event. Serial is *two* or more victims in different locations with some undefined intervening time period. Key point is that serial has some passage of time between victims and it involves separate events."

"So there's a difference," Russell said, glancing off into the distance, disappointment permeating his tone.

"I couldn't in good conscience call it spree, even if it serves our purpose of protecting our ability to catch the offender."

He grunted. "How about the greater good? Throw him off the scent, kill his story's impact to save some lives of future victims?"

"Greater good." She took in a deep breath and sighed audibly. *My OPSIG colleagues have made that very argument on just about every one of our black ops missions.* Vail shook her head. "I'd rather try to influence him to see it our way without lying."

"I admire your moral compass. Good luck."

"Bar hit the spot. Infused my brain with glucose. I can think straight again."

"Oh, great. Now we're in tro—"

"Adam," she said firmly. "Don't finish that sentence." She winked at him, then got out and made her way into the building.

The facility was aging—it was a structure that was probably showing its years the last time she was in Oahu.

She pushed into the lobby and found that security was surprisingly lax—there was none—but media budgets were under intense pressure these days, so money was cut wherever possible. There were just so many writers and editors you could lay off before you no longer had a viable enterprise that could cover the news. No matter how much of a deterrent armed guards were, they did not pay the bills or increase subscriptions.

Vail made her way up to the *Waikiki Vacationer* offices, which were identified by a small wood sign on the wall beside a nondescript entrance at the end of the corridor.

She tried the knob, but it was locked. After a couple of raps on the wood, a woman in her forties pulled the door open, hair tied back and wearing no makeup. "Can I help you?"

Vail held up her badge. "I've got some questions for a reporter who was at a crime scene today. In Wahiawa."

"Ah. That's Travis."

"Yeah. Travis."

Travis? Not ringing a bell.

Vail was led down a long hallway, boxes stacked on one side and reams of paper on the other. They navigated the obstacles and ended up at a small office. The woman motioned Vail in.

"Travis, you have a visitor."

Vail entered, turned around, and realized they were now alone. She swung back toward Travis, whose mouth was agape with shock.

"Didn't expect to see me?"

"Uh, no. Not after you blew me off."

"Wasn't personal. But that's actually why I'm here."

Travis tilted his head left. "That right?"

"Where do we know each other from?"

"You really don't remember."

"Travis, I can be a sarcastic bitch. So when you ask stupid questions, expect to get stupid answers."

Travis snorted while nodding. "Of course you don't remember, otherwise you wouldn't have asked."

Vail pointed at him. "Exactly. So . . ."

"You used to be a detective. Why don't I let you figure it out where we know each other from?"

"Why don't we not?"

Travis smiled.

Now he's starting to piss me off. But he probably knows why I'm here. He's toying with me.

"Let me get right to the point. I don't want you to print that story."

Travis laughed. A hearty belly laugh, the kind that—at 11:00 PM or 5:00 AM, whatever time it was for her—she did not appreciate.

Vail counted to ten, knowing that Robby would be so very proud of her for not grabbing Travis by the shirt collar and pinning him against the wall. Because then a complaint would be filed and Thomas Gifford, her assistant special agent in charge, and her often unreasonable unit chief, Stacey DiCarlo, would get pissed at her and make her apologize . . . as well as have to pull strings so that the newspaper did not publish a nasty account of the altercation. Which would inevitably be picked up nationally.

Vail realized that she had been daydreaming so long that Travis had stopped laughing.

"You didn't find that funny," he said.

"Oh. Was I supposed to?"

"Look, Agent Vail. You've been around the block a few dozen times, right?"

Seriously? How old does he think I am?

"What's your point?"

"You know how this works. We report the news. We're not in bed with the police. If we compromise our journalistic values, society will lose its faith in us. And I don't even have to get into the First Amendment issues your request raises."

"Whoa. Before you go all US Constitution on me, I'm just asking that you delay publishing your story for a few days."

"Define 'a few.'" He grinned. "Sorry. I'm a writer. Words matter."

"That they do. They matter to FBI agents, too." She grinned back.

"Right. So, to you, a few means?"

"Three days."

"Hmm." He leaned forward onto his paper-strewn desk, steepled his fingers in front of his lips. "What you ask is difficult, Agent Vail."

"Only if you make it difficult."

"Karen . . ." He shook his head in pity. "Can I call you Karen?"

Oh, now he's really getting on my nerves.

She shrugged good-naturedly. "Why not. After all, I'm calling you Travis. If calling me Karen makes you more amenable to my request, of course."

He chuckled. "Sorry. Doesn't enter into the equation."

"Then 'Agent Vail' will suffice."

Travis nodded and smirked—as if thinking, "That one I deserved."

"C'mon. Three days is not too much to ask."

He spread his palms apart. "What if the *News* gets wind of it. Or the *Times*. Channel Four. Or—"

"That's a risk, I get it. And if I find out about it, I'll ask them to delay the story, too."

Travis leaned back in his creaky old secretary chair. "Why is this so important to you?"

"Good question. And I'm glad you asked."

"I'm paid to ask good questions."

Here we go. Moral compass.

"We don't think the offender knows that *we* know these are murders."

Travis squinted, as if that was a stupid comment. "He *killed* the woman. How could he think the police wouldn't realize it's murder?"

Vail bit the inside of her bottom lip. "Active investigation. I can't—"

"How predictable. You want something *from* me but you won't give anything *to* me. One-way street."

"It's not for *me*, Travis. That's where you've got it wrong. I get nothing from it. I'm gonna be out of here in a few days or so. But if I can't help catch this killer, more women are going to die. So do it for your fellow Hawaiians."

He snapped his fingers. "You used the term 'offender.' And you referred to 'murders.' Plural." His cadence increased. "And you're here, and you believe more people are at risk. So it *is* a serial killer."

Vail did not deny it, keeping the needle pointing north.

"Damn, I knew it. Thanks for confirming that." Travis threw his head back and groaned. "You make a compelling case. As much as I hate to admit it."

"So you'll do it?"

He closed his eyes.

"Three days, Travis. That's all I'm asking for."

He sighed audibly and slowly raised his lids, locked gazes with her.

"Be like the Nike goddess of strength," Vail said. "Just do it."

He spread his hands. "How could I not?"

"Do what?"

Vail turned around and saw the woman who had let her into the office standing in the doorway.

Travis sat forward. "Agent Vail has asked me to delay publication of the story on the Wahiawa murder."

"The suspected serial?"

Travis's eyes flicked over to Vail's. "Confirmed serial."

"Yeah," the woman said. "Not gonna happen."

Vail rose from her chair. "And you are?"

"Sorry we weren't formally introduced. I'm Liz Warren, editor, publisher, and owner of the *Vacationer.*"

I don't think she's got enough titles.

Vail took Warren's hand and shook—less than enthusiastically.

"Sounds like you're asking us not to print a story, Agent Vail. Do I have that right?"

"Not at all. I'm asking you to delay it for a few—for three days."

Warren sighed. "Can't do it. I'm sure you understand."

"Funny. I was going to say the same thing to you."

"I understand you're asking me to do something that threatens to erode the public's trust in our paper. We've worked hard every single day to earn our stellar reputation. I'm not going to throw it away by doing you a favor."

"Let's get something straight. This is *not* a favor for—"

"If it gets out that we had a story of interest to the people of Oahu—one affecting their safety and security—and we chose not to warn them that there's a serial killer on the loose, we'll never be trusted in the same way again. Trust affects everything, from people who subscribe and read our paper to impeding our ability to work within the community to investigate and get answers from police, executives, and politicians."

"Adherence to high ethical standards is the first thing drilled into the head of every candidate attending the police academy," Vail said. "But this isn't a question of ethics. I'm asking you to delay publication temporarily, not permanently."

"We understand what you're asking." Warren folded her forearms across her chest. "Many years ago in journalism school at the University of Missouri, my professor and mentor gave us two criteria to use when evaluating a decision we were about to make. First was, 'Can I justify my decision if it's made public?' And the second was, 'How would I feel if my decision made the front page tomorrow?'"

Vail nodded thoughtfully. "Sounds like he forgot to teach you the third criterion: the part where your decision costs the lives of innocent women. Because some of these offenders are inspired by what the media reports on. What you write, what you don't." She stopped and studied Warren's face to gauge if she was getting anywhere. "So let me give you two of *my* criteria to consider when evaluating what to do." Vail held up her right thumb: "Can you justify your decision if more women die because you chose to ignore our request?" She added the index finger. "And second, what if *that* makes the front page tomorrow?"

Warren forced a smug smile. "Agent Vail. Travis and I appreciate you coming by and enlightening us as to your philosophy regarding journalistic ethics. If I ever resign from the university staff or hear of a professorial position open up, I'll be sure to suggest your name to the department chair."

Wow, she took Bitch 101. And 102. She's good.

"I'm in awe of your sarcasm." Vail glanced at Travis with a raised brow. "If you move forward with this story, Ms. Warren, and the offender goes off because of it, I don't think you'll need to *resign* from the university."

"She means you'll be fired," Travis said.

Warren frowned. "Thank you, Travis. I gathered the meaning."

"Very good then." Vail clapped her hands together. "I see this has been time well spent. Thank you so much for your understanding and wisdom." She shot one last look at Travis, again wondering where she knew him from, then turned and skirted Warren's left shoulder on her way out of the room, giving it a gentle brush. It was not much, but it was enough to send a message. A little whiff of testosterone.

All these years working around men in the unit has *been good for something. Go figure.*

17

Scott Meece sat on the floor in the corner of the living room behind the paisley couch. Man after man entered the apartment, each bearing a six-pack of beer.

Nick James, a six-foot-three man who strained the scales at 280 pounds, greeted his friends from the Brooklyn ironworkers union as they passed through the door.

Nick had moved his stuff into the apartment two weeks ago, the latest plaything Mary brought home from a bar off Fifty-Ninth Street. He made himself at home, arriving with a couple of suitcases that he left at the front door and made Scott and Phillip struggle to carry into the bedroom.

"Better get used to him," their mother said. "Nick's movin' in. You'll listen to him like you listen to me. You hear?"

That evening, he gave Scott an intense look, his gaze lingering way too long before Scott got creeped out and ran into his room. A week later, Nick stepped into the bathroom while Scott was peeing. He watched until Scott put himself away and flushed. Nick nodded approval, then left. Scott wanted to tell Phillip but was too embarrassed.

Now, as the small apartment crowded with men who looked and acted a lot like Nick—as if one was not enough—Scott decided to get out before it was too late and they started bossing him around. What's more, he did not care about some stupid football game. In fact, he cared more about a different game, one that he could play *himself* instead of watching other guys, on television, having fun.

He slowly got up, hoping to slip out unnoticed, and headed for his room.

"Hey," one of the men yelled. "Mary—get me a beer!"

"Get it your own fuckin' self, Vinnie. What the hell do I look like, ya maid?"

"Super Bowl's startin'. Don't wanna miss the kickawf."

"Giants and Jets ain't playin', so why do ya care?"

"It's the big game," Nick said, as if that would settle the matter. He held up a bottle. "This shit sucks."

"Ain't as good as Rheingold," his friend agreed. "Miss it."

Barry Manilow sang the National Anthem and the faces of Pat Summerall and John Madden filled the screen as the teams readied for the kickoff.

The Los Angeles Raiders scored first, a blocked punt recovered in the end zone toward the end of the first quarter.

By the third, Nick and his friends were laughing loudly, peeing all over the floor in the bathroom, and lounging on top of—and in front of—the sofa. They were talking nonsense, cheering, booing, and yelling.

Then a commercial during a break in the action caught their attention: some kind of futuristic scene from a movie none of them was familiar with, ending with a fit woman carrying a sledgehammer and hurling it at a movie screen. The impact caused an explosion, the following words scrolling up from the bottom:

On January 24, Apple Computer will
introduce Macintosh. And you'll see
why 1984 won't be like "1984."

"I don't get it," Nick said.

"Yeah," one of his less inebriated friends, said. "Like that book, *1984*. Orwell. That's what that was, like a scene from *1984*. Big brother."

"Whose big brother?" Nick asked.

Mary slapped the back of his head. "*Phillip* is Scott's big brother, you doofus."

Nick looked up, his body swaying left to right in the La-Z-Boy lounger. "I think I had too much."

"You *think*? No question 'bout it," Mary said. "Time for everyone to leave."

"No fuckin' way!" one of the men slurred.

"Game's almost over," Nick said. He held up his bottle. "Jusss like fifteen minutes left. Maybe an hour."

Mary shook her head in disgust. "Last time we do this."

"Gotta pee," Nick said. He pulled himself out of the soft chair and, carrying his half-empty bottle with him, stumbled into the bathroom. After peeing—*in* the toilet, all *over* the toilet, and on the floor—he flushed and walked out. Passing Scott's room, he stopped and heard something. Turned the knob.

Scott was hunched over the Nintendo Game & Watch. He must have heard the door open because he looked up. Nick tipped back the beer and drained the last ounce. He kicked the door closed behind him and locked it. Seconds later, his thick moist right hand was clamped over the boy's mouth and he was pulling down his pants with the left.

He repeatedly jammed the end of the bottle into Scott's rectum.

18

Russell sat back in his car seat and reclined it a few degrees. Vail was still in the office with the journalist. What the hell could they be discussing this long?

He stared at the roof and ran through the facts of the case. As he mulled some of Vail's comments regarding the killer, his phone rang.

He leaned his left shoulder against the door and dug the handset out of his pocket. "Chief."

"We need to talk, Detective."

"Okay, sure. I'm listening."

"Face-to-face."

"I'll be in at nine tom—"

"Not tomorrow. Tonight."

Russell's gaze flicked over to the dashboard clock. "It's real late, Chief. Can't we do this over the—"

"It may be late, but you're still working."

Russell moved his seat back into a driving position. "True. But . . . uh, how do you know?"

"I'm in the car behind you," Ferraro said. "I expect my detectives to have better observational skills."

Seconds later, Russell's passenger car door opened and Ferraro sat down heavily.

This is kind of creepy.

"You just happen to be in the car behind me, Chief?"

"Yeah. That's right. And good thing, too, because we need to discuss your collaboration with the FBI."

"By FBI, do you mean Agent Vail? I, uh, I picked up on something when I introduced her and I hoped I was just reading into it."

"And what did your honed detective skills detect?"

"Well, some . . . animosity on your part."

"Oh," Ferraro said with a sardonic chuckle, "you're mistaken."

Russell paused. He knew he had not misread Ferraro's demeanor.

"Sir, with all due respect, I don't think so."

"Well here's where you're wrong. You sensed a lot more than *just* animosity. She's a cancer. I don't want her within two states of any of our cases. But since you already made the request and the taxpayers incurred significant expense to fly her here, I'll give you a pass. Just make sure she doesn't fuck us over."

"She's been helpful. No problems."

"Give it time."

Russell was not sure what to make of that comment. "Sir, if you can provide me some details as to what happened, I can be better prepared to handle—"

"Nothing I care to discuss. Just watch your back."

"She was referred to me by an inspector with SFPD. I was there in San Francisco when she helped with a serial case. Couldn't have broken it without her."

"I don't trust her. And I don't know about you, but I value my career."

"Thanks for the advice," Russell said.

"It's more than advice. It's a warning." Ferraro turned away and looked out the windshield.

Russell was quiet, staring—without realizing it—at his boss's profile. When Ferraro turned to face him, Russell asked, "Can I ask why you don't trust her?"

"I don't owe you an explanation."

"Of course not, but—"

"That said, I've been very happy with your work, so I'll give you the courtesy of an answer. Let's just say that I'm not comfortable with her working one of my cases."

Russell did not think much of that explanation. He shook his head. "I don't understand, sir. Like I said, she's been helpful. What's the issue? Is it personal?"

Ferraro turned away. "That's not a question for you to ask. And it's not something you need to be concerned with. All you need to know is that she'll cause problems."

"I've obviously kept her in check. And I'll continue to do that."

"You'd better." Ferraro swiveled and grabbed hold of the handle. "Don't say I didn't warn you."

A moment after Ferraro left his car, Vail returned. She slammed the door closed. "Bitch."

"I take it things didn't go as you'd planned."

"Since I didn't really expect much, I guess I can't say I'm disappointed. Per se."

"How's that?"

"Disappointment is when reality falls short of expectations."

"Ah. And yet you're reacting as if you *did* expect a different result."

"I had the journalist ready to say yes, that he'd hold the story for three days."

"So a moral victory? No white lies?"

"No white lies, black lies, purple or blue. I told the truth. And I had him. I *had* him!" Vail slammed her right foot against the floorboard. "But then Queen Bitch walked in and shoved a rusty stake through my heart."

Russell cringed. "That's quite an image."

"Kind of how I feel."

"Wow."

Vail turned to face him. "Wow? What's that mean?"

"I didn't take you as someone who'd admit defeat so easily."

"You've known me . . . how many hours?"

"Doesn't matter. I've seen you work. In San Francisco, remember? And here. You don't let anyone or anything stand in your way."

Vail grunted. "Yeah."

"So we'll deal with it. Okay?"

She nodded. Then yawned. "I'm just . . . very tired. That protein bar wore off."

"So let me get you in bed." He held up a hand. "So to speak."

She yawned again.

He waved a hand in front of her face. "Sexually provocative Freudian slip. And no retort. Man, you *are* tired."

She let her eyes close. "I wasn't lying."

He twisted the key and turned the engine over. "I set you up at a place in Waikiki. My buddy's got an apartment in one of those high rises that's mostly time-share condos."

"Does it have a view of the beach?"

"Well not now. It's midnight."

Vail cracked open her left eye and pointed at him. "I deserved that."

"I'll leave it a mystery. You'll see when you wake up."

19

Vail's lids fluttered open at 5:30 AM. It was still dark out, so she made a cup of coffee, showered and dressed, then spent some time thinking about the case. When the sun rose, she pulled open the patio curtains and slider, stepped outside—and smiled. It was seventy degrees and the bright ball of orange was shimmering along the rippling surface of the Pacific Ocean.

Beach view? Check.

She stood there sipping her coffee and letting her mind wander somewhere out among the rolling waves. Her phone vibrated and she turned and retrieved it from the coffee table. "Hey honey. How's it going?"

DEA Special Agent Roberto Enrique Umberto Hernandez laughed. "It's snowing and twenty-one degrees in DC. How's it going there?"

"About seventy. Sun is rising over the ocean and I'm enjoying a cup of rich Kauai coffee on the patio."

"Sounds like life's tough. Was that info on Hancock helpful?"

Vail laughed. "For sure. Now I know why the assistant chief of Honolulu PD hates me. Before it was just a mystery."

"Sounds like you're off to a great start."

"Par for the course."

"I'm glad you said it, not me. How's the case going?"

"Different. Got us a poisoner. Another vic last night. But I think we're making headway."

"How long you expect to be there?"

Vail took another sip. "Who knows. As soon as I can get a better handle on what we're looking at, where I can feel confident in what I'm seeing, I'll give them my assessment and get the hell out of here. Doing a back-to-back isn't my idea of a good time. I just want to feel your body next to mine."

"Amen to that."

"How's *your* case going?"

"Eh." Robby grunted. "Change the subject. Something happy."

"I can do happy. Let's talk about our wedding. How about doing it in Oahu?"

"You want everyone to fly to Hawaii? Like . . . a ten-hour flight? Kind of expensive."

"Well we *were* talking about getting married out of town."

"New Orleans. Or Boston. Or Rhode Island. An hour or two by plane."

Okay, fine. "Have you seen Jonathan?"

"Had a late dinner with him last night. On campus. Big test coming up so probably won't see him till after."

"Miss you."

"Steer clear of the serial killer, okay?"

"Don't I always?"

"No, Karen, you don't. That's why I felt the need to say that."

"Fair enough. And you—DEA Special Agent Roberto Hernandez—just say no to drugs."

"I do, every day. Love you."

"Love you too."

Vail hung up and spent another moment watching the sun clear the horizon, then phoned Russell.

"Like the view?"

"What view?"

There was a second's hesitation before Russell said, "The beach."

"That's cruel," she said, gazing out over the Pacific. "My room overlooks a parking lot."

"No way. He told me it was one of his nicest units in—"

"It's fantastic. The ocean is so . . . I don't know . . . calming."

"Unlike your personality."

"Ow. That hurts."

"You're such a liar," Russell said. "But I still want your help. I'll be by in half an hour."

"Make it a couple of hours. Pick me up at the beach."

"Negatory," Russell said. "Half an hour. Out front by the valet stand."

20

Vail reluctantly bypassed the beach and instead headed to the elevator, mulling the particulars of the case and the paucity of behaviors the UNSUB exhibited. Was she wrong about the gender?

No. Could I defend it in the unit's Wednesday morning roundtable? No again.

If there was a rock nearby, she would kick it.

As she exited in the lobby, she saw a stack of *Waikiki Vacationer* newspapers on the concierge counter. The bold headline screamed at her as if it had a voice:

Famous FBI Profiler Spotted
At Local Crime Scene
Serial killer loose on Oahu

I'm famous?

Vail snagged a copy of the issue and looked at the byline: Travis Sharkey. She now had his last name—but still could not place him. Google, however, gave her the answer within thirty seconds: Sharkey was a longtime journalist who cut his teeth in Napa County on the Crush Killer case, which Vail not only worked, but it was one that had significant implications for her personally and professionally.

Regardless, she did not remember him. Maybe there was nothing more to it than that: he covered the case for his newspaper. Perhaps they had a passing interaction—or altercation. And perhaps not. He could be trying to get inside her head by implying there was something more between them. Or he was merely trying to establish familiarity so she would talk to him.

Joke's on you, Travis. Didn't work.

But Sharkey and Warren got the last laugh, because they published the piece despite her pleas not to. Time would tell whether or not the offender would react.

She realized she was clenching her jaw.

Take a breath, Karen. Nothing you can do about it now. Cat's out of the bag.

Which made her wonder . . . why was the cat in the bag in the first place?

Humor did not help. She scrutinized the photo of her, which was an old one from her early Bureau days.

Damn, I looked so much younger.

She started to read the article while slowly making her way to the front of the resort, taking care not to trip on the granite steps.

A few moments later, she heard, "Hey, babe. Come take a walk on the wild side."

She looked up, ready to slug the asshole. But it was Adam Russell, leaning over in the driver's seat and peering through the open passenger window. A broad smile spread his lips.

Vail climbed into his sedan and held up the paper.

"What?" he said. "We knew that was coming. Don't act so surprised."

"I'm not. I'm pissed. Frustrated. Because now the UNSUB knows the cops are keyed in to him."

"Not exactly," Russell said as he turned left onto Ala Moana Boulevard. "All he can conclude is that we realize this wasn't a natural death. For all he knows, you're here on vacation."

"Nice try. Unless he's dumb as a sack of hammers, there's no way he won't put two and two together. Profiler at a crime scene—*his* crime scene—and multiple victims in one city. This is what we used to call an organized offender. A bright planner. I were him, I'd be heading for the airport, if he's not already on the way."

"I've put TSA on alert. They've increased the number of frisks on males over forty."

Vail looked at the article again.

"At least they chose a nice photo of you."

She snorted. "Yeah from about twenty years ago. Just reminded me that I don't look like this anymore."

"I could comment here, give you a compliment, but then you could sue me for harassment."

"Do you really think I'd sue you for harassment?"

"Fine." He shrugged. "So yeah, I think you look pretty hot in that photo. And you look damn good now, too. You've got nothing to feel bad about."

"Really? Are you kidding me? I can't believe you'd call me *hot*. Do you think women are just objects? That's so inappropriate. Pull over and let me out. I'm going to call my attorney."

Russell turned to her, unsure. She winked and he let out his breath, shaking his head. "You."

"Just so we're clear. I am *not* making fun of women who've been harassed."

"We're clear. Just give me a minute for my heart to return to a normal rhythm."

"Sorry. Sometimes my mouth moves faster than my brain. I've been working on it."

"Obviously with mixed results."

"Do you like your front teeth?"

Russell glanced in the rearview mirror and pulled up his top lip. "Yeah, kind of fond of them. I use Crest whitening gel. I think it's helped."

"Then you might want to consider being nicer to me."

Russell hung a left, doing his best to stifle a grin.

They drove for a minute in silence.

"I think we need to be creative," Vail said.

"I take it you're not talking about sex."

"Now *that's* harassment."

"Whatever."

"I think we should compile a list of all women named Mary on the island in their mid-fifties to sixties and seventies."

"And then what? Go door to door to the houses of all these women named Mary and warn them not to wash their hands or take showers?"

"Exactly. Well, not exactly. Tell them not to buy any handmade soap. Stick to Dove and Caress."

Russell laughed.

"What? We'd explain that we can't tell you why but it's extremely important—and equally important that you don't tell anyone about this. Don't post anything on Facebook about it, don't blog about it, don't talk to reporters from the *Waikiki Vacationer*, and—"

"You're not serious."

"No, the part about the *Vacationer* I made up. I'm just pissed at them. But the part about not telling anyone, posting about it, yeah."

"Too risky."

"Is it?" Vail asked. "We're not real close to catching this asshole. We know his victim pool. Why not warn them?"

"There could be women named Mary we don't know about. Friends, relatives, tourists. It's impossible to cover everyone—and it'd take a lot of manpower. Chief may not go for it."

"And it could frustrate the offender. If he can't find what he's looking for, he could try to leave Oahu, go hunting elsewhere. But we have a tool at our disposal. Don't we have to try?"

Russell stared out the windshield. After a long moment, he said, "I guess it makes some sense. There's a lot of risk, but it's incredibly frustrating not being able to do something to stop this guy." He pulled out his phone. "I'll call Ferraro, make the ask." As it rang, he said, "Oh. I told a couple of colleagues to start going through the credit card transactions of all three vics."

"Makes sense. And?"

Russell held a hand up and asked to speak with the chief. While he waited, he rotated the handset away from his mouth. "And early this morning I got a text that only one of them had a charge at a health food retailer. Dawn Mahelona. I sent a uniform over to the store so they're there when they open in an hour. Maybe one of the employees knows something about our offender without realizing it."

"Worth a shot. But it should be us."

"Why?"

"Bachler gave us some good background about homemade soaps, but someone who deals with these distributors and manufacturers may have inside information. That kind of insight could set us down the right path."

Russell nodded. "The employee might have even interacted with the killer and a beat cop may not know what questions to ask."

"Could even be worse than that. Remember we talked about the UNSUB needing to be in contact with the victim? If that's the case, the only way that can happen—if Dawn Mahelona did buy soap when she shopped at that store—is if the offender works there. A cop walks in and starts asking questions? That'll be the last we see of our UNSUB."

Russell sat up and spoke into the phone. "Yeah, Chief." He told him of Vail's idea of going door to door. After listening a moment, Russell said, "But—" and then waited as Ferraro apparently kept talking. Russell glanced sideways at Vail, then sighed in resignation. "Right. Okay. Yep, got it."

"What?"

He dropped the device to his side. "Thinks it's a waste of resources. Says we'd need a lot of officers but a few large events are going on this week. Can't divert the manpower."

"We'll deal with that later. At least we can have a staff person assemble the list. What we do with it . . ." She pointed at his phone. "Right now call your people and tell that officer to back off—the one going to the store. He or she shouldn't go anywhere near it."

"You do the talking while I head over there in case we can't reach him in time." Russell hit a button on his phone and handed it to Vail. He hung a left and accelerated. "See? Your wish is my command, Karen."

Vail lifted her brow and grinned mischievously. "Then I better choose my wishes more carefully."

21

They arrived at Ola Health twenty minutes later. They sat in the parking lot of the strip mall, thirty yards from the store's entrance.

"You have to go in."

Russell pursed his lips. "Sounds like you've got a reason."

"My very memorable photo was in the *Vacationer* article. Can't take the chance."

"Right. But you realize the *Waikiki Vacationer* is not exactly the most widely read paper on the island."

"Sharkey, the journalist, writes for AP. So yeah, it was in the *Vacationer*, but it could also be picked up by the *Honolulu Tribune*. It's a high-profile story. Hard to pass up unless there's something better to feature."

"Not like they had a lot to report on at the crime scene."

"Since when has that stopped the media? They find ways of filling space."

They watched as a man crossed the lot and walked up to the front door of the store.

"Here we go."

"Whaddya think?" Russell said, keeping his eyes on the suspect. "Hard to say. Look like a poisoning serial killer to you?"

"Ted Bundy looked like the all-American guy."

Russell popped open his door. "Right."

* * *

Russell removed his sport coat and slipped his badge in his front pocket, then shoved the pistol in the small of his back.

He pushed through the door and saw the suspect behind the counter busy with the cash register. It was a modest-size space, no more than seven or eight hundred square feet.

"Aloha."

"Aloha." Russell glanced around, looking for soaps. He saw bottles of shampoo and conditioner, vitamins and minerals, herbal remedies—and bottles of body gel.

"Help ya?"

"Looking for soap," Russell said.

"About three feet to your right."

Russell wanted the guy to come out from behind the counter and interact with him, so he made a lame attempt to miss the products. "Yeah, um . . . I'm—not seeing any."

"Look down about—oh, hang on a sec. Be right there."

Russell kept his gaze on the shelves as the man approached. "Adam," he said, extending his hand.

"Martin."

His face was weathered, like a beach native who saw too much sun and too little sunscreen. Older than what he had thought when viewing him from a distance.

"Thanks for your help, Martin. Wife wants a natural kind of soap. No chemical stuff in it." He laughed. "I do as I'm told."

"Hear ya." Martin leaned forward and selected two products, one featuring olive oil and the other coconut oil.

"Which is better?"

Martin shrugged. "Like 'em both, tell you the truth. Been carrying the olive oil soap for 'bout fifteen years. People seem to like it. But the coconut one, that's a little newer, maybe four or five. Customers like that one, too. So . . ." He shrugged again. "Either will work for the missus."

Russell did not think Martin was their killer. If he was, he would likely prefer one product over the other. Then again, that might only be true if Russell was a sixty-something woman named Mary . . .

"Any of these handmade?"

"You mean homemade?"

"Yeah."

"Doubt it. We got a rep who comes by. Not one of them huge companies, but big enough. Homemade products don't usually have sales reps. Know what I mean?" Martin laughed. "Guess the ones we carry would be considered 'natural.' No chemical stuff in 'em. Seems to me that's what people care about these days."

"What's the sales rep like? He new?"

Martin twisted his lips as if he had bitten into a wedge of sour lemon. "Known her about five years, I'd say. Maybe a couple more. Nice lady. Knows her products, if that helps."

Russell pulled out his phone and texted Vail:

come in. not our guy

Martin turned to walk back toward the counter.

Vail entered and made eye contact with Russell. "Hey, honey." She walked over to him and received a quick, quiet summary of what he had learned.

"Martin," Vail said, stepping up to the counter.

He turned and his eyes lit up. "Can I help you?"

"I'm with Adam. Just curious. I was in here a week or so ago and—was there someone else working?"

"Just a part-timer. She comes in at four and closes at seven. I gotta get home to make dinner for the kids. Wife's got health problems."

"So just you and—"

"Patricia."

"You and Patricia. You have no other employees? No men?"

"Nope." He eyed her suspiciously. "Why you askin'?"

"How old is Patricia?"

Martin canted his head back and examined the ceiling. "Oh, uh, I'm guessing about seventy-one, seventy-two maybe."

Vail glanced at Russell, then reached into her right pocket and pulled out her credentials. "Working a case. Doesn't look like you sell any homemade bars of soap."

"Nope. I was tellin', um, Adam there. We got two really good natural ones, though, no chemicals an—"

"Yeah. He told me." Vail slipped her creds back in her pocket. "Ever see bars of homemade soap around town?"

Martin shrugged. "Not that I know of. Possible, though. Probably be a local thing. You know, sold in small shops like mine. But not just health food stores. Gift shops, tourist shops. They're more likely to be able to sell those things for more money. I mean, if you sell them from a store, you got another mouth to feed, so the store owner's gonna double the price. And then it's not really competitive with a natural soap, which is pretty much the same thing as homemade."

"All good points, Martin."

"Been in business a long time. Only way to survive is to use this." He jabbed a prematurely arthritic index finger into his temple.

Vail thanked him and they huffed it back to Russell's car. "He's got a point."

"About using his smarts to stay in business that long?"

Vail stopped outside the sedan. "No, Adam. About selling homemade soap. It doesn't make sense our offender would sell it out of a store."

"So how is this guy selling it? Craft fairs? Gift shops, like Martin said?" Russell turned the engine over. "Health food stores was too damn easy."

"Let's go back over their credit card statements, see if there are any gift shops or craft fairs or farmer's markets on them . . . anything like that where all three women shopped."

"And what if they used cash?"

Yeah. What if?

"Do one thing for me," Vail said. "Stop asking questions that I can't answer."

22

On the way back to the station, Russell called and asked that four officers in each jurisdiction be tasked with collecting samples from all stores and markets on the island that carry homemade soaps.

Vail and Russell went through the charge records of all three Marys and forwarded relevant information to the respective police departments for their follow-up. However, there were no common purchases among the three women, which made the task more difficult.

Within a few hours they had a dozen samples to test. Bachler and a colleague started their chemical analyses while Vail and Russell retreated to a break room.

"Humor me," Vail said as she stirred some milk into a cup of coffee. "Let's check HPD history and see if there've been other asphyxiation-related heart attack deaths."

"What are you thinking?"

Vail looked at the swirling tan liquid in her cup. "We know there's a chance our offender lives in Hawaii. But if he doesn't, what if he has a relative here and he comes and goes from time to time? I'm gonna touch base with the other PDs in Chicago, LA, Dallas, and Atlanta. Maybe they've had other 'cases'—not necessarily deemed murder—years before, or after, the ones they sent us."

Russell rose from his chair. "Nothing to lose. I'll make a call, check into it."

A few moments later, while Vail finished speaking with her contacts in Chicago and Los Angeles, Russell threw open the door and poked his head in.

"Gotta go."

Vail followed him down the hall, his rapid pace making her jog to catch up to him.

"What gives?"

"New vic."

Vail slowed and cursed under her breath. But getting angry was not going to get her any closer to finding the offender.

23

"Where we headed?"

They entered the parking lot, Russell's quick pace persisting. "Got a call from KPD."

Vail galloped a few steps to catch up. "KPD?"

"Kauai."

"There's a town on Oahu called Kauai? Or the island?"

"The island. Next one over to the west. I put out an alert, in case our killer wasn't limiting himself to Oahu."

Vail stopped walking. "So he's gone? He's left Oahu?"

Russell shrugged. "Looks that way."

"Shit. This is not good. Not good at all. He could be on his way back to the mainland."

"All we can do is take a look at the crime scene. Do our thing. Could be this is just a garden variety cardiac arrest."

"So why'd they call you?"

"Because it didn't look like a garden variety cardiac arrest. Vic was coughing violently and—well, you know the story." Russell chirped his remote and the sedan's doors unlocked. "So we're going to Kauai. Got a helo warming up."

"As long as I don't have to rappel out of one. Did that once or twice. Crossed it off my bucket list."

"I fully expect to land on solid ground." He started walking again and they got into the car. "Ever been there? To Kauai?"

"Nope."

"My favorite of all the islands. Peaceful, scenic beyond belief, great hiking and waterfalls. And not touristy."

"How long a flight?"

Russell shrugged. "Forty-five, give or take. Depends on traffic."

Vail squinted confusion. "Traffic?"

He started the engine with a twist of his wrist. "Kidding."

They arrived at the helipad twenty minutes later and climbed onto the Black Hawk police chopper. They pushed the audio headsets down over their ears and tuned to the correct channel.

"So where are you taking us?" Vail asked the pilot.

"I can set you down in a clearing right in the town."

"*The* town? There's only one on Kauai?"

The man glanced back at Russell, his expression saying, "Is she kidding? Or just stupid?"

Russell apparently thought Vail's question was valid because he tilted his head and asked, "Which one, Greg?"

"Hanapepe."

"Ah." Russell turned to Vail. "They call it Kauai's biggest little town."

Charming.

They flew in silence, Vail snapping a few photos out the side window of the helicopter. The view was spectacular. She was glad the pilot had a flight plan that took them out over Oahu rather than the expansive, though monotonous, ocean.

But as soon as that thought cleared her brain, the island below disappeared, and blue green water rolled beneath them.

So much for picturesque views.

24

Scott and Phillip walked along the plaza separating the two towers of the World Trade Center. It was late in the afternoon on a Saturday and people milled about. But one person caught their attention: a soldier in fatigues walked by with his young daughter and gave both boys a wink.

"I'm gonna serve in the army," Phillip said, twisting around to get another look at the man.

"Yeah?" Scott asked.

"Yeah. Maybe fly planes. Air force. Or the navy. I dunno yet."

"When?"

"Three weeks. When I turn eighteen. Been thinkin' a lot about it. Gonna go see a recruiter."

A recruiter? Scott realized this was not just a passing thought, but something that actually might happen. "But . . ." Scott pursed his lips with quivering sadness.

Phillip craned his neck back to look at the top of the north tower, 110 floors above—and swayed left, nearly falling over. "But what?"

"But what about me?"

Phillip regained his balance and faced Scott. "You'll finish school and join up, just like me."

Scott bit the inside of his bottom lip. He did not think he could join the military. He didn't want more people bossing him around, yelling at him, telling him what he could and couldn't do. Berating him. But he still had four years. Maybe by the time he turned eighteen, he would feel differently. "Does Nick know?"

"Was his idea. He wanted to serve in Vietnam but he broke his leg in a car accident the day before he was supposed to report. Didn't heal good. That's where he got his limp."

Scott did not know this story, but he had always wondered about the limp.

"His ankle doesn't work right. Army wouldn't take him."

"But why do you want to go?"

"I think it'd be bitchin'. Defending the flag. Standing up for democracy."

Scott thought about that. "You not afraid of dying?"

Phillip stopped in front of the large bronze sphere. The jets were off and the black surface of the water surrounding the sculpture was slick and glasslike, reflecting the blue sky.

"Everybody's gonna die at some time. Hopefully my day will be later. But if it's sooner, and it's doing somethin' I love, then that's what was meant to be. Besides, it's in our family. Grandpa Manny?"

"What about him?"

"He fought in World War II, battle of Normandy. He's buried at that big military cemetery in Hawaii. You should be very proud."

"Didn't know him."

"You just don't remember. You were young when he died. He had this scratchy beard and was very proud of his time serving. Said America was the greatest nation on earth. Something like that. Didn't really want to talk about the war, though. Said war was bad but there was nothing you could do about it because it was just the way people were. Always gonna be arguments. Sometimes war was the only way to solve it."

Scott thought about that for a while as they walked toward the subway.

"You're not happy I'm leaving you. You'll be alone with Mom and Nick."

Scott did not answer.

"You need to stand up for yourself. I'm turning eighteen, bro. You knew I was going to leave sooner or later."

Scott nodded that he understood, but he didn't really want to think about it. Things were bad enough with Phil around, but with his brother no longer living at home . . . what would happen?

He never did have the courage to confide in Phil about the things Nick did to him. The bad things. Maybe that was a mistake, but he just could not face what Phil would say. Would he call him a coward, as Nick did? No. Phil loved him. He would never insult him like that. But still. He could not bring himself to tell him.

With Phil headed off to better things, Scott knew he had a problem. He was not big enough to fight off Nick—unless he grew a foot in the next few years and gained a hundred and fifty pounds.

His mother was still mean to him, but he no longer cared when she hit him.

His sole coping mechanism was going to another place in his mind when Nick bothered him. It worked because it had to, but how much longer he could continue like that, he didn't know. Sooner or later he wouldn't be able to take it anymore.

Could he last another four years until he was old enough to move out, like Phil?

He did not look forward to finding out.

25

Scott unfurled the camouflage uniform top, then started to drape it over a hanger. He stopped and held it up in front of his chest, looking in the adjacent mirror.

He liked the idea of blending into the background, of not standing out. If only he could do that at home so he could avoid being the object of abuse for his mother and Nick. That was his motivation for getting this job in the surplus store. But it was not the only reason.

It made him feel closer to Phillip, who had done exceptionally well during his first year in the army. His last letter mentioned that Phillip had his eyes on the Rangers, an elite unit of the military tasked with special operations.

As a Ranger, he would secure strategic locations and reconnoiter enemy positions prior to a military offensive. Scott had no doubt Phillip would make the grade: he had both the physical and mental toughness to compete with others vying for the position. As Phillip described it, the Rangers comprised one of the finest special operations units in the world.

Scott wished he had those qualities.

But as Nick was fond of pointing out, he did not. A few months ago, while Scott was sitting in the kitchen fingering an arm patch Phil sent him, Nick walked in.

"What're you doin' with that?"

The muscles in Scott's jaw flexed repeatedly—but he did not answer.

Nick placed both hands on the table, getting close to Scott's face. Too close. "Thinking of enlisting like your brother?"

Scott lifted his gaze, reluctantly making eye contact. "And what if I was?"

"I'd laugh. Because you're too much of a fuckin' coward to carry a gun, let alone fire it against someone trying to kill you."

Scott put his head down and leaned back in the chair, shoving the embroidered logo into his pocket.

He was not really thinking about following his brother into the military. He would like to—if nothing else, to get back at Nick. He would shove his written orders into the bastard's face. *Then* who would be laughing?

But Scott knew that was not going to happen. Instead, he toiled in the dusty storefront of a military surplus shop, holding up uniform tops and playing soldier in the mirror.

He shook his head, breaking his reverie. He grabbed another camo shirt and placed it on the rack.

The job gave him another important advantage, however: it kept him out of the house and away from Nick and his mother. Nick took the money he earned. Luckily, Scott anticipated that would be the case, so he asked the owner to pay him in cash. The guy probably thought he was ducking taxes—which he was—but it afforded him the ability to skim off some money to stash under his bed.

Scott had entertained thoughts of running away, of escaping his life—but he was surprisingly pragmatic about it. He knew he would need to be able to care for himself, to earn money and buy food—and pay rent.

The retail and customer service experience he gained working in the shop would look good on his resume and, hopefully, provide him with the skills necessary to find a job in whatever city he ran away to.

Would he tell Phillip of his plans? Could he trust his brother not to disclose what he intended to do? Yes—unless Phillip thought it was too dangerous for a sixteen-year-old to be living on the streets alone. In that case, he might think that telling Nick and their mother would be the lesser of two evils.

Evil was the operative word. He hated his mother. Hate was a strong word, but it was truly how he felt. Intuitively he thought he should have some love, buried somewhere, deep down, for the woman who gave him life. But he experienced none of those emotions. He would just as soon push her out the sixth-floor window as stab her between the left fourth and fifth ribs.

Yes, he had looked it up in the library. That was where the heart resided. Physically, at least. He did not believe his mother had an *emotional* heart. She did not care about him. She did not have any feelings for him.

Worse than that, she embodied evil.

Mary was why Nick lived with them. Mary was why Nick abused him. Mary knew what Nick was doing to him. And she said nothing.

"Hey, kid."

Scott spun around. The store owner was there, cash in his hand. He counted off some bills and slapped them into Scott's palm.

"You're doin' good work. See you tomorrow afternoon?"

Scott nodded, dividing the stack and shoving half the money into his left pocket. That was Nick's cut.

The rest of it—which Nick would never know about—he stuffed into his right.

26

Scott was exhausted from work. He had turned off the light when he realized he had not read the new letter from Phillip. He turned on the dim night table bulb and angled it so he could make out his brother's scrawl.

Hey bro. I've got some exciting news. I've done real good here and got promoted a few times since I wrote last. Sorry it's been so long but the days are so fucking long that when training's over I crawl into my bunk and go to sleep. But I had to write to tell you I'm now a corporal and score! I made a really cool unit I'd been trying out for. It's called the Rangers. I think I told you about it. That's the Special Forces part of the army. We do shit no one else can because we're better than all the other soldiers. We get better training and they send us on more dangerous missions because they know we can handle it.

That's why we train so hard. If we're sent somewhere, it's to make sure things are ready for the rest of the army to come in. Stuff behind the scenes, make targets softer, that kind of thing.

I can't really tell you where I'm going but they're getting ready to ship us out to a fucked up place they like to call a hot zone. Some kind of civil war and we got to play the cops. America to the rescue!

Am I the shit or what?

You hang in there. I want you to follow me here. You're better than most of the guys who sign up. You can do it! I know you can. I believe in you.

Take care. Fist bump. Phil.

Scott had just finished the letter and was about to start rereading it when he fell asleep.

Suddenly his bedroom door swung open. He startled awake and noticed the clock as he lifted his head from the pillow: 2:00 AM. His light was off, but he didn't remember shutting it. Phil's letter. Where was it?

The door swung open further. A large figure was silhouetted against the dimly lit hallway.

Scott knew that shape anywhere.

"Whaddya want, Nick?"

"Shut up and turn over."

"No."

Scott never saw it, but he sure felt it: the solid fist of Nick's right hand smashed into his eye socket. Everything went black.

But only for a moment. Or maybe two. Because the next thing he felt was the familiar lancinating pain in his rectum.

Scott was now seventeen, and although short for his age, he was no longer a small boy. He was not going to take it, not anymore.

He pushed up and swung his right elbow back, striking Nick in the face. Nick's head recoiled and blood spurted in Scott's eye. He tried to get off the bed, but Nick groaned loudly and punched Scott in the right kidney.

Pain gripped him and took his breath away. His body went limp.

Nick forced his face into the mattress and as Scott started to recover from the blow to his back, his rectum was on fire.

"Fight back."

"What?"

"Don't give in to it, Scotty."

Scott shook his head. "Dad?"

"I'm sorry I can't be here for you. I'm sorry I died."

"Dad, I need you. Phil's in the army and—"

"You can't let people push you around. Take control and show them who's in charge. That's what Phillip is doing."

He turned his head and saw his father standing in his room. He nodded at Scott, urging him on.

Scott whipped his head back and slammed it into Nick's nose. He squirmed out from his grasp and grabbed a baseball bat he kept by the bed. A well-worn Louisville Slugger. He swung it hard and smashed Nick in the head. His stepfather stood upright, stunned. Scott hit him again and again.

Nick started to cry, the tears smearing the blood that covered his left cheek. He held his hands up, fending off additional blows, as he backed—and stumbled—out of the room.

"I did it," Scott said. He turned to his father and grinned.

"Yes you did, Scotty. I knew you could."

27

There was a knock at the door.

"Scott!" Mary said from the kitchen. "Get it. I'm busy."

Scott gritted his teeth. Yeah, she was busy watching TV. He tossed the dishrag down and headed into the foyer. He grabbed the knob and pulled it open. Two uniformed men stood there, hats under their arms.

"Is Mary Meece at home?"

"I'm Scott Meece. Who are you?"

"We're from the army. Is your mother here?"

"I'm Mary."

Scott turned around and saw her standing about a dozen feet behind him.

"May we come in, Mrs. Meece?"

"What's this about?"

"Important government business. Information about Phillip. Better if we talk inside."

Scott felt sick to his stomach. He knew this was not going to be good news.

They walked into the kitchen and took seats. The men were stiff and formal and wore solemn expressions. "Mrs. Meece, I'm Captain Wenke. Your son Phillip was involved in a US Army offensive and we're very sorry to report that he was killed in action. I can't disclose the details of what happened because he was on a classified mission.

But I can tell you he exhibited extreme bravery, bravery that made his unit, and the US military, very proud. I realize that's of little solace. This is Father Mulrose and he—"

"I saw it on the news," Scott said. "It was Somalia. The battle of Mogadishu. Wasn't it?"

The officer cleared his throat. "I can't say one way or another. But . . ." He shrugged, then nodded.

Scott fought back tears. He walked out of the kitchen, out of the apartment, and found himself wandering the street. It was sunset and although he had the day off, he ended up at work. He stepped inside and surprised the owner.

"What're you doin' here today?"

"I, uh . . . I just found out my brother was killed in action."

The man's face sagged in sadness. "C'mere, son. Have a seat." He grabbed a folding chair from behind the register and set it in front of Scott. Then he flipped the sign on the door to CLOSED and took a seat opposite Scott. "Very sorry for your loss. Bullshit words, but I honestly mean it. I know what that's like. I served in Nam and lots of my buddies were killed."

Scott nodded.

"Tell me about him. Your brother."

Scott took a deep breath. He did not know where to start. One thing he did know was that he could no longer stay at home. He was moving out tomorrow, or the next day, or the day after that.

How, he didn't know. But he felt alone now. All alone. And although nothing had changed in his day-to-day life—Phillip had been away for years now—he felt different.

Responsible. A man.

It was time to take control. Sooner or later he was going to show them who was in charge.

28

The helicopter set down in a clearing—no helipad in the largest small town that Kauai had to offer—and Vail and Russell deplaned, or dechoppered, or whatever the hell it was called.

As long as she did not have to jump out tethered to a cable, Vail was happy.

She removed the sweaty, bulky headset and fluffed her curly red hair—but a gust of wind struck her from behind and sent it flying in all directions. *Glad I bothered with the pomade. Should've used rubber cement.*

She and Russell turned in a circle, taking in the terrain. Single family homes surrounded them.

A Kauai PD cruiser sat idling off to their left. The driver's door opened and a uniformed officer unfolded his tall body. "Detective Adam Russell?"

"That's me," Vail said, extending her right hand.

"*You're* Adam Russell?" the cop asked.

"I'm Russell." He bumped Vail aside with a not-so-gentle brush of his left shoulder. "She's . . . a pain in the ass."

The officer nodded at Vail but withdrew his hand. He clearly was not sure *what* to call her—but concluded that *Ms. Ass* was not a good option.

"Is Detective Opunui on scene?" Russell asked.

"Follow me."

They strolled through the streets of the neighborhood. Teens were on bicycles, gawking at the Black Hawk, whose rotors were still whipping around, competing with the violence of Nature's wind.

As they turned a corner, they saw a group of people—residents, no doubt—and an area sectioned off by crime scene tape. The officer whistled and asked for a clear path. The men and women parted and Russell and Vail soon saw the sides of a modest-size tent. They entered and saw the center of attraction: a woman in her sixties lying on her side, her face having been lacerated and abraded against the asphalt when she collapsed.

Vail and Russell introduced themselves to Opunui, a grizzled, graying man who had to be past common retirement age. They knelt and looked over the victim, then stood up.

"What's her name?" Vail asked.

"Mary Kelleher. Sixty-nine. Worked at the airport as a ticket agent."

"And why do you think this wasn't a natural death?" Russell asked.

"For one, she just had a physical two days ago. Doc said it was great—she was in really good condition. She worked out four days a week. Never smoked a day in her life. Vegetarian. No family history of stroke or heart attacks according to her internist. Hiked four days a week."

"Four days a week?"

"Kauai's gorgeous, Agent Vail. Very little development or tourist contamination. Hiking trails here are full of Nature's beauty. They cleanse the soul, balance out the anger, and straighten the moral compass."

"Whoa. Guess I could use some of that soul cleansing."

Opunui looked at Russell, who shrugged.

"Shoulda kept that to myself," Vail said. "Sorry."

"The doc spoke to you without a court order?" Russell asked.

"He and I go back a ways," Opunui said, giving Vail a dubious side glance. "What he told me—that was off the record. When her husband mentioned the physical, I asked if I could speak with her doctor. Found out it was my Ohana."

"Ohana?" Vail asked.

"Close friend," Russell said. "Like family."

"Doc was upset when I called him," Opunui said. "First thing he said was, 'Impossible.' Mrs. Kelleher just wasn't the kind of patient he would've bet on to have a massive heart attack."

"Where's the husband?"

"At their house, a couple blocks away. Kind of in shock."

"Let's get a tox screen on Mrs. Kelleher ASAP. What about CSU?"

"Haven't come yet."

"You wanna see anything else here?" Russell asked.

Vail stepped outside the tent and surveyed the immediate area. "Where are the witnesses?"

"Sent them home. Got their statements and contact info."

"And?" Vail asked. "What'd they say happened?"

"She started coughing. Real bad. She stumbled into the street and grabbed for something to hold her up. But she dropped to her knees and then fell onto her side. A woman ran over and took a pulse but there wasn't any. She wanted to do CPR but she didn't know how. She called an ambulance but we've only got one, and it was out on a call. Sent one from Waimea. Took 'em fifteen minutes to get here. No need to transport at that point."

"Probably gone the minute she hit the ground," Russell said.

Vail gestured at Opunui. "Why were you called?"

"Paramedic knew the victim. Friend of his mom's. He knew how fit she was. He called KPD, asked for me."

"Why you?" Vail asked.

"He's my nephew."

Vail glanced at Russell. "Does everyone know everybody else in this town?"

"We're close," Opunui said. "Only about twenty-five hundred of us. Whole place is one square mile."

"Let's go take a look at the house, talk to the husband."

They hoofed it a couple of blocks to a two-story, well-maintained home. Opunui knocked on the door and announced himself. "Got a couple a questions, Ted."

Ted Kelleher pulled open the screen. It squeaked and creaked. His face was ashen and he looked like he had been hit with a brick across the cranium. His eyes sat at half mast, his cheeks moist from tears.

"I'm Karen Vail with the FBI. This is Detective Russell, Honolulu PD."

"FBI?" He glanced from one to the other. "I don't get it. Mary had a heart attack."

"Yeah," Vail said. "About that. We're not entirely sure what happened yet. That may be exactly what took Mary, but we have to cross all our t's."

"What else could it be?"

Vail and Russell looked at their shoes, then Vail sighed and said, "We really can't say. That could be all it was. We've got an ongoing investigation, so we can't say any more."

"Mind if we look around the house?" Russell asked.

Kelleher shrugged in a slow, lazy manner, as if it took all his effort. "Sure. Fine. Whatever. Ain't gonna bring me back my Mary." He waved a hand behind his left ear as he trudged away.

Vail and Russell fanned out inside the home, Vail taking the ground floor and Russell going upstairs. She cut right to the chase, checking the bathroom first.

There was no bar of soap—and no soap dish. In its place was a foaming pump bottle. Not wanting to accept the obvious, she pulled over the garbage pail from beneath the vanity and, after slipping on gloves, sifted through the contents. No wrappers. Nevertheless, it would go back to the lab for further analysis.

Vail pulled aside the shower curtain and looked over the tub. She groaned, then padded out of the bathroom and found the husband. "Mr. Kelleher. There're no soap bars."

"Nope."

"How come?"

"Dries us out. We use shower gel and that foamy liquid stuff."

"Any chance Mary bought a bar of soap recently, in the past few days?"

"Doubt it. She was the one who insisted we not use it anymore."

"You sure about that?"

"I know my—*knew* my wife, Agent Vail." He stopped and bit his bottom lip.

"I'm very sorry, Mr. Kelleher. I don't mean to upset you."

Russell walked into the living room. "Nothing. No so—"

"Yeah. We were just discussing that. Mary hated soap. Wouldn't have bought any."

Russell's look mirrored Vail's thoughts: *Shit.* And, *Is this our offender or not?*

"Did you or Mary ever shop at a health food store?" Vail asked. "Or a farmer's market or craft fair—even a roadside stand?"

Kelleher rested both hands on the high-backed wood chair, then glanced at the ceiling for a moment. "Couple years ago we bought some pineapples from a guy by the side of the road. Other than that, no. Why?"

"Something we're looking into," Russell said.

"There are four or five gift shops in the area. We walked through a few of 'em over the years. Never bought anything."

"You sure?"

"Sure, Detective. Money's tight, sometimes it's a challenge to make our house payment. If we don't need something, we pass it up. Mary's always on my case, makin' sure I don't buy stuff we don't need."

Vail and Russell moved off and huddled a couple dozen feet away. "I still want crime scene to go through this place. Probably a waste but can't ask for a do-over a week from now if we realize we missed something."

"I agree." Russell glanced over her shoulder at Kelleher. "Let's go chat with Opunui."

"Mr. Kelleher," Vail said, heading back into the kitchen. "We need to have crime scene technicians collect evidence. There someplace you can go and wait till they're done?"

"Why can't I stay here? In my house?"

"There could be evidence here. And the more you, or anyone else, walks around, moves things, and so on, the greater the chance evidence could be disturbed—or destroyed."

"You—you think Mary was killed?"

"Don't know," Russell said. "It's possible."

Kelleher licked his lips, absorbing that. "How long this gonna take?"

"We'll ask them to be as fast as possible. I don't think it'll be that bad. Maybe a couple of hours once they get here."

Kelleher glanced around, then grabbed his car keys off a hook in the pantry.

They walked out together and Russell waved Opunui over.

"We need this place sealed off till CSU arrives."

Opunui pulled out his radio and asked an officer to post himself out front while Russell requested that the crime scene unit double-time it to the Kelleher house.

As they watched Kelleher's 1980s Chevy pickup disappear down the roadway, Opunui turned to Russell. "Was he helpful?"

"Not a whole lot. But he did give us some potentially useful info."

Vail looked out at the coastline. "If this is our offender, how'd he get here?"

Opunui shrugged. "Most likely, he flew. Short flight from Oahu." A squawk came over the detective's radio. "Excuse me." He turned and walked off.

"But flying means going through security, being scrutinized by law enforcement personnel," Vail said. "That's the opposite of what he wants, his whole reason—we think—why he came to Kauai to kill."

Russell nodded slowly. "Let's say that because of that article, he knows that *we* know these weren't natural deaths. We're suspecting homicide, a serial killer. If anything, he wants to be more careful. Not less. So he island hops to Kauai, a rustic place with little crime and a sleepy police force."

"Even if we find that Mary Kelleher is one of his victims, he's thrown us a sharp curve."

"Yeah," Russell said. "We can no longer just focus on Oahu. That makes our job a lot harder."

Vail stared off into the distance. "What if he doesn't fly? How else would he get here? Can you rent a boat?"

"You mean like a fishing boat or a motorboat?"

Um, is there a difference?

"Let's say either."

Russell chuckled. "No. Not really. The channels around the islands are very rough. Smaller boats wouldn't be able to handle it."

He thought a moment. "If you're not going by plane, it'd have to be cruise ship or ferry."

"Ferry?"

"Something called the Superferry ran about a dozen years ago. Company spent tens of millions of dollars on heavy-duty ships designed to carry cars as well as people. Great idea—and definitely needed. But story I get is that they had all sorts of legal trouble. I think they skipped an environmental impact report, and as you can imagine, in these parts that caused an uproar. Hawaii Supreme Court ruled against the operators and the ferry shut down in '09. Kept getting resurrected and shot down until some other company found a financially sustainable model. Hawaiian Island Ferries started up a year or so ago. HIF carries three hundred cars and about nine hundred passengers."

"How long's the trip from Oahu to here?"

Russell bobbed his head. "I'd guess about three, three and a half hours."

"So he could've come and gone the same day?"

Russell considered that. "He needed to find his target, right? Who knows how long that'd take. No, I'd say he was here a couple of days at least. Hell, he could still be here."

"Problem with that," Vail said, "is that we know approximately when he was last in Oahu. We know when Mary Grant died."

"Right."

"No." She shook her head. "Not right. We can't establish a time-line because we don't know when he came into contact with his vics. We only know when they died, meaning we—"

"Only know when the Marys opened the bar of soap. I mean, a lot of people may open it right away, but others might not."

This time Vail found the rock she was pining for earlier and gave it a good solid boot. It went flying and nearly hit Opunui in the back of the head.

"Starting to get frustrated?"

Vail stood there as a gust blew her tightly curled locks across her face. She did not bother to clear them.

Russell used an index finger to gently uncover her face. "You've had cases like this before. I know you have."

"Yeah. So?"

"What'd you do on those?"

"I found a rock and gave it a good kick."

Russell could not help but laugh. "I mean about the case."

Vail took a deep breath. "I kept moving. One foot in front of the other."

"So let's do that. I'll put a call through to whoever operates the HIF, ask them to get us a list of all passengers for the past couple of weeks. Have them include method of payment."

"Since we have no idea who we're looking for, you want to narrow the list of potential suspects by sorting by cash payment."

"Right." Russell pulled out a pad and started jotting notes.

"We could be dealing with thousands of people. So first we eliminate by gender—toss out all the females—and then we get rid of all the males who used a credit card."

"Male cash customers. Okay."

"These days, I'm willing to bet that'll drop the number."

"Yeah, but two weeks, potentially a thousand or more people per trip, a few islands . . . a couple ferries per day per island. This could take awhile."

"Then the sooner you get some people on that, the better."

Russell rooted out his phone. "I also want to get an undercover detective on every ferry that leaves any of the islands headed for Oahu. *If* he's headed back to Oahu. What's your gut say?"

Another blast of wind buffeted Vail's body and shoved her off balance. She stumbled back a foot. "Jesus." She sorted out her hair and saw Russell doing the same. "Obviously I'm winging it a bit because of this time of death thing. Until we find someone who's actually seen this guy, we have no idea if he's even in Hawaii."

"Your gut," Russell said. "I realize you could be wrong. I promise not to get on your case about it. 'Cause I got nothing better."

"My gut." Vail closed her eyes and stood still for a moment, clearing her mind, filling her lungs with clean sea air. "I think I need to go find one of those hiking trails."

"Seriously, Karen."

"I *was* being serious. Okay, here's my best guess. UNSUB's familiar with Oahu. He's been there before, we know that. It's comfortable for him. He knows his way around. And he's confident killing there. Could be other reasons, too, that we don't know about. So yeah, *if* he's still in Hawaii, I think he'd go back to Oahu. At least before he leaves for wherever he lives year-round."

Russell punched a button then brought the handset to his right ear. "So the question is, is he going back to Oahu to kill?"

Vail did not answer—but she did not need to. Judging by Russell's slumped shoulders, he knew the answer to his own question.

29

Vail's and Russell's helicopter landed and they returned to their vehicle. Her hearing was a bit off, the headset muffling the din of the rotors fairly well. But after forty-five minutes the incessant, droning white noise got to her.

In the quiet of the car, after assimilating the information they had absorbed, they received a call from one of Russell's colleagues.

After hanging up, he summarized what he had been told: "No charges by any of the four victims. The Kellehers' credit card records haven't been looked at yet. The others? No gift shops, farmer's markets, craft fairs, that type of thing."

"So they either paid cash or they didn't buy it from any of these types of places," Vail said.

Russell sighed. "And there's some more bad news. The ferries don't keep a passenger manifest. If someone uses a credit card, yeah, they'll have a name—of whoever's card was used—but anyone who paid cash, they were just admitted into the queue. No record of their names."

"Great."

They were each alone with their thoughts.

Finally, Vail bit her bottom lip and faced Russell.

"What?"

"I was thinking."

"Always advisable."

"I can't decide if Mary Kelleher is the work of our UNSUB."

"Kind of obvious, isn't it?"

"You mean because her heart attack is suspicious? Because if it is murder, it's unlikely we've got two killers in Hawaii using the same kill methods? Because her name's Mary like the other victims? And she fits the victimology?"

Russell pursed his lips. "Yeah. All that."

"But she doesn't use soap. And we found no soap bars and no soap bar wrappers."

"The absence of something can't prove something isn't what it appears to be."

"You're butchering what I said earlier," Vail said with a chuckle. "I once had this argument with my ASAC. But the bottom line is we'll have to wait and see if Bachler finds any aconite on the Kelleher body."

"Which would be a first. What if he doesn't?"

"That's what I've spent the last forty-five minutes thinking about."

"And despite all that effort—and knowledge and experience—you don't have an opinion?"

"I have an opinion. But I was hoping for a smoking gun."

"How often have you had one of those?"

"Every time I fire my Glock."

Russell gave her a look.

"What?" Vail said. "Do you only shoot rubber bullets on Oahu? Is that an 'aloha' thing? No real ammo?"

"That's funny. Didn't Bruce Willis once say, 'Aloha, asshole!' right before he blew the guy away? In one of the *Die Hard* flicks?"

"I don't think so."

"Well, he should have. Great line." A moment later, Russell pulled into the crime lab's parking lot.

It was dusk and Vail fretted that they were farther away from answers than they were two days ago. "I feel like a salmon."

Russell got out of his car and removed the sealed bag containing crime scene evidence from the trunk. "I don't even know what to do with that comment."

"Not making any headway. Swimming upstream. Against the tide."

"Yeah, but don't the salmon always make it and lay their eggs?"

Vail drew her chin back. "I'm FBI, not Fish and Game. How the hell should I know?"

"You're exhausting, Karen."

They walked in and caught Bachler before he clocked out for the night. "Guess what we've got for you," Russell said, holding up the bag.

"Not for me," Bachler said. "I'm going home."

"As long as it's processed PDQ," Vail said, "We don't care who does it. We need to know if there's any aconite. Body is en route on another chopper. Should be here already."

"Yep. It's in the morgue. ME is slicing and dicing as we speak."

"Good." Russell rubbed his eyes. "Can you ask them to text me if they find anything? If it's our killer, that means he's left the island. And that means we *really* need to know."

"Left the island?" Bachler asked.

"Body's from Kauai."

Bachler's lips parted. "Crap."

"Yeah," Vail said. "Crap."

Bachler reached for the wall-mounted phone and pressed a button. A few seconds later, he said, "It's Harry. Priority is aconite. You find any, Adam Russell needs to know immediately." He listened a second, then nodded. "Great. Thanks."

Russell gestured at the phone. "That was Kuoko?"

"Yep. Said he's already ahead of us. Should know something in a couple of hours."

Russell patted Bachler's right shoulder. "Thanks Harry. This case feels like it's in danger of spiraling out of control. We need to get a handle on it. Or we're not gonna be sleeping much."

"I hear you. That's part of what makes you such a great detective."

Russell gave him a half-grin, then turned and motioned Vail after him as he headed out. "Remember you said you were thinking about the case?"

"A few minutes ago?"

"Yeah."

"I'm not senile yet. Of course I remember."

"Good," Russell said, scratching the back of his head. "I was reading last night about something that might help us."

"Oh yeah? Like a crystal ball?"

"Tried to order one last week. Amazon was sold out."

Vail laughed. "So what's this thing that might help us?"

"I hope you don't think I'm crazy, but I found—"

"That train's left the station. I wouldn't say 'crazy,' but maybe mentally—"

"Karen."

"Sorry," she said, holding up a hand. "Go on, Adam."

Russell pulled the exit door open. "I found something called geographic profiling. Some guy named Kim. Uh, Kim—"

"Jong-un."

"Who?"

"The weird North Korea dude."

Russell stopped and looked at her. "I'm being serious."

"And I'm not. Again, my apologies. If you're talking about geographic profiling, you're referring to Kim Rossmo."

He snapped his fingers. "That's it."

"And why do you think geo profiling would help us?"

Russell shrugged. "We're on a small island and yet most of our vics are concentrated in a relatively small portion of it."

Vail squinted sideways at him. "How far did you get into your research?"

"I wouldn't call it research exactly. It was a case study. I used it to put me to sleep."

"Ouch. I won't tell Kim you said that."

"You know this Kim Rossmo guy?"

"I've worked with him on a few cases. But I don't think his methods are gonna help us with the Soap Killer."

"The what?" Russell squinted and tilted his head. "The Soap Killer? Did I miss something?"

"Adam." She shook her head in pity. "You've missed a lot of things."

Russell nodded, conceding defeat. "Feel better?"

"Not really." She bobbed her head. "Maybe a little."

"The media's really started calling him the Soap Killer?"

"No. I just made that up. But it fits, doesn't it? He's so slippery we're having a hard time catching him. Just when we think we've got a grip on things, he squeezes through our grasp."

"Nope," Russell said with a frown. "Soap Killer doesn't do it for me."

"How about the Aconite Slayer?"

"Now you're going *Game of Thrones* on me."

"Just be thankful the media doesn't know enough about the case—or how he kills—to brand him."

"So you were saying." He began walking again and pulled out his keys, chirped the remote. "About geographic profiling."

"You're right that it's useful," Vail said. "If you have a killer who finds his vics by going in search of them, it would have more relevance. Rossmo classifies his killers according to how they go about selecting and trapping them. He calls them poachers, hunters, trollers, and trappers. Each one goes about finding his prey in different ways. He further categorizes the offenders by the way they approach their prey: ambushers, raptors, and stalkers."

"I think I'm glad I fell asleep when I did. Otherwise I'd have been up all night."

"Point is, our offender isn't really any of these—because the victims come to *him*—at least, that's my current thinking. Wherever it may be, they buy the soap from him. Maybe he's got a little raptor in him, but he doesn't really attack. He gives them a ticking time bomb. He probably gets his jollies during the interaction with the vic. And he gets an additional rush when he sees the obituary. I wouldn't be surprised if he clipped the obits from the local paper—or took a screenshot and saved them as a trophy."

"Unconventional."

"Everything about him is unconventional."

Russell nodded, got into the car, then slumped in the seat.

"So you see why I'm not sure a geo profile would help us?"

"Thought I had something."

Vail was staring at the interior, working through a thought, then finally sat down. "Maybe you did. Sort of."

"You trying to make me feel better?"

"No. You forced me to rethink something that's been bothering me. Not only doesn't he hunt for his victims, but he only interacts with them minimally. And not at all after death. This 'distance' flies in the face of a core principle of what we see with these offenders."

"I thought you sorted that out."

"I did. But that doesn't mean I've accepted it. I don't want to make the facts fit our model. I want to go with the facts and see where they take us. That's the best approach. The long held, accepted model *should* guide us. It's done well by us for almost four decades. But new types of offenders and trends do come up. They inform our model and help us improve it as more data becomes available."

"Makes sense," Russell said, shoving his key into the ignition.

"But the underpinning concept still needs to be addressed. How's our UNSUB getting off on these murders? These offenders need to *feel* something. Not in the emotional sense—because most of them are psychopaths—but they have to get something out of the murders. That's the part that's been eating at me. And I think I just figured it out."

"I thought the selection of the victim is what stirs his drink."

"Yes. Not sure that's enough. Even if he sees their obituary and collects them as a trophy, he's not . . . fulfilled."

"Fulfilled?"

"Sexual fulfillment. Reliving the murder, fantasizing about it."

"Okay."

"That's why I'm thinking he might go back to the scene after he sees the obit."

Russell twisted his torso in the seat to face Vail. "That could be huge."

"Could be. Yes."

"We could put an undercover at the crime scene and scope it out in case he shows up."

"Worth the manpower expense, I think. This time don't mention my name when you make the request."

Russell chuckled. "No shit." He pulled out his phone and asked for Ferraro. After a moment of explaining what he wanted, Russell glanced at Vail. "Nope, my idea . . . Completely . . . No, she's out getting java." He rolled his eyes. "Thanks, Chief." He hung up and shook his head.

"Sorry I came back empty-handed," Vail said. "Starbucks was all out of coffee."

"He's really got a hard-on for you."

"I think we should send forensics back to the crime scenes."

"All of them?"

Vail chewed on that. "Maybe not all. The homes. The ones that are easy for our UNSUB to get to without anyone seeing."

"What are they looking for?"

"Semen."

Russell cringed. "What?"

Vail popped open the door.

"Where you going?"

"Back inside. Gotta pee."

Russell followed her toward the building. "You think the killer's jacking off at the thought of the woman having died there?"

"I do. Fulfillment. Sexual release."

Russell contorted his mouth, as if he had bitten into a bitter lime. "That's sick."

"Par for the course, Adam. Welcome to my world."

30

Vail headed to the restroom while Russell intended to use the time to catch up on his emails. But as he opened the app, his phone started vibrating.

It was the deputy chief. Good news or bad?

"Chief."

"We've got a lot more heat on us because of that damn news article. Reporters calling from all over the country. I told you Vail would fuck things up for us."

"Wasn't her fault. The media was already there before we—"

"Not interested in excuses. Are we any closer to catching this knucklehead?"

After Russell quickly updated him, Ferraro expressed his displeasure with the "lack of progress."

"Not sure what more we could be doing, sir. Actually, though, I'm glad you called. Something's been bugging me. Agent Vail."

Ferraro sneered. "Had enough?"

"Huh? No. Not what I mean. Nothing like that. I haven't had any issues with her. I just wanna know what happened between the two of you. Just so I can keep an eye out, be ready."

"I gave you fair warning. That's all you need."

"All due respect, I—"

"If you're half the detective I know you are, you'll figure it out. Maybe even before it's too late."

"Too late for what?"

"Joan was supposed to call you but she's been fielding the media calls."

"Call me about what?"

"Vail's going home. Tomorrow morning. There's a flight at 9:00 AM and there are seats available. I want her on it."

"What?" Russell stopped pacing and craned his neck toward the ceiling. "Let's take a breath here, Chief. Everything's fine. Everything *will* be fine."

"And you're guaranteeing that?"

"I am."

Ferraro was quiet for a long moment. "She's got two more days. And then I ship her back. Anything happens, it's on you."

Russell swallowed hard. "Two days?"

"Two. Got it, Detective?"

"Yeah. I mean, I guess so. But why don't we see how things are going and then reass—"

"Two days." He hung up.

Russell stood there staring down the empty hallway, thinking. He was perturbed by Ferraro's attitude toward Vail and had been worried he would pull the plug on her involvement at the slightest mistake they made—or even the perception of one. Now that worry was realized.

He needed all the help he could get with this case. Surely Ferraro understood that. Vail provided a unique perspective, a different way of looking at homicide, even if the "Soap Killer" did not fit the traditional serial killer model in terms of behavior. That might render her experience less relevant, but he liked the way she thought and processed facts.

Russell heard someone approaching. He turned to see Vail.

"Ready?"

"Yeah." He forced a grin.

"What's wrong?"

"Why do you think something's wrong?"

"This isn't my first rodeo, Adam."

"All's good. Just feeling some pressure to catch this bastard."

Vail held his gaze for a long moment, then nodded—unconvinced but apparently letting it drop.

He started walking toward his car. "So how many rodeos have you ridden?"

"Enough to leave me with a number of broken bones. A perpetual pain in the ass. And a lot of bulls that would like to skewer me through the heart."

Given his conversation with Ferraro, Russell had every reason to believe that assessment was true.

31

V ail lay awake in bed, the balcony window open and the waves washing in and out, a calming rhythm as she stared at the ceiling, hoping to feel the pull of sleep on her eyelids.

At least the ocean's relaxing repetition stood in contrast to the drone of cacophonous rotor noise they endured in the Black Hawk.

Her phone rang a bit after 11:00 PM. She grabbed for it, hoping it was Robby.

It was Russell.

"I got the list of Marys that fit our killer's MO. That's the good news."

"We've got a list of *names*? That's what constitutes good news these days?"

"Well, that's only because there's also bad news, so it's good by comparison."

"What's the bad news?"

"Techs didn't find any aconite-infused wrappers in the house or neighborhood. ME didn't find aconite on her clothing or skin. Still checking for the metabolytes."

Vail sighed. "How'd you know I was awake?"

"Seriously?" He laughed. "How could you sleep?"

Vail sighed. "Yeah."

"So now what? Obviously, we're left to wonder. I hope at some point it'll all add up and make sense."

"We weren't expecting there to be aconite on the body, Adam. And other than her name and age, I mean, it could just be that an older woman had a heart attack and dropped dead. Genetics. Fate. Karma. Whatever you want to call it."

"Right. Just a coincidence her name was Mary and that she happened to be the right age."

"You have to admit that it's not much to base an investigative theory on." She heard rustling on the other end of the phone. "What are you doing?"

"Looking for a rock in my house to kick."

That made her smile. "You said it yourself. You can't rule something out based on the absence of evidence. It was super windy. What if the soap wrapper blew away?"

"Wasn't windy inside her house. And they didn't use bars of soap, remember?"

"Yeah." Vail yawned. "So maybe you're right. Just a coincidence. But I don't really believe in coincidences."

"Me either."

"I'm tired."

"So am I."

"But I want to solve this. I'll be up if you want to run anything by me." She waited a moment, but Russell did not reply. "Adam? Yo. Adam."

Vail heard a snore, hit end, and went back to staring at the ceiling.

32

The *Daily News* headline was bold and screamed at Scott Meece as he passed the stand packed with unsold papers:

Chief Justice William Rehnquist To Preside
Over President Clinton's Impeachment Trial

Scott continued on to the rear of the store. He did not concern himself with politics. That had been Phillip's domain, an interest he adopted when he joined the army. Scott had more problems than worrying about whether or not the president had oral sex with an intern in the Oval Office. Or whatever it was.

Christmas music was playing in the bodega as Scott rummaged through the refrigerated section. Goddam Christmas. People happy, celebrating with family and friends, buying presents for others, going to parties.

Scott was not happy.

He had no family to celebrate with.

He had no friends.

He gave no presents and received none.

The fucking music made him crazy.

He checked his watch—just past 11:00 PM. He started to look away but kept his gaze on the timepiece. It was a black G-Shock, nothing special—except that it was worn by Phillip every day he served in the military. It even had a piece missing in the black bezel where, presumably, a round nicked it. It wasn't there the last time he had seen the watch when his brother was home on furlough. Maybe the damage was from the shot that killed him.

But the damn thing still worked. Even if it didn't, Scott would still wear it. He slept with it, showered with it. He had not taken it off since the army delivered it to the house along with Phillip's other personal effects.

A jingling bell in the background jarred him from his reverie. He pulled open the glass refrigerator door and grabbed a six-pack of Corona from the shelf. Seconds later, he hoisted it onto the counter. The man made small talk and they exchanged cash. Scott reached for the beer.

"Merry Christmas."

Scott stopped and looked at the guy. "What did you say?"

"Merry Christmas."

In the background:

Ring, ring, ring the bells,
ring them loud and clear . . .

"I'm so fucking sick of hearing about Christmas!" Scott slammed the six-pack down on the counter. "Merry Christmas," he mimicked. "Happy music. Happy this and happy that. Well, *I'm. Not. Happy!*"

The man held up his hands and took a step backward. "Okay, okay. I get it. Want me to shut the radio?"

Scott grabbed his temples. "I just want everyone to leave me alone." He swung his body right and lurched out of the store and into the frigid night air. He pulled his jacket around him but instantly felt the nineteen-degree chill nipping the top of his ears.

He wandered down the street, then two or three or four . . . he was not paying attention. He leaned his right shoulder into a door and pushed into Lefty's, a neighborhood bar.

It was loud with chatter. But thank god, no Christmas music. He made his way to the counter and sat down.

"I'm Gary. What can I get ya?"

"Blanton's. Straight from the Barrel. Neat."

"You got it." Gary moved off to prepare the drink. Scott closed his eyes and clenched his jaw. He had a few days off from work, but it was doing him no good. Left him alone with his thoughts. His anger and frustration and loneliness.

"Here ya go," Gary said.

Scott opened his eyes and watched as Gary placed the tumbler down and poured from the decorative squat, deep honey-colored bottle. Scott took the glass of high-proof bourbon and threw it back. The burn against his throat lifted some of the numbness and fog clouding his thoughts. Reminded him he was alive. "Another."

Gary squinted—no doubt wondering why his customer would order expensive, flavor-filled alcohol and guzzle it without savoring it. But that was not his job. He shrugged, gathered up the bottle, and did as requested.

Scott drained the drink.

"You okay?"

Scott felt the pull of alcohol on his lids. "One more."

"Sure you don't want to take a few minutes? That's a hundred twenty-five proof." Gary grabbed a bowl of nuts and slid them in front of Scott.

"Don't want any a that." He lifted his empty tumbler and set it back down. Hard. "Another."

Gary hesitated, then nodded.

Scott knew that the barman had seen a lot of people get drunk in front of him. He did not care. But at ninety-five dollars a bottle, perhaps Gary cared—as in being concerned that his customer had the money to pay.

The man next to Scott brushed against his arm. Once, twice. The third time harder. He laughed and high-fived his buddy. "Good one!"

"Hey," Scott said to his back, not loud but not to himself, either.

The bald bar mate—in his thirties and sporting a few tattoos on his head and thick neck—did not respond.

"Hey," Scott said again. Louder.

The man turned, glass in hand. "Yeah?"

"You keep bumpin' inta me."

"Oh. Okay. Thanks for tellin' me." He laughed and clapped hands with his friend again.

"Good one, Tony!" his buddy said, getting in his own chuckles.

"No," Scott said. "You don't understand. I don't want you fuckin' bangin' into me. Not in the mood."

"Heard ya the first time," Tony said. "Chose to ignore you."

Scott looked at the tumbler in his right hand. Anger built. Bourbon-fueled frustration flushed his face.

Another bump—which nearly knocked Scott off his stool.

Before he knew it, Scott's arm was moving. He smashed the glass against the back of Tony Asshole's skull.

Tony cringed in pain, fingers blindly reaching for his head, which was liberally oozing blood, then swung his torso around.

Scott felt the crush of a fist against his nose. He flew backward and hit the ground with a thud.

Tony was atop him but before he could land a blow Scott kneed him in the groin. Tony contracted, his head involuntarily slamming into Scott's cheek.

With the alcohol settling in his bloodstream, Scott tried to get off a punch. But his movements were sloppy and impotent. In response, Tony swung a pointy elbow into Scott's left eye.

Several blows to his face followed. In his blurry haze, Scott was vaguely aware of men pulling the assailant off him.

But that was the last thing Scott saw as his lids closed and he descended into darkness.

33

Hey. Get up."

He heard the voice far away, a hazy fog enveloping his thoughts. But then he felt a kick to his ribs: not hard but more of a firm nudge.

"Move on, buddy. Find another doorway to sleep in. I gotta open my deli. I'm goin' next door for a cup a joe. You still here, I'm a call the cops."

Scott shielded his eyes against the bright morning glare. "Where am I?"

"Broadway. In the way of my front door. Now git." He turned and walked into the adjacent Starbucks.

Scott rolled onto his left side. His ribs hurt. His face hurt. His nose was crusted and swollen closed. As was his left eye. Broadway. *How'd I get here? What time is it?*

He cleared his parched throat and checked his watch.

But it was not there.

Scott patted his pockets, his shirt, his pants. Nothing. He tried to get to his feet—maybe it was wedged underneath him—but it was nowhere to be found.

He dropped to his knees and sat there, staring at the ground, trying to remember what happened and how he got there. He vaguely recalled going to the bodega. The bar. That guy who kept banging into him. A fight.

Except it was not much of a fight. A beat down. That was all he could remember.

But the G-Shock. Phillip's watch. That was irreplaceable.

A tear dropped from his right lower lid, landing in a small puddle of dried blood. He knelt there, shoulders slumped. He lost track of time . . . literally.

"You still here?"

Scott slowly swung his head to the left. He looked at the guy, standing there holding his steaming tall coffee. No clue as to the loss he had just suffered.

He pushed to his feet and trudged off in the direction of his apartment.

"Hey, you got blood all over da gawddam entrance . . ."

Scott continued walking, pain in his ribs with each breath, his left eye tearing and blurry, the swelling making it tough to see. He was concentrating on putting one foot in front of the other—then realized he had better check to see if he still had his wallet. If they stole the watch . . .

It was gone too.

Scott made his way back to the bar to see if anyone had turned in his G-Shock. He figured there was nothing to lose. He was assuming he was robbed, but maybe it had come off in the fight.

But Lefty's was closed, locked up tight. He realized that it must be earlier than he thought. He glanced around and saw a woman approaching. "Miss—what time is it?"

She cringed at the sight of him, stepped to her right, giving herself a wide berth. "'Bout seven," she yelled, hurrying off.

"I—I was robbed. They stole my watch." He held up his bare wrist.

She glanced over her right shoulder, checking for oncoming cars, and added distance between them by crossing the street.

He walked all the way back to his place on Thirtieth Street. It was a typical New York City apartment—old, outdated, and small, though not tiny like others in the area. He had a shade over nine hundred square feet, plenty of room for one person. In fact, he had no right owning an apartment at all. But the market had been in a prolonged downturn since the eighties and he lucked onto a foreclosure owned by a bank that also had financial trouble.

Not only had Scott inherited the money Phillip socked away while in the army, but Phillip had listed him as the sole beneficiary to his military-issued group life insurance. Scott did not get rich off it, but it facilitated him putting a roof over his head. Even in death Phillip had taken care of his younger brother.

All this virtually guaranteed that Scott would never have to see his mother and Nick again. As long as he got a decent paying job to cover property taxes and homeowner's association dues—with enough left over to put food on the table—he was self-sustaining.

As it turned out, the housing market started rising shortly after he made the purchase and he now had some equity in the apartment. Even though everything else in his life was a mess, this was a steadying influence. No matter how bad things got, he had a place to call home.

He walked in and stood in front of the wall of picture frames: most were of Phil with a number of his buddies. Different poses, locations, friends, and times. Some were serious, official army pictures. Others were casual snapshots taken with his rifle in full tactical camo gear, mugging for the camera.

Scott could not help but notice the watch in every one of the images. He hoped the G-Shock was still at the bar . . . but he figured that was wishful thinking. Either the guy who beat him up took it, his friends—or someone who saw him passed out in front of the deli.

He walked into the bathroom and pulled off his filthy, smelly clothing. No wonder the woman had freaked out when he asked her for the time. He looked like the bums on the Bowery who dragged their greasy rags across your windshield in hopes of getting a tip. He poked at his swollen and bloody face. There were two large bruises covering his ribcage. He could feel the bones moving under his fingers. Two were busted for sure.

After turning on the shower, and wincing from pain as he bent over, he slowly pulled off his underwear and began peeing in the toilet. He closed his eyes. Took a deep breath—or tried to.

And flashed back on the moment when Nick had walked in on him while he was in the bathroom . . . and then the first time he had jammed the bottle up his rear end.

Scott finished and flushed, but stood there reliving the moment, anger building. He felt impotent, useless, weak.

He hated Nick James. But worse than Nick was his mother.

She had abused him, physically and emotionally. She poisoned him, bullied him, and made life miserable for his dad. And her ultimate sins: she brought Nick into his life—and failed to protect him from that scumbag.

Somehow, some way, someday, he had to make her pay. Maybe even both of them.

34

Vail stood in the resort's lobby yawning repeatedly before shaking her head and hoping it would somehow wake her up. She caught a guy ogling her, so she pulled back her thin leather jacket and deliberately exposed her holstered Glock and brass FBI badge.

The man looked away faster than a Rottweiler can snatch a hunk of steak.

A moment later, her phone rang.

"Good morning, Adam."

"Not really."

"Why?" she asked. "Not enough sleep?"

"Not enough sleep. And."

Vail waited a beat, but Russell did not finish the thought. "And what?"

"And we've got a list, remember?"

"Last night the list was good news."

"Only by comparison to—"

"Yeah, yeah, yeah. Whatever. But I thought Ferraro said we couldn't go that route."

"He said we couldn't devote manpower to go door to door. Didn't say *we* couldn't do it."

"When are you picking me up?"

"I'm parked out front."

"You could've said so."

"I just did. Get your ass out here."

Vail strode into the sunlight and saw Russell's car parked near the valet stand. She descended the steps and climbed into his sedan.

A moment later, they were pulling out of the resort.

"So when we visit these women, I don't think I should introduce myself as FBI. Might freak them out."

"You mean freaking them out more than the police coming to their doors and telling them not to wash or shower . . . until further notice?"

Vail shrugged. "Yeah."

"We're not seriously going to tell them that, right?"

"No, Adam. We're not. You're going to introduce yourself as HPD Detective Adam Russell and then say, 'This is my partner Karen Vail.'"

"Thanks. I couldn't have figured that part out."

"The key is not saying FBI."

"Do you think I took a stupid pill this morning? Move on."

"Right. So we tell her that we've gotten an anonymous tip and she should not buy any homemade soap."

"And you don't think they're gonna wonder about us?"

"How so?"

"Like maybe we're imposters—or cops who've lost touch with reality?"

"Sell it. You want me to give you a script?"

Russell frowned at her. "No thank you."

Vail tried to hold back her smile but failed.

"So which Mary do we visit first?"

"Might as well save time. Go by proximity. Which is closest?"

Russell pulled to the curb and looked over the list he had printed out. "This one. Mary Pollard."

A mile later, they parked in Pollard's driveway. Russell took the lead and knocked on her front door, which featured a wreath made of wine corks and silk flowers.

"Pretty," he said.

"If you like that kind of thing."

They waited, then rapped on the wood again.

"Now what? Leave a note?"

"No," Vail said, pulling the list from her back pocket. "We've got phone numbers. Let's call. Maybe she doesn't hear us."

"Are those cells or landlines?"

"You're asking me? It's your list."

"Don't know."

He dialed and they waited. They did not hear the phone ring inside the house, but Mary Pollard answered. Russell explained who he was and went through the spiel they had agreed on. After hanging up, he turned and headed back to the car.

"Well?"

"Good news is she's still alive. And she hasn't bought any soap."

"How'd she take it?"

"There was some pausing. Like she was trying to figure out if I'd escaped from the looney bin."

"I've been trying to figure out the same thing. What'd she decide?"

Russell snorted. "That I was legit."

"For the record, *I'm* not convinced yet."

He ignored the dig. "Let me see the list," he said, wiggling some fingers. "Next one up."

She handed it over and he scanned it as they climbed back into the car.

"That one," he said, tapping the page. "Mary Wingate."

Ten minutes passed. They parked and Vail and Russell strode up the center flagstone path to the front door. Russell knocked. They waited.

Russell pulled out his cell. "I'm gonna call."

"You hear that?" Vail moved closer.

"Hear what?"

Inside, the phone began ringing.

"That's me calling."

"No," Vail said. She pressed her ear to the wood. "I hear—I hear noises. Scuffling or something. Groaning? Moaning?"

Russell chuckled. "Really? C'mon, Karen. I thought you were better than that."

"What?"

"Every cop knows that trick and—"

Before he could finish his sentence, Vail unleashed a firm side kick and the jamb splintered. She followed the door in, Glock now in her right hand.

"Shit. What the hell are you doing?" Russell followed, having exchanged his phone for a pistol.

Vail wound her way to the back of the house where a small Italian greyhound was lying across a woman, her body prone on the back patio deck.

She whistled and the dog turned and snarled, baring his teeth. A low growl rumbled from deep inside his throat.

"I'm betting she's dead and he's freaked out," Vail said. "Thinks we're gonna hurt her. Or him." Vail holstered her weapon and got down on her knees.

"What are you doing?"

"I'm not gonna shoot the dog, Adam. He's confused and upset." Vail made a kissing noise with her lips and smiled, held her arms out and talked soothingly. "It's okay, boy. Good boy."

The dog's growl morphed into a whine. His ears drooped.

"Adam," she said softly. "Put your gun away."

Russell hesitated. "What if he charges?"

"Once he realizes we're not a threat, he'll be fine. Put it away."

"What are you, the dog whisperer?"

"Now."

"Fine. Good thing I'm a quick draw. And if he charges, I am gonna shoot him."

"C'mere guy. It's okay." Vail wiggled her fingers. The greyhound hesitated, watching her, then rose from his haunches and stood. He remained in place as she continued to speak to him, using a high, sing-songy voice.

He advanced on her slowly, keeping a watch on Russell, who had mimicked Vail in getting on his knees.

"No quick moves, Adam. Smile."

"Smile? You're shitting me."

"Smile. Dogs read human facial expressions. Do it."

"I feel like an idiot."

"Socrates said to know thyself. And Shakespeare wrote, 'To thine own self be true.'"

"You're really quoting Shakespeare?"

"I have a personal connection. Someday I'll tell you about it."

The dog began wagging his tail, but his ears were still pinned back. Vail reached out slowly to let him sniff her palm. "That's it," she sang. "See? I'm here to help."

"Can I go check on Mary?"

"Hang on a second. No quick moves. Let me build some trust. Unfortunately, Ms. Wingate isn't going anywhere."

Vail began petting his head gently, stroking it, talking softly. "I'm sorry, guy. I know, this is very difficult for you."

"You have a dog, I take it?"

"I do. A standard poodle."

Russell chuckled. "Wouldn't have taken you for a poodle owner."

"And I wouldn't have taken you for someone who knows anything about profiling dog owners."

"Just a good judge of character."

"Well I can't dispute that. You obviously like me." As she rubbed behind his ears, she checked the dog's collar. "Oscar. Good boy." Vail turned her head toward Russell. "Call animal control. Maybe they can locate next of kin who'd be willing to take Oscar."

Russell slowly pulled out his phone and began poking at the display.

"And see if there's a leash around here somewhere. No quick moves."

Russell rose and began moving about. He located Oscar's lead and brought it over to Vail, who fastened it to the dog's D-ring. "Okay, boy, let's go for a walk, okay?"

Oscar wagged his tail harder. Vail got to her feet and started toward the door. But Oscar stopped and turned back to Mary.

"You want to say good-bye to mommy?" She led the way to Mary Wingate's body. Oscar sniffed it, gave her face a lick, and then looked at Vail.

"I know. I understand." She turned and walked out under Russell's watchful eye.

Vail walked Oscar and waited by Russell's car, getting down on a knee and petting the dog, calming him. A moment later, Russell exited the house and joined her.

"So?"

"So it looks like Ms. Wingate is another of our aconite vics. No one else home. Soap wrapper in bathroom. Freshly opened. Bar looks new."

"We were, what? Ten minutes too late?"

"The way it goes, Karen. We can't be everywhere at all times. We do our best."

"Yeah, yeah, yeah. You'd think that after all these years I'd be used to it."

"Used to blaming yourself or finding dead bodies?"

Vail harrumphed. "Both."

"Jesus," Russell said. "If I'd chosen her address before Pollard's, she'd still be alive."

"Now you're blaming yourself?"

"Dammit."

"Look at it this way. It's probably all Ferraro's fault, not ours. If he didn't have an attitude toward me and allowed a bunch of cops to go door to door, she'd still be alive. Think about that."

Russell ground his molars.

"How about animal control?"

"Crime scene's an hour out." He reached down and stroked Oscar's head. "Animal control will be here in fifteen."

"I hope Wingate's got kids or siblings. He's a really sweet dog."

"He is beautiful."

"Always been attracted to greyhounds. But I'm a dog person. There aren't many breeds I don't like."

"Carrie and I thought about getting one, but we got a divorce instead."

"Oscar's gotta be only about twelve to fifteen pounds. So dainty."

"Listen to you," he said with a laugh.

Oscar reached over and sniffed her ear, then gave her cheek a lick. "Let's see if we can track down Mary Wingate's friends, in case they were with her when she bought the soap."

"I checked around. She had two more bars."

"One was apparently enough."

Ten minutes later, animal control pulled in behind Russell's vehicle. Vail explained the situation and they took down the information.

"I'm Karen."

"Vanessa."

"So what's the next step?"

"We'll look into it," Vanessa said.

"And what if you can't find a relative or friend willing to take him?"

"We'll check with the local rescue organization. They'll try to get him a home."

"And if they can't?"

"You're getting way down the road. Let's take first things first."

Vail bent over and gave Oscar a pat behind the ears. "Take care, boy. You're in good hands."

35

The forensics unit arrived and began the process of documenting the scene. Russell was on the phone with Ferraro, who called the moment he was informed there was another victim.

Vail made use of the time by canvassing the neighbors. None knew anything of value. A couple expressed shock at Wingate's death while others did not know her.

As she made her way back to Russell, she noticed that he was still on the phone.

"This is getting out of hand," Ferraro said. "We need to make some progress."

"I understand. I'm—we're doing our best here, Chief."

"That hasn't been good enough, Detective, has it?"

"I don't know what you want me to say. If you think we've missed—"

"Missed? I don't know what you've missed. But you seem to be missing more than you're catching. 'Cause you sure as hell haven't caught *the killer*. You don't even have a suspect."

Russell rubbed his right temple and glanced at Vail, who was approaching.

Vail read his expression, gave his shoulder a reassuring pat, then walked away. This was not an argument she should be involved with . . . one she could not win.

She went for a short walk, then stopped and closed her eyes. Took a deep breath, trying to clear her mind and mentally work the case backward in case she had missed anything.

She felt a tap on the shoulder. "Sorry to interrupt."

She turned and opened her eyes. It was Russell.

"Chief wants to see us. Now."

As they walked back to the car, Vail glanced over at Mary Wingate's house.

"Didn't sound happy," she said.

"Nope."

"Sorry. You're taking the brunt of it, for our failures."

"I don't know what more we could be doing."

"I agree. But a boss doesn't want excuses. He wants results."

Russell frowned. "Yeah." He was a quiet a moment. "You were deep in thought when I came over."

"Just trying to see if we overlooked something."

They got into the sedan and buckled up. "And?"

"And the way he kills—almost passively—it makes it tough to set a valid timeline. We don't really know when he made contact with his vics, when they bought the soap. If they don't open the bar right away, they could've bought it a week ago, two weeks ago."

"And since we don't know if Mary Kelleher's death is one of his victims, that makes it even tougher to evaluate the frequency of the murders."

"His MO," Vail said, "makes that almost impossible to figure out anyway."

Russell groaned. "Smart son of a bitch."

"You know, you're very likely right."

"That he's smart?"

Vail reclined against the passenger door. "That he's a son of a bitch. His mother musta been a real doozy. 'Course, that doesn't excuse his behavior."

"You mean every guy who's been abused by his mother isn't a serial killer?"

"Something like that."

Russell's phone rang. He answered it and Bachler's voice filled the speakers.

"You got something for us Harry?"

"Am I on speaker? Are you with Agent Vail?"

"Yes to both. Why?"

"You're both gonna want to hear this. Found semen at the crime scene you asked us to check. On the outside deck of Mary Burkhead's house."

Russell elbowed Vail. "No shit. You were right."

"You know what they say."

"Miracles happen?"

"No," Vail said with a frown. "That even a broken clock is right twice a day."

"Any hits in CODIS?" Russell asked, referring to the Combined DNA Index System.

"Just got the report. Give me a second." Bachler hummed a few seconds, then said, "Umm . . . negative. So we got his DNA but not his identity. Best I can do right now."

"Let us know if you find any at the other homes. And please send that sample to Tim Meadows at the FBI lab."

"Copy that."

Russell hung up. "Does this change your opinion of this guy?"

"Nope," Vail said. "I still think he's scum." She cringed. "So to speak."

"Seriously."

"I'm being serious. It just confirms what I'd been thinking, what had been gnawing at me. He avoids confrontation—which is why he poisons from a distance—and yet needs some connection to the victim to get off."

"Apparently, literally."

They drove in silence for a few moments. "Any other thoughts while you were . . . meditating?"

"Yeah. He could've modified his MO. If Kelleher is his vic, he still could've used aconite but delivered it in some other way."

"No soap."

"Right. No soap."

"And hard for him to go back to Kauai to jerk off."

"True," Vail said. "Maybe he took a trophy from her. Something to remember her by, so when he saw the obituary in the paper, he could manufacture some kind of deeper connection—even if it's only in his head."

"Do serial killers change their MO?"

"Definitely. They adapt, learn, develop better, more successful ways of finding their vics and, obviously, killing. But their ritual doesn't change—and that's exactly why it's so important for us to evaluate the behaviors. Which is why this case is so damn frustrating."

"The lack of behaviors. No interaction with the vics' bodies."

Vail was staring out the windshield. "You're learning."

"These offenders aren't the only ones who can adapt."

Vail let a smile tease the corners of her lips.

"I guess this new victim will tell us a lot." Russell nodded slowly. "If we don't find aconite and this is really one of his vics, we need to figure out how he's doing it."

"Yeah."

"Well . . . I'll shut up now. Keep thinking, Karen. We've got another fifteen minutes till we get there."

36

They walked into HPD and Russell announced that the chief was expecting them.

His back was to them when Vail and Russell entered.

"You made quite a mess of the crime scene," Ferraro said.

Vail and Russell shared a confused look.

"Oh," Russell said. "That was the dog, sir. Ms. Wingate had a small greyhound—"

"Not the dog. The front door." Ferraro turned around slowly and faced Vail.

"I heard a noise."

"A noise. What do you think, that I never drove a beat?"

Vail squinted. "I don't understand what you're getting at—"

"Did you have a warrant?"

"No. But like I started to say, we heard something inside."

"Exigent circumstances," Russell said. "Agent Vail thought the offender might be in there."

"Really," Ferraro said. "And why would he be in there? I thought he poisons from a distance."

"I didn't think he was in there. I was afraid the woman was choking."

"You were afraid." Ferraro laughed sardonically. "Yeah. Now *that* I believe."

"You know what I mean."

Ferraro sucked his bottom lip. "And if the woman was choking from this poison, what would you have done? Administered the antidote?"

"There is no antidote," Russell said.

"Oh, right," Ferraro said derisively. "There is no antidote." He mock-slapped his forehead. "So what were you going to do, Agent Vail?"

"Render aid and assistance. That's what police officers do."

Ferraro pursed his lips and nodded thoughtfully—but not really. "And exactly what aid and assistance were you going to render? What was effective against this poison?"

Asshole. He knows there's nothing I could've done.

"I was acting on instinct. To save a life."

"So you weren't thinking."

"Look, Chief. You can twist my words and their meaning all you want. I was doing my job. That's it. Even if you were behind that door, I would've done the same thing."

He worked his molars, pissed—and measured his response. "How touching. You would've used your clairvoyant talents to determine that I was lying there dead in the back of the house."

One can always hope.

"I'm proud of what I did. And I'd do it again."

"That's what I'm afraid of."

Asshole. You're the reason why she died! No—don't go there, Karen. Keep your mouth shut.

"I wonder if your unit chief would approve of your actions."

Is that a threat?

"My chief," Vail said with a laugh. "I'd hope my chief wouldn't have penny-pinched and played a petty game with other people's lives."

"Come again?" Ferraro asked, his face reddening.

"If you'd deployed officers to do check-ins on all the Marys on our list, Mary Wingate would probably still be alive. But because I suggested it, you rejected the idea outright."

"You know what, Agent Vail?"

"Sir," Russell said, holding up both palms. "Playing the blame game isn't getting us anywhere. Let's all take a deep breath. These killings are getting to all of us. We're *all* doing our best to catch this guy. Let's not forget we're on the same team here. And right now, all our energies should go toward finding him before he takes more lives. You said so yourself half an hour ago."

Ferraro frowned, then swatted at the air. "Get the fuck out of here, both of you. Go do your jobs."

That's what we were doing.

37

Vail and Russell stepped out into the building's parking lot.

"Not sure that was wise, Karen."

"Wisdom did not enter into the equation. It was emotion. Anger. His bias is not helping us." She snorted. "Maybe he's right. Maybe I'm hurting more than helping."

"Bullshit. You know that's ridiculous."

"I tried to keep my mouth shut, Adam. I really did."

"Water under the bridge. We need to focus now, right?"

Vail sighed. "Yeah."

They were approaching Russell's car when a cop called to them from across the parking lot.

"Yo! Adam, they got another for you."

"Another what?" Russell asked, starting back toward the building.

The officer waited until Russell reached the door. "Another body."

A particular four-letter word fluttered through Vail's thoughts.

"Where?"

Ferraro walked over and handed them a slip of paper. "Sunset Beach."

"Pūpūkea?" Russell asked.

Vail read Russell's consternation. "What's poop pooh keah?"

"A small town. Different from what we've dealt with."

Vail frowned. "Let's go. Wasted time is our enemy."

"Wasted time is our enemy," Russell said as they started back toward their vehicle. "That's pretty good. Mind if I use it sometime?"

"If it helps you catch bad guys, use it all you want."

They arrived at the crime scene thirty minutes later: a tight-knit community known for surfing, snorkeling, and relatively uncrowded beaches. Now there were three police cars and yellow tape ribboning around an area bordering the two-lane road.

Off to the side were a couple of news trucks. Travis Sharkey was standing by one of them, watching as Russell and Vail drove by him.

They parked across the two-lane road in a public lot and crossed the street. They donned booties and gloves and checked in with the crime scene officer. Directly to their right was a mud brown Chevy van, circa 1960—and looking every decade of its age—brush painted with "Fruit Smoothies" across its front and sides. The tire treads were just about bare, worn down to their base rubber.

Vail and Russell introduced themselves to a woman carrying a large Nikon camera: Cynthia, the head criminalist. She gestured at the covered body that lay sprawled on the ground a dozen feet from the truck. "Several witnesses. All had the same story: vic started choking, eventually dropped to her knees and then stopped breathing."

"Find any bars of soap nearby?" Russell asked.

"Bars of . . ." Cynthia looked at Russell, then Vail. "Soap?"

"Sounds like a strange question," Vail said. "But it's not. Did you? Yes or no?"

"No."

Vail glanced around the area, looking for the nearest restroom. There was one across the road, near where they had parked. But why would you buy a bar of soap and then use it in a public beach bathroom? *Unless you're a local and you know there's no soap there.*

"Do we have an ID?"

Russell's question pulled her back to the discussion.

"Yeah," Cynthia said, "but it's gotta be verified. Her name was printed on a homeless shelter card. No photo."

"Let me guess," Russell said. "Mary something?"

"Guess again. Haley Anderson."

"Haley?" Vail squinted at the nondescript sheet draped over the victim. "Gotta be someone else's ID."

"Could be," Russell said. "Someone named Haley must've given her the card to use. Or she took it off someone. Or found it."

"I sent a photo along with her name to HPD for confirmation," Cynthia said. "Hopefully we get a hit."

"Good." Russell knelt down and looked under the covering. "Whoa." He drew his chin back and glanced up at Vail. "Not sure what to make of this." He pulled the drape off the woman's head and torso.

Vail leaned forward and rested a palm on each knee. The deceased woman was disheveled, with leathery, severely sun-ravaged skin.

"Looks elderly," Russell said, "but I doubt she's much older than forty."

"At most," Cynthia said. "The constant unprotected UV exposure causes dramatic premature aging."

Vail examined the corpse's fingers. "No osteoarthritis. Could be in her mid to late thirties."

Cynthia held up her phone and said, "She's thirty-eight. ID just came through. That *is* Haley Anderson."

Russell straightened up. "What the hell's going on?"

Yeah. What he said.

Vail realized Russell was staring at her. Of course he was. He had no explanation—and limited experience as a detective. She was the serial killer expert. Which meant she was supposed to have the answer. Or least *some* answer.

"Karen?"

"Yeah. I know, Adam. I'm thinking."

I got nothing.

"No soap," she said, more to herself. "Again?" *Unless Kelleher wasn't one of his vics.* She began pacing. The near-pristine beach was to her right, a wide expanse in the cove creating a haven of paradise.

Except for the dead body.

"Vic doesn't fit our theory."

"I know," Vail said. "Well aware of that."

After a long moment of reflection, Russell cleared his throat. "There's something you should know. I've wanted to tell you but I didn't know how."

Vail looked at him. "This is not sounding promising, Adam."

"Ferraro. My chief? He doesn't like you."

Vail snorted.

"I asked him what the deal is, but he refuses to discuss it."

"I think I already know."

"You—you do? I thought you—"

"My fiancé looked into it. A former colleague of mine, Chase Hancock, is Ferraro's brother-in-law. Hancock was a crappy agent and wanted into the profiling unit. My boss asked my opinion, I told him what I thought, and Hancock didn't get the gig. He blamed me. As if that wasn't bad enough, we ended up squaring off during a case a few years ago. He was out of the Bureau and working private security for—well, for a state senator. She assigned him to my task force and that didn't go so smoothly. He didn't know his ass from his elbow."

"Hard to mix up those two body parts."

"That's my point."

Russell chuckled. "But this Hancock guy, he thought he was the foremost expert, right?"

"Yep. And I didn't hesitate to call him on it. Anyway, we didn't play well together and it all went south from there."

"So it's personal, this animosity Ferraro's got toward you."

She shrugged. "Never met the man before, so it's gotta be."

Russell looked out at the ocean. "The part I didn't want to tell you is that he wanted you outta here tomorrow."

"Tomorrow?"

"I talked him into giving us a couple of days."

Vail shook her head out of disbelief, not sadness. "What if we're making headway and have a bead on—"

"Doesn't matter. This is emotional, not logical. Like your outburst a little while ago. He wants you gone whether we've wrapped things up or not."

"I didn't exactly help my case, did I?"

"Probably not."

Vail sighed. "I'm here to help you guys out. So if he doesn't want the help . . ." She shrugged. "Nothing I can do about it."

"I'm not giving up so easily. I want you here. I need you here."

"Nice thought."

But I've been gone for almost three weeks. I could go home, see Robby, start planning our wedding.

She checked her watch. "Let's make use of whatever time we've got left."

Russell frowned. "Yeah." He got quiet for a moment, then said, "So is the killer changing? Devolving or something? Because of yesterday—"

"No."

"No? How do you know?"

Didn't I tell him to stop asking me good questions?

She kept her gaze out on the breaking waves. A gentle breeze ruffled her red hair—but she hardly noticed because a thought was formulating.

"Karen?"

"He didn't mean to kill Haley."

"How do you get that?"

"Haley was a mistake. Why, I don't know. Maybe he gave the soap to someone else, who lost it. Haley found it and . . ." She shrugged. "Wasn't her lucky day."

"That's your best guess?"

"For now. Give me a few minutes and maybe I'll come up with something better."

"That's not funny."

"I'm not joking."

"Detective!"

Russell turned and saw an officer standing by the mud brown smoothie truck. He started toward the cop, followed by Vail.

Vail trudged along the pavement. "Another possible scenario is that someone named Mary bought the soap, saw Haley, or knew her—or knew she was homeless—and gave it to her. As a gesture of goodwill."

Russell gave Vail a look, but his face was silhouetted against the sun and she couldn't make out his expression.

He stopped in front of the officer. "What's up, Kahale?"

"You're gonna wanna hear this."

Russell and Vail ducked beneath the crime scene tape, following Kahale, who led them to the van.

"This lady's a witness," Kahale said. "Says she saw the whole thing."

What's there to see? Woman starts coughing, drops dead. End of story.

Kahale stepped aside as Vail and Russell craned their necks to look through a window cut into the side of the old panel van, where a woman was wiping pineapple and mango remnants off a well-worn butcher block countertop that looked like it had seen many years of continuous use.

"You see what happened?" Russell asked.

She stopped and set the sponge down. "Crazy. Never saw anyone die before. Haley was here one minute, the next she started coughing and just dropped—well, dead."

"You knew her?" Vail asked.

"Everyone around here knew Haley. At least, the locals. She's homeless, we all kinda looked out for her. Sometimes we wouldn't see her for weeks, then she'd come by and sit on the beach. I give her one of my old knives and she sits there carving wood that washes up onto the sand."

"Was she doing that today?" Russell asked.

The woman shook her head. "She'd waited, like she always does. Very polite. Never cut the line. Anyway, she got up to the window and I asked her what she wanted. I make some special drinks for her. Never charge her. She needs the nutrition, ya know?"

Vail nodded. "Very nice of you to look after her."

"Yeah, so she said she wanted an OJ with pineapple juice. I started to cut the fruit when she sees this chocolate bar I had on the counter. And she said, 'Wait. Can I have that instead?' I told her the smoothie would be better for her, but she said, 'Just this once.' I figured, hell, we all have our weaknesses, so I told her of course. I gave it to her, she walked away, and well, the rest you know."

"How long after you gave her the chocolate bar did she start coughing?"

"Not that long. Maybe a couple of minutes?"

Vail turned to Russell. "We need that chocolate—including the wrappers."

Russell swiveled around in the direction of the criminalist and brought two fingers to his mouth. The loud whistle made a dozen heads turn. He waved Cynthia over and told her what they were looking for.

"We bagged a bunch of stuff in the area. I'll go take a look."

As Cynthia walked away, Vail huddled with Russell. "I know this doesn't fit the UNSUB's ritual. But we follow the evidence and see where it leads us, right?"

Russell shrugged. "Guess so. Really thought we were onto something with the soap. I mean, in spite of Kelleher."

"We were—we *are*. Don't let this shake you. It'll all make sense once we figure it out."

Listen to me! So calm. Rational. What if it doesn't *make sense?*

"Yo, Kahale," Vail called to the officer, who was standing with his fingers locked in his belt loops staring out at the ocean.

He turned and trudged toward them. They met him halfway.

"Extend the crime scene tape around the van," Vail said. "You didn't secure a large enough area."

Kahale dropped his hands from his belt and apologized. "I'll get right on it."

Russell jerked a thumb over his right shoulder at the fruit smoothie van. "And get that witness's contact info."

"Already got it."

Vail and Russell headed back to Haley Anderson.

"So what the hell, Karen? I know you said I shouldn't let this bother me, but . . . I gotta admit. It's officially bugging me. Between Kelleher yesterday and now Haley Anderson, I feel like we're back at square one."

Vail sighed. She had thought the same thing—but kept rejecting the notion that she had gotten this all wrong.

Did I? Did I fuck this up?

"We're not wrong. I had my doubts last night, around 3:30 AM, I think. But I'm right. I mean, I don't know for sure what the hell's going on, but we're close. We have to be. I just . . . I feel it. There *is* an explanation here. We haven't found it yet, but we will."

"Yeah, but what if the explanation is that we're on the wrong road and—"

"Hang on a second." Vail jogged back over to the juice truck. But the woman they had spoken with was gone. Vail spun in a circle and located her about thirty yards away on the beach. "Hey! Hold up."

Vail took a step onto the sand and stopped. *Fuck it. Sand isn't gonna kill me, even a city girl like me.* She pulled off her shoes and socks and waded into the warm silica.

The woman waited for Vail to get closer. "The officer said my van is now a crime scene so I couldn't stay there. This is gonna kill my business."

"At least you get to live for another day. Haley, she's laid out on the asphalt back there."

She frowned. "Sorry. Just frustrated. I didn't ask for any of this."

"Neither did Haley."

Another frown. "What do you want?"

"Let's start with your name."

"Really?" She looked off at the ocean. "I already gave it to the officer."

"Look," Vail said. "I get that you're pissed off and that you're losing business. But I've got a job to do and, at the moment, that job is serving Haley Anderson by finding her killer."

The woman recoiled. "Killer?"

"Don't waste anymore of my time. Your name."

Seemingly mesmerized by the breaking waves, she said, "Mary Alana."

Bingo.

"That chocolate bar you gave Haley. Where'd you get it?"

Mary swung her gaze back to Vail. "Why?"

Now you're pissing me off.

"In case you didn't notice, Mary, I'm the one with the badge. So *I* get to ask the questions."

She frowned. "Some guy in a wheelchair. I've seen him around town."

Vail noticed that Russell had come up alongside her.

"Everything okay?"

"More than okay. Adam, meet Mary, the woman from the smoothie truck."

Russell instinctively held out his hand to shake—but his head whipped back to Vail. "Did you say Mary?"

Vail faced their witness. "Tell me about this guy in a wheelchair."

Mary shrugged. "Full beard, bushy. Starting to gray. Hair, too. Black, graying at the temples. Maybe forty, forty-five. Sign on his wheelchair says he's a veteran of the Iraq War."

Iraq War? Doubt that. A poisoner avoids confrontation. A soldier is taught to run toward a fight, not away.

"And he sold you this chocolate bar," Russell said. "Homemade?"

"That's what his sign said. And something like 'boutique' and Ecuadorian cacao beans. It was small, only like two ounces."

"Did he also sell soap?"

"Yeah," Mary said, drawing the word out, surprise permeating her expression. "How'd you know?"

"Have you used it?" Russell asked. "The soap?"

"Didn't get any. I bought like a gazillion bar pack at Costco. Last thing I needed was soap."

"Where'd you see him?"

"Waikiki, on one of the corners where they have all those fancy stores."

"Fancy?" Vail asked.

"Kalakaua Avenue," Russell said. "I know the place. Luxury Row. Chanel, Coach, Gucci, Tiffany's—you get the idea."

"Yes," Mary said with a nod. "Lots of rich Chinese and Japanese women shop there. Tourists."

"Doesn't sound like a place you'd find a guy in a wheelchair selling homemade soap and chocolate bars," Vail said.

"Not the kind of place you'd normally find me at, either," Mary said. "I obviously don't have that kind of money. But it's fun to rub elbows with the rich. A thousand bucks for a purse? Give me a break." She snorted. "And they've got some great restaurants down a couple of alleys. An authentic Korean hole-in-the-wall that I love. But I don't think Luxury Row's the only place this guy sells his stuff."

"Why's that?"

"Pretty sure I saw him somewhere else, maybe a few days before that."

"Where?" Russell asked.

Mary sucked on her bottom lip. Her eyes canted toward the sky for a moment, then she shook her head. "Can't remember. I buy my fruit and supplies all over the island. I—I was driving at the time, that's all I can tell you. Wasn't anywhere around here." She glanced up at the sky. "High traffic area. Which I guess makes sense because he needs people to sell to. Maybe closer to downtown?"

"What time of day was he out there?"

Mary shrugged. "Both times I saw him it was late afternoon. Four-ish. By Luxury Row, a little later because it was getting dark. Maybe he's there for a few hours. I don't know. He's not only catching tourists in the area but people getting off work."

Yep. That's what I was thinking.

"This guy," Russell said. "You get his name?"

"I think he said it was John."

John. Mary. Jesus. Couldn't their parents choose less common names? Like Latoya? Almudena? Constanza? Aurelia? Wilfred?

"Can we set you up with a forensic artist, see if we can get a likeness of him?"

Mary shrugged, then hooked a fingernail beneath a lock of hair that had blown across her face. "Sure."

"Did you open the chocolate bar?" Russell asked.

"Never got around to it. Bought it last night and stuck it in my purse. Forgot about it until I was here this morning. Figured I'd eat it after lunch. I took it out so I wouldn't forget about it. That's when Haley saw it."

"So the chocolate *was* meant for Mary," Russell said.

"Looks that way."

Mary looked from Russell to Vail. "What do you mean?"

Vail sidestepped the question. "You're sure you bought it last night?"

"Yeah. Why?"

"Oh," Russell said, "that's music to my ears."

"You know his name," Vail said, "so the two of you obviously talked. Any accents?"

"Southern. Or, I don't know, maybe back east. It was distinctive."

"Those are very different," Vail said. "Which was it?"

Mary thought, her eyes canting up to the sky. "Back east. New York. Or Boston. I'm not good with accents."

"What'd you discuss?" Russell asked.

"Small talk. He asked me where I was from, if I had any kids. If any of them served in the military. You know, stuff like that."

"Any of the questions seem odd? Did he seem off in any way?"

Mary stared out at the ocean. "Nothing I picked up on. Just making conversation. He did ask a lot about me, though. I didn't get to ask that much about him."

"How'd he become disabled?" Vail asked. "Was he missing any limbs?"

"No. He—he said he was in a Humvee accident outside Baghdad. Spinal cord injury. Didn't seem like he wanted to talk about it so I didn't push it. Had something wrong with his left hand, too. Wore a glove."

"A glove?" Russell asked.

"Yeah, not a thick, winter one. Thin, like a cotton one."

"Did he say anything about his mother?" Vail asked.

"His mother?"

"Yeah, like, 'Wow, you really remind me of my mom.' Anything like that."

"Actually, now that I think about it, he may've said something like that. Wasn't a big deal." She studied Vail's face. "Was it?"

"Yo!" Cynthia was approaching, sand flying off her shoes as she slogged toward them. She lifted up a clear evidence bag. "Found a chocolate bar wrapper. Among a bunch of other crap. But this is what you wanted, right?" She held it in the direction of Mary.

"That the one you gave the vic—uh, Ms. Anderson?" Vail asked.

Mary leaned forward and examined it, moving slightly to avoid the glary sunshine. "Yeah."

"No sign of the chocolate," Cynthia said.

"It was small," Mary said. "She probably ate the whole thing in a couple of bites."

Great.

"Spoke with Harry Bachler at the lab," Cynthia said. "He'll run this soon as I get back, check it for that toxin."

"And have him check her stomach contents," Russell said.

"Ten-four."

"Can you have someone bring it over there now? Rather not wait till you finish out your day?"

"I'll make it happen." Cynthia turned and headed back the way she came.

"Other than the red handwritten 'Mary Alana,'" Russell said, "looked like the wrapper was printed on a LaserJet. Black and white text. Did you catch what it said?"

"Seventy percent dark, homemade, small-batch premium chocolate from sustainably farmed Ecuadoran cacao beans."

Russell squinted at her.

Vail shrugged. "I like dark chocolate. A lot."

"She looked like she really, really wanted it," Mary said. "Haley. Her eyes were riveted to it. I—I just felt bad for her. I mean, how many happy things does she have in life? So I gave it to her. And you people are saying that that's what killed her? I killed Haley?" She brought a hand to her mouth, cupped it.

"No," Vail said, "you didn't kill her. We're looking into a number of things. You did the right thing in helping her out."

"But she ate the chocolate and then—then—"

"Mary," Vail said. "Listen to me. We don't know what happened yet. But even if it was something with the chocolate bar, it was someone else who was responsible. Not you."

Mary bit her lip and nodded slowly. Vail had not convinced her—that was obvious—but there was nothing more she could say.

Mary certainly won't feel any better when she realizes the toxin was meant to kill her, *not Haley.*

Vail and Russell thanked her, then left her alone with her thoughts—and guilt.

38

Vail and Russell stood roadside, waiting for a passing line of cars with surf boards bungied across the top, then headed back to their vehicle.

Vail took one last look at the beach over her left shoulder. "We need to ask Bachler if there are any chocolate bar wrappers in the crime scene cache they collected from Hanapepe."

"You know what *I* was thinking?"

"Lemme guess. That the description of the chocolate sounded damn good?"

"Nope. I was thinking that you were right. The offender's a male."

Vail took a long deep breath of moist sea air. "Looks that way."

"Speaking of chocolate," Russell said as he poked away at his phone. "If there *was* a wrapper, it could be who-knows-where. That wind on Hanapepe was relentless."

"At least it gives us some hope for linkage. We know Kelleher didn't buy soap. But now that we know he's also using chocolate, it puts her back in play."

Russell spoke with Bachler and made the request.

As he hung up, Vail said, "Think we can get a couple of undercovers to circulate Luxury Row, check out the intersections for a guy selling stuff from a wheelchair?"

Russell pursed his lips and nodded, then started dialing again. "Why do you think he switched to chocolate from soap? Is it related to the news article? Does he think it'll help keep the cops from finding him?"

"Mary told us the reason, even if she had no idea what it meant. What if John—if that's his real name—sees a woman who excites him, but she doesn't want a bar of soap? Chocolate gives him a completely different option. It's a pretty universal indulgence. I once read that ninety percent of people like chocolate. Don't remember how scientific that study was but sounds about right to me."

"I guess if you're gonna pick something to sell, our killer made a wise choice."

The call connected and Russell put in the request for immediate dispatch of undercover detectives to Luxury Row.

"Let's also use that 'army,'" Vail said. "Ask if any of your patrols have seen a bearded veteran in his forties selling soap and chocolate bars from a wheelchair."

Russell passed it along and asked that any officer with information text him—or call if they have a current location on the suspect. He also requested a review of traffic cam footage, though while on hold he told Vail that not many of the island's camera views would be helpful since most of them were mounted on freeways to monitor congestion. "We just don't have that many urban areas to worry about."

"We'll work with what we've got."

Vail's phone vibrated. She motioned to Russell and walked off.

Caller ID told her that Tim Meadows was calling.

"Tim."

"Got some good news and bad news for you."

"Bad news first."

"Nope. Gotta give you the good news first."

A grin cracked Vail's lips. "Deal."

"So what would you say if I told you I got DNA off one of the inner wrappers of the bars of soap?"

"I'd say you're playing a cruel game. Teasing me."

"And you'd be wrong. My eagle eyes picked up a ripple in the wrapper."

"A ripple in the wrapper? Really racked and wrangled your brain on that one."

"Huh?"

"Sorry. The alliteration threw me off."

"Focus, Karen. Yes, I saw a *ripple* on the inside *wrapper*. I checked, just to make sure it was water and not something else. It was saliva. And that contained DNA."

"Saliva? From what?"

"My guess, a sneeze."

"Okay. But could've been the victim's."

"Ah, but it wasn't."

"How do you know?"

"Because it was a male's DNA profile."

"Oh."

"Oh? Karen, I just gave you the key to solving this case."

"You did? Got a hit in the DNA database for the offender?"

"Well . . . not quite *that* key."

"Not to diminish the 'ripple on the wrapper' find—which was truly genius—but did you get the package of semen?"

"Karen. A package of semen? That sounds gross."

"The CSU team here found semen at one of the crime scenes. I had them send it to you."

"I'll look for it, compare the two profiles when I get it. But I may have something better. How about a physical description of the UNSUB who killed this victim known as . . . uh . . . Dawn Mahelona?"

"That would be very awesome."

"Damn right it would be."

"And how would you do that?"

"DNA phenotyping. My system is able to draw up a picture of the offender. So to speak."

"I forgot all about that. Email the picture to me."

"A picture—*so to speak*. There's a reason why I included that phrase, my dear Karen. Because it's not really a photo. It's . . . a figurative photo."

"Tim . . . Tim . . . please stop talking in circles. Do you have a picture of this guy or not? Figurative or literal."

"Yes. Figurative."

"So *figuratively*, what does this guy look like?"

"Hazel eyes, with a golden ring around the pupil."

"Hazel eyes? That's it?"

"That's not it. But before you toss that in the garbage as useless info, that type of pattern is very rare: only about one percent of the world population has it."

"From a practical point of view, Tim, that's of minimal assistance. Even a DMV description on a driver's license may say hazel eyes. It sure as hell isn't going to say, 'hazel eyes with a golden ring around the pupil.'"

"You know what, Karen? You're being ungrateful again."

"Sorry. I don't mean to minimize your work. Go on."

"A few caveats here. Height is only about eighty percent dependent on genetics and eye color may not be that accurate. Brown and blue eyes are easy to predict, but colors like hazel are a lot more difficult."

"Caveats noted. So the hazel is—"

"Somewhat accurate."

Vail shook her head, unsure as to how much this was going to help. "Go on."

"He'll have brown hair, most likely straight with a slight wave."

"Unless his hair is clipped short."

There was a brief silence, which Vail herself broke. "Sorry again. Continue."

"I was kidding about the wave. We don't have that ability yet. 'We' as in science, not me and my unit."

"Of course."

"Well, we have some ability to predict. So I was only half joking. He might have wavy hair."

Is there a glass pane I can put my fist through?

"He'll be a Caucasian male, about five foot eleven, somewhere in the range of thirty-five to fifty years old."

"That's a big range."

"Really, Karen? Glass half empty?"

"What glass?"

Meadows groaned. "You're looking at the negative. How about the positive of what I've given you?"

"You're right again. Wow, how often does *that* happen?"

"You're the best, Karen. The best at making me feel like shit about outstanding work that any investigator would kill to have. So to speak."

"I'm very grateful for this info, Tim. Do you think—can you render some kind of computer-generated photo of what this guy might look like—given the physical parameters of what you've just told me?"

"Check your inbox. I sent it right before I called."

"Jesus, Tim. You could've just told me that right up front."

"Then I wouldn't have had the opportunity to chat with you. But before you cut the call here to look at the rendering, you should understand a few more things. Our current technology can tell us certain things with relative certainty: ethnicity, gender, eye color—subject to the limits I mentioned—and hair color. But as far as height and age, I have to leave myself some room for error."

"Meaning you could be wrong."

"Meaning," he said with tension in his voice, as if Vail were starting to test his patience, "that the information might not be one hundred percent accurate. Same goes for baldness, hair texture, whether it's curly or straight—like the waviness I mentioned—and the shape of his teeth."

"How much can we rely on this computer rendering?"

"Consider it ballpark accurate. Enough to narrow your suspect pool."

"Our suspect pool is not very deep. It's more like a wading pond."

"So you have no suspects."

"Yep, that'd be accurate."

"So my phenotype is incredibly helpful."

Vail hesitated. "Potentially. I'll wait to answer that until we catch him. Fair enough?"

"I guess."

"Tim—thank you. Really. This is outstanding work. I'm sure it's going to help."

"Are you yanking my chain? Because you, well, you know you like to do that."

"As do you. But I'm serious. I can circulate this photo to the airports, update our BOLO," Vail said, referring to a "be on the lookout" alert. "And make sure anyone even close to this rendering is pulled aside and held for questioning."

"Glad to help."

"As always. I kid you, Tim, but you're a valuable member of my team. And no, I'm not being sarcastic here."

"Then let's end this conversation on a high note."

"Wait, what's the bad news?"

"That I already gave you the good news."

So much for a high note.

"Thanks, Tim. You came through for me again. Big-time. Talk soon."

Vail ended the call, then walked over to Russell, who had finished his call. "You ready for this?"

"For what?"

"I've got a ballpark accurate photo of our offender."

"No shit."

"Serious." She explained what Meadows had sent her.

"I've heard of phenotyping, but I've never used it on any of my cases. Didn't they use that a few years ago in North Carolina on a cold case?"

"Yeah—but it was South Carolina. So you're familiar with how it works?"

"I know just enough to butcher the science."

"DNA phenotyping is pretty simple," Vail said. "You know about DNA being the building blocks of life. The genetic instructions determine everything that makes us human. And the phenotype part of it is newer technology that keeps getting better as we learn more. Phenotype is what a person looks like based on her genetic code, plus any effects the environment has on her."

"But we don't have the killer's DNA."

"We didn't *think* we had it. But we do. My crack forensic tech noticed a ripple in one of the soap wrappers. Could've been just a drop of dried water, but it wasn't. It was saliva. And based on the DNA he extracted from that, he determined it was a male, so it wasn't from our victim. It gave us an approximate rendition of our UNSUB."

"How approximate?"

Vail shrugged. "Guess we'll find out when we catch the knucklehead."

"Helpful answer."

"Thanks. I try to be helpful."

"And you fail a lot. Like—how do we know the male DNA isn't from someone else who used the soap?"

"Because it was on the inside wrapper. And since I believe the offender is working alone, the only male who would've handled that—without dying—is the UNSUB."

"Probably."

"Probably," Vail said. "Yes. Send the rendition over to HPD and have some officers see if anyone where Dawn Mahelona worked looks like the phenotype image. If not, that just increases the odds it's our offender."

Russell sighed. "Fine. Send it to me and I'll get it over to the chief, ask him to have a guy run down to the palace. And I'll have him update the BOLO and get it out to the entire force."

She emailed it to him. "Meantime, let's test it out," she said, heading back toward the beach. "See if Mary Alana recognizes him."

Moments later they were trudging through the sand heading toward Mary.

She was sitting near the water's edge staring out at the ocean.

"Mary," Vail said.

She swung around, revealing tear-stained cheeks.

"Sorry to bother you, but we've got a photo for you to look at. Of the guy who might've sold you the chocolate bar."

Mary gathered herself and rose to her feet.

Vail held out her phone. "Keep in mind this is an approximation. It may not be completely accurate."

Mary took the Samsung and shielded the screen from the bright sunlight. "Hard to say. He had a beard. I mean, I think so. Yeah. Could be."

Think so. Could be.

She handed the phone back to Vail.

Dammit.

"Thanks, Mary," Russell said, taking Vail by the elbow and giving a gentle tug. "Appreciate it. Sorry again for your loss."

As they walked away, Russell sighed. "You were hoping for a slam dunk ID."

"I was."

"That'd be too easy."

"I would like to get back home this year."

If Ferraro gets his way, that'll be happening sooner rather than later.

A few moments later, Russell and Vail got in their car. "So now what?"

Vail pulled the shoulder harness across her body. "Let's join the Luxury Row party. Our offender shows up, I assume you wanna be the one to present him with his new set of silver Louis Vuitton bracelets." Vail winked at him.

"You assume correctly." He twisted the key and the engine turned over. "I just want you to know, Karen, that regardless of what Lance Burden said about you, you're definitely not as dumb as you look."

39

Scott Meece had been planning this for months. After not finding what he was looking for, he continued hunting—until he realized the answer had been in his own high-rise office building the entire time.

The woman reminded him of his mother, at least when he was young. Mid-thirties with a similar gait, build, and constitution. At first, when he noticed her in the elevator, his jaw went slack as she glanced over at him because he had neglected to move aside to make room for her. It was the same evil look his mother gave him when he did something she did not like.

Scott had checked his watch—a used G-Shock he bought from a pawn shop near Broadway that looked a lot like Phillip's—and noted the time. Each day he waited in the lobby for her. Like a spy, he used a copy of the *Wall Street Journal* to shield his face from view. Fortunately, she was fairly consistent in her schedule, give or take a few minutes.

He had decided he knew her routine fairly well. This was going to be the night. He packed a dopp kit filled with items he might need, then slipped it into the backpack he brought to work. It was difficult to concentrate all day as he watched the attack unfold in his mind.

Now, as he followed her down to the subway to take the N line near Forty-Ninth Street, his heart was racing, his breathing shallow.

He kept his distance, but among the crowd of rush hour commuters, it was not difficult to blend in. At one point he was standing at her left elbow as the train swayed and rocked while picking up speed between stations. He felt an erection swell in his pants as he thought of putting his hands around her throat.

The train hit its next stop and two dozen people moved toward the doors. Scott followed the woman—Nanette, according to someone who acknowledged her on the street.

They passed a few dog walkers until she hung a right several blocks later and ascended three black brick steps to an anteroom, fished out a key, and continued inside. Scott followed a moment later, then stopped at the entrance. He had not thought that her building would require a key to get in. He should have expected this, but there were so many kinds of apartments in Manhattan. He realized now he could not anticipate everything. He should have previously followed her all the way home. Then there wouldn't have been any surprises.

As Scott stood there, another woman excused herself and followed the same procedure Nanette had.

He laughed. "Forgot my key. Thanks." She held the door open for him and he "piggybacked" her, sliding in behind her.

Dodged a bullet there. Except that he had not looked to see what apartment Nanette lived in. He cursed himself. How could he be so stupid to think that he was ready to do this?

Scott thought about postponing it until he was better prepared. But he had come this far. What if he chickened out again? There were always excuses not to do something.

No, he was going to do this. Tonight. He needed to prove to himself he was capable.

He waited as the resident ascended the steps, then went back to the anteroom and looked at the various buzzers on the directory. Only first initials and last names were listed. There were five Ns.

He fisted his right hand and pressed it against his closed lips.

Stay or go? Try again another night?

No. Think this through.

He started at the top. Pressed the first N, waited. No answer. One more time. Again, nothing.

Moved on to the next one. A male voice. "I have a delivery for Nanette."

"Who?"

"Sorry. Wrong apartment."

But that got Scott to thinking. What if there was a husband or significant other? Or a roommate? Nanette did not wear a wedding ring, but that was not an absolute.

Tapped the next one.

"Hello?"

"Delivery for Nanette."

"Delivery?"

"UPS."

"Leave it by the mail room. I'll get it later. In the middle of making dinner."

"You got it." And so, apparently, did Scott: apartment 5B.

But now he lost his reason for knocking on her door. It would require a little more effort.

He rested his back against the wall and took a deep breath. All this thinking on the fly was exhausting. He thought he had done his homework. He thought it'd be easy.

Scott closed his eyes and again wondered if he wanted to do this. He was afraid that if he didn't do it, and do it now, he never would.

Could he live with that? He did not know . . . nor did he want to find out.

He needed to push forward.

Scott began climbing the stairs—then had an idea and stopped. He went back to the front door and crumpled a small piece of cardboard and shoved it into the female end of the lock's strike plate. He tried opening and closing it, but the male "tongue" of the knob did not catch. Perfect. He would be able to get back in.

He did the same thing to the outer door and then left to find a street vendor or store that sold what he needed.

Upon returning, he found that his security workaround was still intact. When he hit the fifth-floor landing, he took his backpack off and rummaged through it, pulling out the flowers that he had just purchased. He pulled on a white baseball cap and pressed on a fake moustache and goatee he brought from home, then stepped up to the door. Knocked, keeping the large arrangement front and center.

An eye covered the lens and after a second's hesitation the door swung open and revealed Nannette, her left hand cradling a mixing bowl against her hip. "Can I help you?"

"Yes, ma'am," he said in a bad southern drawl. "I've got a flower delivery for you from George Simon."

Nanette scrunched her nose. "Who?"

"George Simon. All I know is what the delivery instructions were. Could be wrong, I guess. Office mighta screwed it up."

She sighed. "Fine," she said, extending her free hand.

"It's real heavy and they overfilled the water. Here," Scott said, pushing his way past her and heading for the nearby table. He set the glass vase down then turned toward her and hooked his foot behind her ankle. With a shove against her chest, she went down fast and hard, landing on her back. The bowl went flying, sending its creamy yellow egg-and-flour concoction into the adjacent wall.

He leaped atop her and grabbed her neck with both hands.

"Bitch! I'm gonna kill you. For what you did to me. Made my life a living hell!"

Nanette's eyes bulged. She bucked and squirmed—anything she could do to dislodge him. Her face began shading red, a choking gurgle emerging from her throat. But she continued to struggle.

Nothing worked—until she swung her right fist into Scott's left eye. It stunned him and he released his hold. She followed with her other hand and connected with his nose. Another to his mouth, whipping his head backward.

He saw stars.

Scott sat there, stunned, trying to make sense of what was happening. He tasted blood and then another punch to his mouth and he was on his back.

rolling around
pain exploding from his face and
blood spurting everywhere

He was not quite sure where he was. He ducked his chin down and covered up, then swung his arms blindly. He struck something—and then the pummeling stopped.

He steadied himself, saw his backpack—grabbed it—and stumbled sideways out of the dining room.

Scott somehow made it into the hallway. The woman was yelling . . . somewhere behind him . . . was she coming after him?

He started running, sort of, down the stairs. His thoughts were still foggy, but he knew enough that he was in trouble.

He had to get out of the building . . . into the fresh air . . . away from the screeching. To safety.

Scott hit the street and the damp, cool night slapped him across the forehead, restoring some sense of self.

He remembered now. Nanette, the ruse to get into her place.

The metallic taste in his mouth nearly made him vomit. He brought a wad of blood-tinged saliva onto his tongue and spit it toward the curb. It was then that Scott realized he was missing part of a tooth.

Damn bitch. This was not supposed to happen.

He turned down the next street and did not stop until he saw a subway entrance. He scrabbled down into the station and hit the turnstile hard. He gathered his body over the top and somehow rolled over it, landing on the other side.

The train came seconds later and he stumbled on and sat down, keeping his face hidden as best he could. Last thing he wanted was for someone to call and report him to the police. He had no idea what he looked like—until he caught a glimpse in the window across the car.

Holy shit. His face was swollen and bloody and bruised, as if he had been worked over in a street fight. That was not far from the truth. It brought back painful memories of the bar brawl a few years ago. In a night of anger, frustration, and personal woe, he had asked for that beating. But that was not his intent tonight. He expected to have the upper hand, the advantage.

He was not Phil. He could never be.

He was a coward. An inept one at that.

As the subway sped forward, rocking slightly side to side, he realized that no one could ever find out he had been pulverized by a thirty-something woman. No.

No one could ever know.

But *he* knew.

He closed his eyes and cried.

40

Scott called in sick for a few days following his run-in with Nanette, then worked remotely from home for a week after that. His position as a computer coder afforded him such flexibility.

His facial swelling cleared up with repeated rounds of ice, and makeup covered the residual bruising. He got his front tooth bonded. It looked good as new.

But his ego had been battered beyond repair. He could not speak of what happened to anyone—for obvious reasons. Beyond the criminal nature of the attack, he could not stand the embarrassment. He would rather jump off the roof of his apartment building than face the pain and ridicule.

That night scared him. He was a wimp, plain and simple. He was the polar opposite of his brother, who dodged bullets in foreign countries. Who died a hero.

Nope. Scott Meece was a goddam coward, just as Nick had said when he told him and his mother that he was moving out. Leaving.

During the months after his encounter with Nanette, he pondered his next steps. His anger toward Mary intensified. He decided he would no longer think of her as his mother. He did not want to be identified with her in any way. He was not a *part* of her. And he sure as hell did not *want* any part of her.

He wanted to kill her more than ever. Over and over and over.

But he could not go through that trauma again. It was like reliving his childhood. It put him in a bad place, back when he felt worthless. There was no Dad, no Phillip to talk to, hang out with.

No one who understood what it was like living with Mary.

Scott spent weeks trying to think of a way around his dilemma. He kept a list by his night table and added to it whenever he had a new idea . . . which usually came while he lay awake in bed, unable to sleep. Once he identified an acceptable target, he could proceed in a variety of ways:

1. Hit it with a hammer from behind. Don't give it time to fight back.

2. Shoot it in the face with pepper spray, then attack.

3. Choose an older target. Can't fight back.

4. Stab it with a knife. As it bleeds out, choke it.

Scott looked over his list. All the possibilities held promise, but . . . blood. It did not matter whether it was his or not. He didn't like blood.

And what if it turned around right before he hit it with the hammer? Or stabbed it? Could he look in its eyes and still do it?

Probably.

Probably? Not good enough.

He slammed a fist into the mattress. This is who he was. He hated being a wimp.

He hated himself.

And so it went for weeks at a time, penciling out ideas and then rejecting them. They all held risk—risk of failure. Risk of embarrassment. Fear of confrontation.

As he stared at the copy of the *Daily News*, splattered all over the back page was the shame of a Yankees loss to lowly Texas, 13-3 . . . a thrashing by Bronx Bomber standards as Jeter, O'Neill, and Posada all took o-fers. They were still in fine position with an exceptional record, on pace for another mid-ninety-win season. Good enough for the playoffs if not the World Series.

Scott tossed the paper to the table. Engrossing himself in the sports pages was escapism; he knew it . . . and yet he did not know what else to do. The stress was becoming untenable. He had to figure out a solution before he walked out onto the roof and jumped.

Did he have the guts to end his meaningless, pathetic life?

If he did not think of something soon, he would find out once and for all just how much of a coward he was.

41

Scott sat in his easy chair watching the news. There was little else on TV other than unending reports of the 9/11 attacks. He had been in Connecticut the day the planes hit and was not able to return home until three days later.

His employer had canceled work for a week, so even though he had transitioned to working remotely most days, his boss told them all to take time to reflect. He said it didn't feel right to produce when others were mourning.

Regardless, most of his life was consumed with the tragedy. Everyone in New York City had been deeply impacted. Many knew someone who had died in the towers. The mass hysteria and confusion that followed was unlike anything he had experienced. He had difficulty empathizing with them, with feeling what others felt. He didn't know why. Other than anger toward Mary, he was kind of numb, as if he was living with the mute button permanently activated.

He learned how to feign concern, as that seemed to be essential to relating to his coworkers.

Even now, seven weeks or so following the attacks, the news was dominated by reports. Follow-up reports. New information discovered. The president talking about going after those responsible.

He closed his eyes and reclined, a beer in his right hand. Enough already. Move on to something else.

Please.

Grabbed the remote. Kept blindly pressing the channel up button until his finger got tired. Stole a look at the screen. He had stopped on CNN.

The story was the same here. Tossed the clicker down as the anchor droned on: "The Environmental Protection Agency has sent dozens of polarized light microscopy testing kits to Ground Zero to test bulk dust samples for the presence of asbestos fibers. According to Dr. Paul Zantar at Maimonides Hospital, there is a real danger of chronic airway disease afflicting the firefighters who were exposed to toxins during the 9/11 rescue. Because of the size of the toxic particles, the poison could . . ."

Scott's eyes shot open. He listened a second, then abruptly sat up.

Poison.

His mother had poisoned him when he was a kid. That's how he ended up in the emergency room. He had blocked it from his memory but sometime later he remembered his father coming to the hospital, the doctor explaining what had happened.

He stared ahead, seeing nothing. Whatever it was, she had to have put it in his food, mixed it in his breakfast. The . . . uh . . . oatmeal. It was oatmeal. It tasted too sweet.

What if he tried poison? On his targets? That way, if he did not want to risk it, he did not have to be even in the same room with them. No face-to-face confrontation. No chance of embarrassment, no blood, no chickening out.

Scott turned on his Compaq desktop and waited for Windows 98 to boot up. Like a watched pot taking its time to boil, the software took forever to load. Finally, Scott dialed in to the World Wide Web and listened as the modem noises whooshed and buzzed while making the handshake to the server and authenticating his account.

He opened Alta Vista and began a search for poisons. He needed something that would work quickly but not be obvious as a toxin. If the police knew it was murder, he would have to leave town. He didn't want to move, so it had to be surreptitious. It'd be better if no one—except him—would realize his target had been killed.

After poking around for an hour, he was not finding what he was looking for. Maybe you weren't supposed to put on the web the kinds of information he wanted to know. He shut down the computer and decided to go the old-fashioned route.

That Saturday he went to TR Dhanes, a well-known used bookstore in Brooklyn that a coworker had once told him about. They improperly bought advance readers, or bound proofs, that publishers gave out free to reviewers to help promote a book in advance of its release. Scott did not know if his colleague was right, but he did not care. If it was cheaper, who cared where it came from?

He walked in and saw a sign that advertised fifty tons of books—a statement that seemed grandiose. The place was dusty and old . . . probably an atmosphere the literary, intellectual types of Manhattan treasured.

To him, though, the musty smell was irritating and reminded him of a damp basement.

Scott perused the stacks—metal bookshelves stuffed with used hardcovers and paperbacks. As he walked through the store, he was beginning to think their claim was possible. Tons? Good. The better the chance he could find books on poisons.

Two hours later, he had settled on three that drew his interest: two on toxins and their effects on the body, and one that chronicled both famous and little heralded cases from the files of a former New York City medical examiner, including the methods the killer used and how police ended up catching the person responsible.

As he paged through the chapters, he realized that most of those who had been caught were women. Did that mean most poisoners were women? Or were they the only ones who got arrested and convicted?

He shook himself out of his fugue and dug out cash from his pocket. He paid and caught the subway back to his apartment.

By Sunday evening, he had assembled a list of potential poisons. Each had its advantages and disadvantages, but the first concern—even more important than being able to disguise it—had to be whether he could get his hands on it.

One caused malignant ventricular arrhythmias due to an accidental intoxication—essentially the person suffered a fatal heart attack that appeared to be a death by natural causes.

Yes. This poison ticked off all the boxes on his list of needs: Aconitum napellus.

Also known as aconite.

He found some additional details in the third book and discovered the toxin was derived from a plant. He could buy one, keep it in his apartment, and grind up the roots when needed.

Aconite was commonly used in herbal medicine for treating musculoskeletal pain, but the margin of safety between analgesic and toxic doses was very low. In Southeast Asia, where it was widely used, aconite-related deaths were not uncommon . . . at least at the time the reference text had been published.

The purchase would not be difficult—and it would not be questioned. This was it . . . the solution he had been looking for.

As Scott continued reading about it, he turned the page and found a few color photos of the plant. His jaw dropped. He recognized the blue violet flowers because of their unusual shape, which the text described as resembling a monk's hood.

It was a plant his mother kept by the sink in their kitchen. She nurtured it, watering it religiously, trimming it often. She gave more love and attention to that thing than she ever showed him.

Holy shit. Is this what she used on me? Or had she bought the plant afterward?

Wait.

His father had supposedly died a natural death. But was it? Was it really? Impossible to know.

But Scott knew.

His dad's heart attack was likely not an act of God or poor health or bad genes. It was a bad wife. A very bad wife.

Mary had killed him.

He knew that now.

The anger built inside Scott's chest. He wanted to grab a bat and smash the nearby window. And the television. And anything else within reach.

Instead, he grabbed his coat and walked out of the house in search of the plant known as Aconitum napellus.

42

V ail's phone vibrated. She thought about ignoring it but checked the caller ID and it was the assistant special agent in charge of the Behavioral Analysis Units, Thomas Gifford. Her boss's boss.

She could not send it to voice mail.

Vail groaned aloud.

"Problem?" Russell asked.

"We'll see." She brought the Samsung to her ear. "Sir. So nice to hear from you."

"Cut the crap, Karen. We've got a problem."

"With all due respect, whenever you call me there's a problem."

"And I seem to call you way too often."

Touché.

"What 'problem' do we have now?"

"You want to tell *me*?"

"Sir, I'm in Oahu and we've got a major case here. If this is something that can wait till I get back, then—"

"It can't."

Vail glanced over at Russell, whose brow was bunched in concern. She held up an index finger and refocused on Gifford.

"Then let's hear it."

"I'm trying to piece things together, but it looks like DOJ got a complaint," he said, using the abbreviation for Department of Justice—the parent of the FBI, as well as a host of other federal law enforcement agencies.

"A complaint? About what?"

"Not what, *who*. And that who is you."

"Who's the complainant?"

"The assistant chief at Honolulu PD. Brad Ferr—"

"Ferraro." They said it in unison.

"I see. So you *do* know what this is about."

"Not really. But Ferraro is the brother-in-law of Chase Hancock, and, well . . ."

"The asshole who caused all sorts of problems during the Dead Eyes case? The senator's security chief?"

"And former special agent. Yep. Him. Robby did some poking around, made the connection."

"Hmm. Okay. So what's that got to do with you?"

"Hancock and I didn't exactly end things on a positive note."

"Oh yeah." Gifford laughed. "I remember now. 'Positive note' is pretty funny."

"I didn't mean it as a joke."

"And this complaint certainly isn't. Best I can determine, after drawing it up, Ferraro sent it to the attorney general's office. And *he* referred it to the DOJ's inspector general. After a few phone calls he opened a case. They're starting an investigation."

Government bureaucracy moves like a snail. Except when it runs like a cheetah.

"An investigation into what?"

"Haven't seen the paperwork yet. Just got a verbal heads-up."

"If you can give me some clue as—"

"All I know is it has something to do with unlawful entry."

"Are you fucking kidding me?"

"Do I have to answer that?"

"No." She sighed loudly. "Can I talk off the record? As your future daughter-in-law?"

"You're putting me in a very tough spot, Karen. Only spousal privilege means anything in the eyes of the law. In-laws don't enjoy the same protections."

"Fine. Then you're not hearing this." She waited a beat and he didn't stop her, so she continued. "The complaint is bullshit. We're dealing with an offender who poisons his vics. From a distance. We determined there might be a way to predict who his next victims are, so my partner and I were checking in on those women. Second one on our list, I heard something inside the house. A groan, or something, maybe someone coughing—a precursor to death from this toxin—and I went in. Turns out she had a dog and he was growling or moaning. We were too late. She died."

"Will your partner corroborate?"

Vail glanced over at Russell, who'd been alternating his gaze between Vail and the road ahead. "Yeah. Of course he will. He was right there with me. I mean, he didn't hear the noises I heard, but—"

"Jesus Christ, Karen." He was silent a moment. "This could be trouble."

"Can't you call Knox?" she asked, referring to the FBI director. Knox knew Vail well because of her involvement with OPSIG, the Operations Support Intelligence Group—a covert ops division Knox had been instrumental in starting. He seemed to have her back.

"Who do you think gave me the verbal heads-up?"

"So we're good, right?"

"No, Karen, we're not good. Because the attorney general is Knox's boss and I'm pretty sure there's a limit to the director's reach."

Vail closed her eyes.

I have to focus on this killer. I don't need this shit now.

"Wish I could tell you how this is gonna shake out. But I've got no feel for it. We just have to let it ride."

Vail sighed. "Do I need an attorney?"

"You *could* call FLEOA," he said, referring to the Federal Law Enforcement Officers Association. "But I really can't advise you on this. It's a conflict, even if this conversation isn't really happening. I mean, on a personal level, if I tell you to get an attorney and it ends up backfiring, Robby will be pissed at me."

"I think he'd understand. But regardless, don't say anything to him. Let me tell him what happened, okay?"

"Of course."

"He knows I was having a problem with Ferraro. He's the one who found out about the connection to Hancock." Vail pinched the bridge of her nose. "Anyway, I'll take care of it. But if you hear anything else—"

"I'll let you know . . . whatever I'm allowed to tell you."

"I understand." And she did. But she still found it frustrating. "Administratively. How does this go down?"

"I've only had a few other cases like this, and it was a while ago, so I may not have this a hundred percent right. But here's what I think will happen. Now that the inspector general has opened an investigation, a couple of agents will be assigned, if that's not already happened. I'll be notified—officially—that a case has been opened. I may then have the option of recalling you home, or the AG could mandate it if he thinks it's a particularly egregious breech of Bureau procedure."

"Is it?"

"If you're asking, you already know the answer. Yes."

"Yeah. If the complaint was legit."

"Have you ever done anything like this before?"

Well, um, yep. In Napa. That was even worse than this. But Robby's life was in danger. And I'd do it again.

"On second thought, I don't want to know."

And we won't even talk about what I've done with OPSIG.

"Probably best."

"Would've been better to keep your mouth shut there, Karen."

"You know I'm not good at that, sir."

Gifford groaned audibly. "It's hard being your boss, Karen."

"I know, but someone's got to do it. And I can think of no one better suited for the job. Certainly not my idiot unit chief. Uh—we're still off the record, right?"

"Karen, I'm concerned about this investigation. Whether you're up to it. You—well, you sometimes don't think before you speak."

"I'm getting better."

Gifford groaned again.

"I'll be fine. I can turn it off whenever I need to."

Hope he buys that, because I'm lying big-time.

"That's BS. You and I both know that. But that's for another time. Right now, since you're in the middle of a major case, I'm going to make the executive decision to run interference for you and leave you there. Don't make me regret it."

"This is where I'm supposed to tell you not to worry."

"Right."

"Don't worry, sir. I won't get into any more trouble."

"And I'll do my best to keep you in Hawaii, but if I'm forced to put you on the rubber gun squad, I may not have a choice."

The rubber gun squad was Bureau slang for administrative duties. And that would suck because all her cases would be reassigned for the foreseeable future.

"Let's hope it doesn't come to that."

"My guess?" Gifford said. "It'll depend on past conduct. If they see any red flags, they'll be more aggressive early on in the investigation."

"Okay."

"Once the OIG decides they've got enough information, they'll want to interview you," Gifford said, using the abbreviation for Office of Inspector General. "The case agent will reach out to schedule something. I'll be notified as well."

"And that's where I get to explain myself and give them background on Ferraro—and stop this stupid waste of time before it goes any farther."

"Karen, put on your Bureau hat for a moment. Hard to do, I know, but separate yourself from this. They'll check out whatever you tell them, but I'm sure Ferraro will deny it. And they're gonna focus on *your* actions, not Ferraro's relationship to a former thorn in your side. Remember, *your* behavior and *your* actions are the purpose of the investigation, not Ferraro's. And once they start opening the can—"

"The worms crawl out. Like my arrest during the Dead Eyes case."

"That and all the other shit I've had to deal with over the years."

Vail tried not to take that dig personally. "So should I just decline the OIG interview? Can I do that?"

"Depends. There are two types of interviews: voluntary and compelled. For voluntary, you can decline. No consequences. But for compelled, you're required to do it as a condition of your employment."

"So I get to potentially bury myself." She shook her head. "Definitely need an attorney."

"You get what I think is called limited use immunity. Whatever you say can't be used against you in a criminal case. Just don't perjure yourself."

"Always good advice, sir."

"I'm not joking," Gifford said.

"Neither am I."

"Just keep in mind that anything you say in a voluntary interview *can* be used in a criminal case against you."

Vail chuckled. "So hope for a compulsory interview?"

"This is the FBI, so nothing's simple. I think they'll try to get you to come in for a voluntary interview first. If you say no, they'll have to go to the assistant US Attorney to ask him or her to decide whether or not the case will be prosecuted. If the case is declined, they can then compel you to be interviewed."

"Either way, I could be screwed."

"Think positive. If you do retain an attorney, he'll have the resources to dig around on Ferraro, find some witnesses who'll support your assertions. But you didn't hear that from me."

"Yeah."

"Karen, there's nothing for you to do about this right now. Focus on your case. This is gonna drag on for a while. You have to compartmentalize."

"I'll put it in a closet."

"Figuratively, yeah. Try to do that. I know this isn't fun, but it's part of the job, right?"

"It is when people like Hancock and Ferraro are involved."

"Don't get into it with the assistant chief, okay?"

"What would I say?"

"Not as worried about what you'd say as what you'd do."

"Like?"

"I don't want you punching him out."

"You really think I'd do that?"

There was silence.

"Guess that's my answer." *Wish I could say he's wrong.* "I'll do my best."

"Make sure that's good enough."

Vail hung up and slumped against the passenger door.

Russell glanced over at her a couple of times, alternating between Vail and the road. "I take it that didn't go well. Ferraro causing problems?"

"Lots."

"Man, what the hell's his deal?"

"Doesn't matter, does it? He made a complaint to the US Attorney General. And that's set in motion an inspector general investigation."

"Jesus," Russell said. "I'm sorry."

"Let's just put it out of our minds and concentrate on the case."

Russell laughed. "Can you do that?"

"Give it my best shot."

"Your best shot while distracted is better than a lot of cops with complete focus."

"Thanks. Appreciate that. True or not. It does make me feel better."

"Sounds like you need to call an attorney. Want to do that now or wait till you're back?"

She thought about that a moment. "Yeah, may help to put my mind at ease. I'll make it quick."

Vail searched her contacts and pulled up the number for P. Jackson Parker, a defense attorney who had been a tenacious nemesis—until he became her best advocate during the Dead Eyes case.

The number connected, and she was expecting to get his voice mail when he answered. "Mr. Parker."

"Karen Vail? Is my caller ID right?"

"I didn't think you had caller ID. Isn't that newer technology?"

Parker laughed boisterously. "You know me too well, Agent Vail. Not sure that's good or bad. But since *you* callin' *me*, I'd say that's good for me and bad for you."

"Always know how to cut to the chase, Mr. Parker. Got a situation here and just want some advice." She related the sequence of events and the facts as she knew them.

"I've dabbled in employment law, but not federal administrative employment law. You don't want to fool around with this. Might be better hiring an attorney who specializes in it. What about the FBI Agents Association? They rep FBI agents exclusively, so they should know their shit."

"Should?"

"Depends on who you get. You know how it goes. Good and bad in every profession."

"I know *you*."

"Be happy to take your money, Agent Vail, but quite frankly, you need someone who knows what he's doing. This federal arena, it's an animal all its own. But I think the world of you, so I'm not gonna let your ass flap in the breeze. Let me cogitate on this and see who I'd want to trust *my* career to."

"I appreciate that."

"I'll have someone dial you up. So don't be screening your calls."

"Thanks Mr. Parker."

"I think it's time to call me Jackson."

"Only if you call me Karen."

"I ever face you in court again, we'll need to change things up again."

"Look forward to it."

"Me too. And good luck with that investigation."

She hung up and took a breath. "We're back in business."

"Let me put you in the right frame of mind," Russell said as he completed a right turn. "Looks to me like our killer's taking a lot more risks. Four victims inside of a week. Five if you count Kelleher."

Vail appreciated Russell diving right back in. He was right: it forced her to focus. "We don't know what the UNSUB's normal pattern is. And we still can't say with any certainty when he sold the bars to these vics."

"I don't know about soap, but if you bought some premium chocolate, would you set it aside and wait days or weeks to eat it?"

"Me? A confessed chocoholic?"

"I guess if someone bought it for an after-dinner treat, they'd wait. But not very long. Regardless, we now know he's probably still on Oahu. He took a side trip to Kauai, maybe because of the article, maybe not. But it's safe to assume Mary Kelleher bought a chocolate bar. So for now, I'm putting her on his tab. *When* he went to Kauai we can't say. At this point, all that matters is that he's still here."

Vail shifted in her seat. "And still killing."

"Until we stop him." Russell made another turn and said, "Got a text while you were on the phone. More semen. At Mary Grant's house. Outside, in the yard. I would imagine he's doing it at night so he's not seen."

"Not surprised. Is it me, or does it feel like we're getting closer?"

"It's you. I don't know about getting closer to catching him, but we're very close to Luxury Row."

They arrived in Waikiki and began a grid-like patrol of the high-end shopping enclave. They kept their eyes on the street as they talked.

"So what do you make of him killing in multiple states?" Russell asked as he made a left onto Kalakaua Avenue and passed masses of people shuffling along the sidewalk.

"I think it's safe to say that he doesn't live in all these places. He moves around. Which reminds me." Vail pulled out her phone.

"To make it tougher to catch him?"

"That'd be the most obvious reason. Probably figures that sooner or later someone's gonna realize that these deaths weren't all accidental," she said slowly while typing on her Samsung.

"Who're you texting?"

"Those PDs, see if they turned up any other asphyxiation deaths that could be the work of our UNSUB."

"Crap. I haven't gotten an answer on that either." He glanced down at his phone and made a call.

The medical examiner, Keiki Kuoko, answered. "Aloha, Adam." His voice filled the car speakers.

"You got anything for us?"

"We're still looking through files. Since they weren't ruled murder, it's a little more difficult. But I've found six so far. And—you'll like this. They're clustered in twos, roughly three years apart."

Vail and Russell shared a glance: a slight nod from Vail indicating they were, indeed, onto something.

"Apparently, he's been at this awhile," Kuoko said. "And we had no idea."

"Keep looking," Russell said. "And if you can text us the names and locations of the six victims, that'd be helpful."

"You'll have it soon."

Vail's phone vibrated. She read the message. "We've got something similar in Chicago."

She replied to the detective:

bet you find more
out here his kills were 3 yrs apart
we think he moves around
different states

Her handset buzzed again while she was typing. She hit send, absorbed the new message, then turned to Russell. "LA just responded. Four so far. A couple in 2015 and another two in 2017. Waiting on Dallas and Atlanta."

Vail looked out the side window as they drove along the avenue. "Without knowing the offender's normal kill pattern, we can't say what his state of mind is. Based on what we just heard about his previous murders, both here and in the other cities, it does look like he's upped his game. It's possible the newspaper article set him off, served as a trigger. But we just don't know."

"The good news is that he didn't freak out and take off even if he saw it."

"The residents of Oahu may not think that's such 'good news,' Adam. Just saying."

Russell turned left. "Those cities where he's killed, they're all big metropolitan areas, or at least they've got decent population density."

"Not quite like Oahu," Vail said. "Definitely different from Hanapepe. Wonder if that's significant. It's clear why he'd choose a large city: the chances of finding a woman in her sixties named Mary are higher. But is there more to it?"

"Like what?" Russell asked.

"He's familiar with these cities. It also tells me he's either got money or an economical way of traveling. Like he uses mileage. Or maybe he has relatives in each city where he can stay when he's in town."

"Accomplices?"

"Probably not."

"Why do you think he might have money?" Russell asked as he cruised, his gaze roaming the streets. "Because he travels?"

"Yeah, but he also has the *flexibility* to travel. Be away from work, or at least an office. Then again, maybe he works from home. After COVID, there are a lot more people working remotely."

"Not likely his work would take him to these cities for weeks at a time."

"Can't really rule it out, but I agree. Unlikely." She thought a moment. "If we take him at his word, he's an Iraq War vet. He could be living on a disability retirement."

"Hard to *live* on a disability retirement, let alone travel extensively on one."

"Except that when he's not murdering his customers, he's making money on his soap and chocolate business to supplement his disability retirement."

"Enough to support a sightseeing-and-serial-murder lifestyle?" Russell shook his head. "Definitely something sick about that."

"What part of being a serial killer *isn't* 'sick'?" Vail let her eyes wander right, checking out the passersby, looking for a wheelchair.

As they left the Luxury Row area, Russell flicked on his signal to circle back.

When they came out of the turn, Vail saw a sign in a storefront advertising a service designed to get people out from under their burdensome time-share commitments.

"This is the tedious part of police work," Russell said. "Drive around for hours looking for someone who may not even be here."

"There's another option."

"Let the other cops drive around and we go grab a beer?"

"No," Vail said, shifting her bottom in the seat to face Russell. "It fits." She nodded.

"What fits? Want to let me in on what you're thinking?"

"What if he's not flush with money, or retired, or working remotely, or disabled."

"We were just brainstorming. All of it could be wron—"

"What if he's a time-share owner? Know anything about them?"

Russell laughed. "Seriously? Waikiki is chockfull of time-share owners. A lot of those high-rise buildings that look like hotels are actually condos. Some are privately owned, but a lot are time-shares."

"How do they work? Is this something our UNSUB could use?"

"Let's say a big company buys up properties all over the world and then sells 'shares' to owners. There are different setups, but a popular one nowadays is where the company gives the shareowners a certain number of points per year to spend on their vacations. The owners use those points to go to any place the company owns property.

"Take DV Squared, the biggest one here on the island. They own dozens of floors worth of condos—suites, basically—and people can come and spend a couple of weeks on Oahu depending on how many points they have in their account and how much those points are worth here. The points are also worth more in winter months because it's not as desirable as being here in the summer. Weather's not as good."

Looks pretty good to me. You should come to Virginia in December.

"So this company has properties in other states where people can use their points?

"Yep."

"What's it called? BV something?"

"*DV*. Diamond Vacation Ventures. DVV. Awkward to say. Cooler to say *squared*. Two Vs, so it's squared. DV squared."

Thanks for the mathematics lesson.

"Call Kuoko back. Those previous asphyxiation deaths, the ones not ruled murder. He said they were clustered in twos, about three years apart."

"What about 'em?"

"Ask if they were around the same time of year."

"You really think the killer is a member of a time-share."

"Hoping. Because he should be in Luxury Row already if he was coming. And if he's not working here today, he could be somewhere else on the island."

"In which case this is a waste of time."

"Right. Unless one of your uniforms happens to see him somewhere, we need another way of tracking him down—sooner rather than later."

Russell dialed Kuoko—and within ten minutes the ME called back and confirmed that the asphyxiation deaths all occurred in December and January.

"Far from a slam dunk," Vail said. "But it's something. You know anyone who has connections with a time-share?"

"A friend at DV Squared. Arranges tours for people, tries to get them to listen to a sales pitch to increase their ownership fees in exchange for more points."

If I'm right about this, I'd like some points. See the Grand Canyon? Get married in Yosemite?

Russell hung a sharp right and accelerated. "Let's go pay him a visit."

43

Vail and Russell left their sedan out front—pissing off the valet—and jogged up the slate staircase of the Ilikai Resort Tower entrance, where Diamond Vacation Ventures Oahu offices resided. They walked through the mahogany-paneled lobby, decked out in Hawaiian decor around a central fountain that shot water twenty feet into the atrium.

"Nice place," Vail said.

"That's the idea. People want to feel like they're on vacation in the lap of luxury."

"I used to know a hooker named Luxury," Vail said.

"Must be where that expression came from."

Vail laughed—but caught a glimpse of the ocean directly ahead and realized what she was missing. "That the beach out there?"

"You should take a walk on the sand if you can before you leave—which could be soon if you're right about this time-share thing."

"Ready to get rid of me?"

"*Definitely* ready to get rid of you."

Vail's phone vibrated as they approached the DV Squared office, a storefront down a wide corridor that was lined with ice cream parlors, cafés, restaurants, gift shops, and high-end convenience markets.

"Text from Atlanta. Looks like the same story we got from Kuoko, Chicago, and LA. Similar clustering of victims over a ten-to-fourteen-day period. Three years apart."

They pushed through the door and entered the sales suite. A long reception desk sat along the back wall, where several large-screen monitors displayed high resolution video of vacation paradises. Vail caught a scene in Dallas, and another in Los Angeles ... not surprisingly, a glam shot of Beverly Hills.

"Adam!" said a man in his mid-thirties sporting a nose ring and black nail polish. "How you doin' brah?"

"Aloha. How's Mindy?"

"Doin' great. She's off today, hitting the waves."

Russell laughed. "And getting hit *on*, no doubt."

"No doubt." His gaze flicked over to Vail.

"Oh," Russell said. "Sorry. Benny, this is a colleague, Special Agent Karen Vail. FBI."

"Whoa." Benny scooted back in his office chair and held up both hands. "I'm innocent. I did *not* rob that bank. I swear."

Vail looked at Russell, her expression saying, "Are you serious?"

"Benny has a strange sense of humor."

Yep. Strange. Let's leave it at that.

"We're hoping you can help us with some general time-share questions," Vail said.

"I invoke my Fifth Amendment rights."

Vail pursed her lips, then nodded slowly. She artfully drew back the right portion of her jacket, exposing the handle of her Glock. "So which bank are we talking about, Benny? Citi or Chase?"

Benny's grin faded. "Huh?"

Vail took a deep breath. "We're here on a murder case. How about you can the ... *attempt* at humor and answer our questions?"

"Everything okay over here?"

Vail and Russell turned to see an older woman.

"All good," Russell said, holding up a hand. His jacket lifted a bit on the left, exposing his badge. Her gaze dropped to the shiny gold surface. "Benny's a good friend of mine. He's helping us with some info on time-shares, how they work, that type of thing. For a case."

She eyed their faces, then turned to Benny. "Anything I need to know about?"

"Everything's fine, Charlotte. Like Adam here said. I'm helping them out."

"It's just that I get nervous when the police show up asking questions," Charlotte said.

Oh, one of those. A helicopter manager.

"He *is* just helping us out," Vail said. "But if we do have to arrest him, you'll be the first to know. I promise." She held up her badge. "FBI agents don't lie."

"Karen," Russell said, covering his eyes, dropping his chin to his chest, and shaking his head.

Vail was sure he was stifling a laugh.

Charlotte did not know what to make of this—or Vail. She gave Benny a dubious look, then turned and walked off—keeping an eye on them over her right shoulder.

"What do you need to know?" Benny's demeanor was instantly serious. More like: "Hurry up and get the hell out of here before you get me fired."

"Sorry if we caused you any trouble," Russell said.

Benny shot a look at Charlotte, who was behind the long desk about twenty feet away, making no attempt to hide the fact that she was monitoring their goings-on.

"We need to know if Chicago, Los Angeles, Dallas, and Atlanta are common areas for time-shares," Vail said.

"DV Squared has properties in all those cities. Anywhere that's a destination for travelers, places people want to go for a vacay, you'll find a time-share."

"How much do these things run?"

"To buy into a time-share?" Benny asked.

"Yeah."

"Varies."

"You wanna get rid of us?" Vail asked. "Give me an idea. A range."

"From thousands of dollars to fifty thousand, or more. And then an annual maintenance fee, which can run six hundred to twelve hundred. Depends on the properties and the number of points, amenities, number of weeks each year, stuff like that."

"They've got properties in all those cities," Vail said, directing the comment to Russell.

He glanced at the photos of the various locations. "But how are we gonna look him up, see if he's an owner? I doubt 'John' would get us anywhere."

"I was hoping we can get a name from this somehow." She swung her gaze to Benny. "You can look in your system and see which of your owners are staying here, right now, in Waikiki. Right?"

"Of course. But . . ." His eyes flicked over to Charlotte, then back to Vail. "I'm not sure I'm supposed to release that info. If you feel me."

"I feel you all right," Vail said. "So you want us to go before a judge, get a warrant, and then serve you. Here. In front of all your colleagues. Not sure Charlotte would like that."

"But I didn't do anyth—" Benny cut himself off, ground his molars, then—as if realizing that Charlotte was still watching—said, "Sure, I can help you with that. Thanks for your interest in Diamond Ventures Vacations."

"Our suspect is in his forties," Russell said. "Full beard. May be a war veteran. Wheelchair."

"Wheelchair." Benny's eyes widened. "I think I may've seen him."

"When?" Vail asked.

"You sure it's our guy?"

He looked up at Russell. "No, I'm not sure. I only saw him once, a couple days ago."

"Then why do you remember him?" Vail asked.

He had this box on his lap. He was selling something. And on the side of the box, there was this sign. Something about being an Iraq War vet. So I asked him where he served and his answer didn't really add up."

"Benny did two tours."

"Ah."

Bet that was before he got the nose ring and painted nails.

"I have serious doubts about that veteran story, too," Vail said. "You call him on it?"

"Nah. I mean, he was in a wheelchair. If he needs to bend the truth a little to make ends meet . . . well, aloha, ya know?"

"Yeah," Vail said. "I'm beginning to understand."

"We need his name and room number."

Benny's eyes flicked over in Charlotte's direction. "Why? What'd he do?"

"You gotta keep this under wraps," Russell said. "Okay?"

"Brah, all you gotta say is *quiet.*"

Russell leaned forward. "We're pretty sure he's a serial killer. And he's already murdered several people on Oahu."

Definitely no aloha in that.

"Holy shit," Benny said, then covered his mouth, his gaze again shooting right, toward Charlotte. "Sorry," he said, grinning and waving meekly at her. "The one in the news?"

"Sooner rather than later," Vail said.

"Right." Benny struck some keys on his keyboard. Then several more. He groaned, then continued to tap away.

The suspense was getting to Vail—she was about to scream when Benny leaned back in his seat. "I searched for single-occupancy rooms that are wheelchair accessible. And I got one. Name's Scott Meece." He swiveled the screen so they could see it. "Room fourteen-eleven."

"You got a photo?"

"Nope. We don't have that kind of info on file."

"How 'bout a home address?"

"We do have that. But in the billing and financial records. I don't have access to those. Lots of laws governing that kind of data."

"Benny," Vail said loudly, "I can't thank you enough." She shook his hand. "You may've just saved a number of innocent people. Thank you for being a hero. We're all indebted to your courage and bravery."

On her way out of the office, Vail saluted Charlotte—the kind used by the military, not the one featuring an extended middle finger.

44

Scott placed the robust, newly purchased specimen in his kitchen, by the window, just like his mother had done. He wanted it to get acclimated to its environment before digging up and pulverizing one of its roots. He could always buy another one but doing so could attract unnecessary attention. Better to try to take care of it. Go slowly. Treat it with care.

That was something his mother never did with him. Funny that she reserved such love and affection for a plant. It obviously gave her the joy she did not derive from her family.

Then again maybe it was not funny at all.

Two weeks later, with the flowers blooming and bursting with bright and rich color, Scott gently dug his fingers into the moist soil and hooked a stringy rhizome. He snipped off half of it and reburied the remaining portion in the dirt.

After drying the cutoff material in a dehydrator for two days, he pulverized the root in a mortar with a stone pestle. Wearing a mask and rubber gloves, he crushed and ground the root until it was nearly a fine powder. He found the gnashing motion strangely calming, yet satisfyingly aggressive, as he took out his frustrations on the plant.

He placed the resulting talc-like dust in an empty Kodak Ektachrome canister and used an awl to punch several holes in the cap, creating a controlled delivery mechanism.

With the poison prepared, he went about prepping for who he would try it on—and when.

Scott decided the best way to test-drive his concoction was to follow accepted medical research convention: try it on an animal. He was in the subway, waiting for the Times Square-Grand Central shuttle when he saw a few rats scurry by down along the tracks.

Perfect.

That afternoon, he stopped at a local pet shop on Thirty-Ninth and bought a rat. He did not bother with a cage or any of the accoutrements, telling the merchant he already had the stuff from a few years ago.

He took the rodent home in a box poked with holes and set it on the kitchen table. After opening the flaps, he watched it scurry from one side to the other, wondering what had happened: he had been in a large terrarium-style environment, playing with his buddies, running on the wheel, eating and drinking, enjoying life.

Now he was in a brown prison. No stimulation other than a rocking motion as he swung to and fro. And finally in this new place, light streaming in from above with a gentle warm breeze blowing on his neck.

"Yep, the heater's on, my friend. I know it was cold outside. But I need a normal environment to run my test properly. Enjoy the toasty air because in a few minutes you'll be joining all your friends in rat heaven."

Scott picked up the small film container he had filled with ground aconite.

"I'm gonna call you Peter," he said, peering into the box at his new pet. "You look like a Peter. So how much should I feed you, Peter?"

Scott held up the canister and shifted his eyes from the fine dust to the rat's body.

"No idea. But that's what research is all about, right? I'll keep a journal. Start with a small dose and observe the reaction. If you survive, I'll try a larger dose. Record the results. Sound good?"

Peter stopped and stood on his hind legs, his two delicate front paws held in front of him, tiny nails projecting from the ends.

"You look hungry. I'll give you some food and sprinkle the goodies on top. Okay?"

Peter looked up, locking his eyes on Scott's.

"I'll take that as a yes. Okay, here goes."

Scott put the mask on and removed a small ceramic bowl from the cabinet. Next came a hard-boiled egg from the fridge. He had done his homework.

After setting it all out, he used a wood stirrer he had saved from Starbucks to scatter the aconite over the yellow yolk. He took a pinch of Swiss cheese shavings and sprinkled it on top. Added a tiny drop of red food dye for that Hawaiian Punch look. Just like Mary did.

"That should do it. Here ya go, Peter. Enjoy."

Scott grabbed his 8mm camcorder and propped it atop a pile of books. He pressed the record button and the tape's sprockets began turning, creating video documentation of what he was about to do.

He set the bowl inside the box and watched, the camera pointed roughly in the direction of the rat. He didn't want to have his face behind a lens. He wanted to witness it firsthand.

Peter sniffed, his tiny nose wrinkling and then twitching left and right. He poked tentatively at the food and began eating.

Seconds later, Peter stopped and stood up on his hind legs. He began convulsing. Coughing?

Yeah. Coughing.

A moment later, his legs buckled. He fell to the bottom of the box and then rolled on his side. Rock still.

Scott stuck his index finger in, carefully, slowly, and poked at Peter's exposed abdomen. It was taut and concave.

He withdrew his hand and stood there observing.

Nothing. A minute passed. The rat did not move.

"Well shit. Maybe I gave you too much. Shoulda started with less."

Scott sighed, then turned off the camcorder. He rewound the tape and watched it.

"Hmm. It *did* work," he said, his right eye pressed into the ocular cup as he viewed his handiwork. "Guess I'm just too hard on myself."

He sat down at the table and nodded. "I did it. It worked. That's all that matters. Now I just have to try it on a real target."

Mary. *I have to try it on Mary.*

45

Having decided to go forward with the next step in his plan—to make sure it worked—he took a part-time job as a waiter at Nevada's Diner. A guy he knew from a local bar, Terrence, had bought his fictional tale of being in financial difficulty and needing a second job. A month later, Terrence hooked Scott up with the boss at Nevada's, where a weekend shift had come open.

Scott had done some restaurant work years ago—busing tables mostly, but he filled in here and there as a server—and a little embellishment never hurt anyone.

After acing the interview, Scott spent a few weeks learning the routine, the menu, and what would be the best way to strategically place the aconite in a patron's food.

Five weeks passed. He was wearing down, working five days a week at his real job and two at the diner. No time off.

He hoped it was worth it.

As January came to a close, he decided he had done all he could to prepare. Today was the day. It was dinnertime on Saturday, so the place was busy.

Two hours passed without the right target anywhere near Scott's station. He patted his left pocket, which contained the small, round plastic container.

With the night wearing on—and ironically none of his customers matching his requirements, he saw a couple in their late fifties being seated at a booth by the window in Terrence's assigned area. It was about twenty feet from Scott's tables, but he would still be able to observe what happened without too much difficulty.

It would likely cause a commotion, anyway, as someone would immediately call for an ambulance.

If it worked. If he did it right.

That was a huge unknown since he really did not have any guide as to how much to use other than a few notes he had found on the web and his small sample size—literally—with Peter.

He stood by the counter under the row of heat lamps, where the cooks set the plates to stay warm until they were served. Scott made sure to watch when Terrence took the order, and fortunately he walked right over to the kitchen and handed in the mint-colored slip. Scott caught a glance at the ticket and was fairly certain he knew which food was going to be his chosen target.

He preferred to be sure, but he had grown tired of waiting. What if no one else matched his desired mark? No. He had to do this now. It was right.

Scott kept an eye on Terrence's orders, a challenge because Scott had his own customers and food to manage.

Twenty minutes later, the cook slid the plate onto the counter, where it was instantly bathed in red-orange warmth.

That's it. Has to be.

Scott made his way over and removed the film canister from his pocket, pulled back a piece of tape he had placed over the holes, then sprinkled the powder onto her New York steak. It immediately disappeared into the fatty grease atop the meat.

He turned on his heels and headed to his right as he slipped the container back in his pocket.

He glanced at the order slips, found the one he was looking for, and scooped up the hot plate to deliver it to his table.

A moment later he set the trout in front of his customer and told her husband he would be right back with the rest of their food. But by the time he returned to the counter to check if it was ready, there was shouting from the back of the diner.

Scott's head snapped left where he saw a woman grabbing her throat. She was coughing violently and pushing against her friend, trying to get out of the booth. Her face was red and she was trying to suck in air.

"Cindy!" screamed her companion. "You okay?"

But Cindy did not reply.

She collapsed and hit the floor with a thud. People crowded in around her. Yelling, shouting. Someone was calling for an ambulance.

Scott pushed his way through and made it to the circle that had formed around Cindy's still body.

Cindy was a lot younger than what he was looking for. And she didn't even look remotely like his mother. Scott had screwed up the order and sprinkled the poison on the wrong food.

Goddam, he said under his breath.

Still, he could not take his eyes off the corpse.

"What happened?" someone asked, the voice off in the distance.

"I—I dunno. She was eating her steak and all of a sudden she started coughing."

"She choked?"

"Shoulda done the Heimlich thing."

"Not choking. Coughing."

"Looked like she had a heart attack."

"Yeah, she grabbed her chest, then fell over . . ."

The voices sounded off in the distance as Scott stood there, mesmerized by what he had accomplished.

But someone yelling snapped him out of his trance. He realized he had to get away from there. This was not his table. There was no reason for him to remain. The woman was dead.

He turned and made his way back to the counter, where Terrence was looking hard at him.

"Holy shit. You see that?" Scott managed to blurt.

Terrence leaned in close to Scott's right ear. "The fuck you do?"

"Huh?"

"I saw you, man. You put something on her food."

Scott swallowed deeply—but his throat was dry and he nearly started coughing himself.

In the distance, the scream of a siren.

Scott gathered up the other plates for his order and delivered them to his table. Doing his job, avoiding unwanted attention.

"What happened back there?" the husband said.

Scott avoided eye contact as he set the food in front of his customers. "Woman up and died. Heart attack, someone said."

"Jesus."

"I know. So young, too."

Too young. Not what he was aiming for, but it was arousing nonetheless.

Scott excused himself and went to the restroom, entered a stall, and pulled out his erection. A moment later, he felt the release. He stood there, leaning against the metal wall, trying to get his breathing under control.

This was exactly what he needed.

Denials aside, Terrence was right. Next time he would be more careful, find a better way of selecting his mark. And a more discreet way of using the aconite.

He washed and headed back into the restaurant, then saw Terrence, who grabbed his arm and led him into the alley by the garbage bins.

"What the fuck, Scott?"

Terrence was angry, that was pretty damn clear. Scott had the good sense to take a second to think. Slow his pounding heart. He had to keep his cool.

And deny, deny, deny.

He pulled out a pack of cigarettes and offered one to Terrence. Stalling. "Smoke?"

Terrence grabbed it and Scott lit it up, then stuck the match against his own, the end instantly catching fire.

"You put something on her food," Terrence said again.

Scott tried masking a grin but could not. It was involuntary; he could not help it.

"She stiff you, too?"

Scott puffed. Shrugged.

"I didn't like her neither," Terrence said. "Nasty bitch. Usually sits at one of my tables. Been stiffin' me on tips for long as I can 'member."

"Yeah?"

"Yeah." He took a drag, then faced Scott. Lowered his voice. "But whatever you did to her food, that was some pretty stupid shit, man. I ain't gonna say nothing to the cops 'cause you're my friend and all. And she deserved it ten times over, but . . ." He took another long pull, the smoke puffing out as he spoke. "You just lucky was me who saw you or you'd be doing twenty-five to life."

Scott tossed the butt to the ground and crushed it under a heel. He did not say anything but gave Terrence's shoulder a pat.

He thinks I'm his friend?

As he walked back through the kitchen, Scott smiled.

I have a friend?

The night was shaping up to be better than he ever could've planned.

46

Scott quit the diner job two weeks later. He told Terrence he had found a full-time job and he could not work seven days a week. The two promised to keep in touch. That would be tough, Scott knew, because their schedules conflicted.

But that was fine, because it was better if Terrence did not know about his future adventures involving Mary. It was dangerous enough that he knew he was involved in the death of Cindy, the diner woman. If he dropped out of Terrence's life, perhaps he would forget about him.

Was Terrence a threat? If the police ever figured out Cindy's heart attack was induced and not natural, would they question all the employees? Would Terrence cave under pressure? Give away some detail accidentally?

Hard to be sure. If that became an issue, he would deal with it somehow. There seemed to always be ways around problems. Sometimes they were not good solutions, but options usually existed.

One thing he was sure of was that he liked what he'd done with Cindy. She was not the intended target, but he could fix that going forward. He just had to give it some thought.

Scott walked through Bryant Park, stopping by the bocce court and absentmindedly watching while he worked through a modification of his MO. He leaned against a tree near the prominent sign explaining how the game was played. He learned it was actually Pétanque, a French game played with steel balls.

He knew what he needed to get out of his aconite exploits and he knew how he was going to carry them out. The questions to be answered were how he was going to find these women without arousing suspicion or attracting attention to himself; and how he was going to deliver the toxin so that he was not in close proximity to the target. One fatal heart attack in his presence was a coincidence. More than that would put him in danger of being discovered by the cops.

Someone off to his right yelled. Scott figured the guy had rolled a winning ball and was celebrating.

Scott turned his attention back to his planning. Once he addressed those unknowns, he could be ready to begin.

47

Scott had thought long and hard about how to deploy his poison without getting caught. He did additional research on the plant and bought more books on the basic principles of chemistry—applied concepts that had more relevance to everyday life than a typical college course. Or at least more relevance to *him*.

He decided to take his time and dot all the i's. His father had once told him to measure twice and cut once. At the time, Scott did not understand what he meant, but in thinking back on that it made perfect sense: plan and get it right . . . because once you make that cut, you can't put it back together. He was sure his dad did not mean for Scott to apply the concept to murder, but if he knew that Mary had killed him, then perhaps he would approve of his son taking revenge and returning the favor.

His father was a practical man.

Or he liked to think he was. Scott did not remember much about him, at least the way adults think of people. He had good feelings about him. Looked up to him. Liked spending time with him. Felt secure around him.

He had none of those feelings about Mary.

He used what he had learned about chemistry to perfect his delivery mechanism for the poison. That was not the most difficult part. More problematic was how to deploy the aconite in a way that he was nowhere near the victim when it took hold.

He had already discounted the concept of directly confronting the Mary he was targeting because he did not want to be caught off guard like the first time.

That was traumatic. He would never do that again.

Well, perhaps once more. But it would be done in a way that would not place him in any danger.

Now, after three years of planning, he was ready to proceed.

Scott knocked on the door. The buzzer still had their names listed, so he knew they had not moved. Still, it had been a very long time since he had talked with them. How would she take to him suddenly showing up?

Shuffling footsteps, heavy, slow. He smiled. He knew that gait. The door swung open.

"Scott?"

"Hi, Ma."

"What the hell you doin' here? Haven't heard from you in years."

"I know. I've been trying to find my own way. Didn't want to rely on anyone." He was impressed by how easy it was to lie to her. He felt no guilt whatsoever. "Nick home?"

"At work."

"Can I come in?"

"I'm kinda busy."

"Just for ten minutes." He waited a second, allowed her to think. "Jesus, Ma, we haven't talked in forever. You can't spare ten minutes for your son?"

She groaned, then stepped aside and Scott walked in. He glanced around, comparing the present to the past . . . rather, to his memories. The place looked pretty much the same. Furniture, wall hangings, carpet . . . nothing had changed.

They walked into the kitchen. Scott looked to the windowsill where the Monkshood—Aconitum napellus—plant used to reside, soaking up the sun. It was not there. But a cockroach was. Those damn bugs. An involuntary shiver shook his torso.

"Ain't gonna bite. Nothing to be afraid of."

I'm not afraid, he said to himself.

"You may be livin' away from home, but you're the same old Scott."

We'll see about that.

"What've you been doing with yourself?"

"Me?" Mary shrugged her thick shoulders. "Working. Part-time. Nothin' important. Nothin' interesting."

Scott waited a moment for her to ask him what he had been doing. She did not, so he volunteered the information. "I'm a computer coder. Completely taught myself how to do it. In the city. That's where I live, too. Bought my own apartment."

"Bought it. Really."

"Yep. Real proud of that."

"Must be doing good."

"I am. I am. And—oh, I brought you a gift."

Mary narrowed her eyes. "A gift. For me? For what?"

He shrugged. "I need an excuse to bring my mother a gift?" He pulled a small item from his satchel.

She took it and looked at it. "What is it?"

"A bar of handmade soap. All natural. Smells incredible, too."

"Like my Dial?"

He inwardly laughed. *Dial. No, this is much, much better.* "Commercial soap's fine. But this is . . . special."

"Yeah?" She turned it over in her pudgy hands. Hands that used to punch him, slap his face, pull his hair, shove him to the ground. He did not think she would dare try that now.

She looked older, her hair graying. He did a quick calculation. She was about sixty-two.

"Open it, Ma. Smell it. I made it myself. And I put a special scent in it, just for you. I bet it'll remind you of someone."

She put the bar to her nose and sniffed. "Lilac."

Scott forced himself to grin. "Yes, Lilac's right! Very good. But that's not what I was referring to."

"Then what?"

"You have to open it. You can't smell it through the wrapper."

"If you wanted me to smell it, why'd you wrap it in the first place?"

"If you like it, I was thinking of making more, selling them. I think they're a great product and people—women in particular—would like them."

"Oh yeah?"

"Yeah. Let me know what you think. You're the best judge. Go on, open it."

She rolled her eyes, slipped a fingernail under the fold and ripped the paper, then unrolled the soap and held it to her nose.

"Still getting lilac. And—" She coughed, cleared her throat, then looked at her fingers, then coughed harder. Her shoulders lurched forward and upward. "I—I can't—breathe."

"I learned a lot from you, Mary. Didn't think I had, but I really did. You taught me good."

Mary tried to stand but began hacking uncontrollably and fell to the floor.

Scott got down on his hands and knees. "The scent you should've smelled was aconite. You know what aconite is, don't you? It's what you used to kill Dad. Brilliant, Mary. Really brilliant." He paused, watching her struggle, crawling along the floor, trying to breathe. "But in the end, you're pretty fucking dumb."

She was moving slower and slower. Struggling.

Scott laughed. "You passed the test, Mary. I can't tell you what this has meant to me. Finally. I mean, it only took twenty-nine years for me to see the good in you.

"Without you, I never would've learned to kill so efficiently. And effectively. If I do it right, the police will never be able to catch me.

"Without you, I never would've experienced the most exciting thing I've ever done in my otherwise miserable life."

He made eye contact, trying to gauge her reaction. She knew what was happening. She knew what he had done to her.

"I'd say, 'rest in peace.' But I'm sure you're going straight to hell, Mary. And peace is one thing you won't have."

Her arms gave way and her forehead hit the floor.

He slipped on a pair of latex gloves, took the soap from Mary's hand, and placed it—and the wrapper—in a plastic bag. He would dispose of it later.

Scott felt the rush build in his chest. He stood up and looked down over Mary's corpse. Then he unzipped his pants and reached inside.

48

Scott left the apartment and went home. He had experienced euphoria in the hour after Mary had died. But then it wore off.

Something was missing.

He went outside and walked for twenty or thirty blocks, oblivious to the outside world. Off in the distance, he heard taxis honking, people shouting and cursing, and trucks rattling amongst the potholes as they whooshed by.

He racked his brain to figure out what was bothering him.

And then it hit him. He needed to see Nick. He had to see him grieve, or at least feel out of sorts. He grabbed a cab and went back to Astoria, getting out several blocks away and hoofing it the last quarter mile.

He walked up to the apartment and knocked. Everything looked normal. Nothing unusual.

And then the door swung open.

"Nick."

His stepfather looked distraught, lost, his face sagging—perhaps from age and fat, or maybe it was anguish.

It took a moment for Nick to put it together. "Scott. What're you doin' here?"

"I had a meeting in the neighborhood and stopped by the bagel shop to eat. I heard. About Mary—about Mom. I wanted to come by, see if it was true."

"It's true." He said it in a voice barely louder than a whisper.

Scott pursed his lips, then nodded slowly. "Good."

Nick squinted. "Good?"

"Good. She was a bitch. Treated me like shit, abused me." He chuckled. "Like you. Only she *let* you abuse me. How could a mother do that? She knew what you were doing. And she let it happen. She brought you into our house. It was all her fault."

"Get the fuck outta my life. Always been stupid. Good for nothin' piece a shit."

Scott snorted. "Apparently I'm good for *something*, Nick." He locked eyes with the man, then turned and walked off. The door slammed behind him.

On the walk back to the subway, Scott realized that he needed some kind of closure with the murders. Perhaps returning to each Mary's house to check in on them, make sure they'd died, would fill that need.

He would have to think on that for a while.

For now, reveling in the knowledge that his poison-treated soap wrapper worked as planned would suffice.

49

V ail and Russell walked briskly down the corridor toward the
elevator bank.

"You think Benny will be okay?"

"Don't know," Russell said. "You laid it on pretty thick."

"Did I?"

Russell was navigating his phone as Vail pressed the up button.
"Just a bit. Hey, something else for you to work on." The line connected and Russell asked for the district attorney. "I need a warrant
to search a time-share suite. Which judge we got?" He listened a
moment, then explained the situation.

While Russell made his call, Vail dialed Del Monaco.

"You know, Karen, this six-hour time difference is a real pain in
my ass. Either that, or you're doing it purposely. Waiting till late in
the day to bother me with some stupid request."

"Yeah, Frank, that's exactly what I'm doing. I'm not really bust-
ing my tail out here to help HPD find an UNSUB. I'm doing all this
just to make your life miserable."

"Pretty much what I thought."

Vail ignored that. "Got a lead on suspect and I need you to find
out everything you can on him—but first see if you can get me a
photo. DMV, military, whatever—recent if possible but at this point
I'll take anything. Gotta get it to all ports and avenues of exit before
he can get off the island."

He groaned loudly. She wasn't sure if he was expressing his displeasure or pulling his bulky frame out of bed. "That it?"

"That's a lot, I know. But Meece has killed a lot of women in multiple states and he may be unraveling."

"Yeah, yeah, yeah. I get it. Okay . . . Scott Meece. How do you spell that?"

"S-c-o-t-t."

"Karen . . ."

"Sorry. I'll play nice. Pretty sure it's M-e-e-c-e. But if you're not finding anything, try other permutations."

"That all you can give me?

"I've got a phenotype image, but hard to say how accurate it is."

"Send it over. Maybe I can run it through facial recognition."

Vail harrumphed. "Didn't think that's possible."

"Don't know if it is. Can't hurt to try. Could get lucky. Anything else?"

"He's disabled. Wheelchair bound. It's possible he served in Iraq—where he suffered an injury to his spinal cord. But I have strong doubts about his service. Can't rule it out though."

Okay, let me get a shot of caffeine into my body and I'll get to work."

"Thanks, Frank."

"Really?"

"Really what?"

"You *never* thank me."

"That's not true."

Actually, it might be.

After hanging up, she emailed the phenotype image to Del Monaco, then nudged Russell's elbow. "So?"

"Got a text from Dr. Kuoko. They found two more vics, one from Oahu and one from Kauai, mid-December, nine years ago. They're still looking for others."

"Makes sense. He's obviously familiar with killing on Kauai. But I meant about the affidavit."

"I'm going to dictate it and email it in."

"How long till we get the warrant?"

"Truth?"

"No, lie to me."

"Hour and a half."

"Oh." Vail waved a hand. "Not nearly as bad as I thought."

"You told me to lie to you."

She looked at him. Daggers.

"Three hours," he said. "Best case. Likely more. Every time I think it'll be faster, some kinda shit happens. Printer goes out. Judge is at lunch or has the runs. Realistically, three hours is the fastest."

Russell began walking down the corridor, dictating the affidavit into his phone as he went.

Vail thought about Scott Meece and his soap and chocolate bars and unsuspecting women. She checked her watch. It was four o'clock, which meant that Meece—wherever he was on the island—could be handing his poisoned products to an unsuspecting woman. If they went public with this info, could they prevent all sixty-something females named Mary from washing their hands or breaking their diets?

Vail called Kuoko and asked if he could talk with his superiors and get an alert issued along with a press release to the media on the island.

"I'll do my best, but I'm a medical examiner. Where's—why isn't Adam requesting this?"

"He's writing up the affidavit for the search warrant."

Kuoko sighed audibly. "Okay, I'll take care of it. But honestly, this is not my job."

Vail did not have time to quibble over that true, but ridiculous, comment, so she hung up—then called TSA and issued a hold on all passengers named Scott Meece. She referred them to the phenotype image they had previously received and asked them if TSA could grab a government ID photo. Maybe they could access one faster than Del Monaco.

Immediately after the call ended, someone else buzzed her handset: a number she did not know. She groaned and answered it.

"If you're selling a Hilton Hotel time-share, now is *not* the t—"

"My name is Dylan Price. Jackson Parker asked me to make contact."

"Oh—sorry. I'm—yeah. Karen Vail."

"Jackson filled me in on the details, so no need to recap them—at least not right now. He said you're in the middle of a case in Hawaii."

"That's true."

"Then I'll be brief," Price said. "You need me to tell you my qualifications or can I get to work ASAP on this? I'll send you my retainer contract and we can go from there."

"Is it as bad as Jackson's?"

"Afraid it is."

"Lucky me. Send it over. May be a few hours before I can get to it. Meantime, can you give me some thoughts as to where this can go? What can OIG do to me?"

Price laughed. "You want me to make you feel better, is that it? Because surely you know that I can't give you any kind of accurate evaluation of the case until I see the complaint, ask you questions, and so on."

"Right."

"First off, some general impressions. OIG doesn't discipline. That'd be up to the Bureau. I assume you're familiar with OPR."

"What agent doesn't know about the Office of Professional Responsibility? The cops for the cops."

"Pretty much. Just understand that there are a lot of ways this can go. It can get complicated and convoluted. I'll give you my best guess—which could change if I find out you really did fuck up and someone's got video."

"I didn't and there isn't any."

At least I hope not.

"Very unlikely something bad's going to happen. Just to be clear, I said, *Very.* And *unlikely.* In the same sentence. Got that?"

"Yes."

"Now that said, OPR could decide to discipline you, which is obviously not good—it'll affect promotions, future placements, and so on."

"Not worried about that stuff. I like being a profiler. No desire to be an administrator."

"That makes it a little easier. Either way, a civil rights violation won't look good in your jacket. But I'll do my best to make sure they close it out without action."

"How long does this thing take? We talking weeks? Couple of months?"

"Months," Price said. "Probably longer. A year? Could be."

"You're shitting me."

"I don't shit. Well, not like that. You, um, you get what I'm saying."

Her phone vibrated. Del Monaco.

"Hey," Vail said, "gotta go. Could be a break on this case."

"Take a few deep breaths and clear your mind," Price said. "Let me worry about this, okay? I've got your back. Jackson told me to make sure I take good care of you."

Take a few deep breaths? Clear my mind? Who the hell has time for that?

50

As Vail switched over to Del Monaco's call, her heart started racing. Never was she so excited to hear from him. But she couldn't tell him that because he would inevitably twist it into something sexual.

"Talk to me, Frank. Good news?"

"Got an address on Scott Edward Meece. Grew up in Queens. Owned an apartment in Manhattan but the info's about twenty-five years old. Still digging, but I figured you'd want to run with that."

"Absolutely."

"Just texted it to you."

"Awesome job, Frank."

"Wow. 'Awesome' and 'Frank' in the same sentence. From your mouth. This is a momentous event."

"More like a *onetime* event. Must be all the 'aloha' going around."

"The what?"

"Gotta go."

Before I say something that'd spoil the moment.

She shoved the phone back in her pocket, then immediately withdrew it. Without thinking—her special talent—she called her friend and past mentor, Captain Carmine Russo. It went to voice mail. Rather than leave a message, she redialed.

"What the fuck? Karen?"

"Sorry to wake you, Russo."

"I'm dreaming, right? A nightmare?"

"Listen. I—"

"You need something. A favor."

"No. Yeah. I mean, not for me. A case."

"Of course it's for a case. I may be half asleep but I figured that much. Whaddya got?"

"I'm in Hawaii. Which explains the late hour in New York."

"Not really. But go on."

"Serial offender. A poisoner. He operates in multiple cities all across the country. But he lived in Manhattan."

"Lived. As in past tense?"

"Don't know. Still investigating. But he did live there several years ago."

"Several? How many does that really mean?"

"Twenty-five."

"I define 'several' differently. But why do you think he's still there?"

"Because I have to start somewhere. And it's where he grew up, in Queens. He knows the area."

Russo sighed. Audibly. "And you want me to . . ."

"Find him."

"You still haven't explained why you've called in the middle of the fuckin' night and spoiled my beauty rest. And at my age, I need all the sleep I can get."

"He's a prolific killer and he's been at it for a long time. I can't even begin to guess how many vics he's got."

"Karen, I'm losing patience. Get to the point. Why now?"

"Because we've now got a name and some leads. And Manhattan is our best lead. And I'm betting you've got some of his vics in your backyard and don't even know it."

"How would we not know it? You mean unsolved cold cases?"

"Very cold—but they're not even *cases* because cause of death was acute myocardial infarction, not murder."

There was silence.

"Russo, you fall asleep on me?"

"Nope. Just realized I'm probably not gettin' back ta sleep. Sylvia's got us theater tickets tonight so I'm gonna nod off before intermission."

"Shit, Russo, I'm sorry."

"Me, too. I usually make it ten minutes into the second half before fallin' asleep."

Vail explained the mechanism of death.

"Well, you've succeeded," Russo said. He was huffing a bit, as if he was moving around.

"In what?"

"In waking me up. I'm making some coffee because I'm gonna head over to the office and snag me a rookie to help me out."

"So you think this is . . . intriguing?"

"No. I think this is a pain in the goddam ass. But yeah, if this guy's killed in my city and we don't know about it, that's a scary proposition. Piss me off, too."

"We know he's been here on Oahu. May still be if we're lucky. Found a time-share suite we think he's using. The detective out here is writing up an affidavit. I'm gonna have him send it to the Honolulu's FBI field office and make sure the doc's also faxed to the New York City division. That'll save time."

"Sleep. I need it to save me some *sleep*."

"Again, I'm sorry. This is important."

"And working with the FBI . . . you think *that* will save time? They'll fuckin' screw up—"

"He's killed four here in Oahu, Russo. I think we're up to ten nationwide. That we know of."

"Jesus Criminy. Ten's enough. You got my full attention."

"I had it the minute you decided to answer the phone."

"You know me too well, Karen."

"I'll keep you posted. Thanks Russo."

Vail called Russell and told him they now had the NYPD pursuing a New York address for Meece. "You know a guy at the Honolulu field office you've worked with?"

"Yeah. I know a guy. But he's a she. You mind?"

"You're asking me, a woman, if it's okay if you bring in another female LEO?" she asked, using the insider term for law enforcement officer.

"I've given up trying to understand you, Karen. Better to be safe."

"Send her the warrant and ask her to fax it to the FBI's New York division. I've got my old mentor, an NYPD captain, on his way over."

"In the middle of the night? Must like you."

"I know. Imagine that." She holstered her phone and walked up to the door of fourteen-eleven. No matter what strings she could pull or favors she could ask, this was not going to be a quick process. And yet lives were at stake.

Sometimes the easiest solutions were overlooked. She made a fist and knocked on the door. Nothing. She leaned in close. "Mr. Meece, I'm a manager with DV Squared. We have a hundred-dollar American Express gift card for you. I'm sorry, I forgot to put it with your paperwork when you checked in."

Vail rested her left ear on the door and waited. She heard no movement.

So much for easy solutions.

At the end of the long corridor Vail saw a maid's cart parked outside a room. She jogged over to it and found the door open. Vail stepped inside.

"Yes?" A man in his late twenties poked his head out of the bath-room. "Can I help you?"

"I did a stupid thing," Vail said with a coy, flirting smile. "I—I was with Scott last night and I left something in his suite."

"Scott?"

"Scott. Scott Meece, fourteen-eleven," she said matter-of-factly. "I just need to get my phone from his room. He was supposed to be back an hour ago. And I have to get to a dinner reservation across town."

"Did you try knocking?"

Nope. Didn't think of that, dumbshit.

Instead, Vail's smile said, "You're the smartest, most handsome man in the world."

"I did."

"And he's not there?"

If he was there, I wouldn't need you, would I?

"He's not. And obviously I can't call because I don't have my phone. Battery's dead by now, anyway. Look, I wouldn't bother you with this, but I really can't exist without my phone. Can you just open the door for a second, let me run in and get it?" She made a pleading pout with her lips.

Shoulda put on lip gloss. Dammit.

"Sure." He tossed down a rag and followed Vail to fourteen-eleven. He tapped his universal key card and the green light glowed.

"I really appreciate you letting me in—" She glanced at his name tag—"Orlando."

Vail stepped inside and let the door swing closed behind her. She looked left and right, taking in everything she could. She had no idea how long she had until Orlando knocked—or entered.

She went over to the coffee table in the large bedroom. A stack of soap bars was neatly corralled into a corner. On the other side sat a box of chocolate bars. And in between were another two piles, not so carefully separated out. Her guess was that the orderly products were the ones containing the aconite.

Vail moved quickly throughout the suite. In the bathroom, on the vanity, was a map of Oahu. Five areas were circled. One was Luxury Row. They were numbered. The fifth was Ala Moana Center.

She rooted out her Samsung and snapped a photo—but a loud knock made her jump and she nearly erased it.

Phone in hand, she pulled the door open and saw Orlando standing there. Vail held up the handset and gave him a big kiss on the cheek. "You're a lifesaver," she said.

"Oh," Orlando said, laughing. "You're just saying that."

"No, I'm serious," Vail said. "Really. Trust me."

51

Y ou did what?" Russell's face turned redder than a farmer's market beet.

They were running down the steps, having taken the stairs because it was faster than waiting for the slow building elevator.

"I got a look at his suite. The maid let me into the room. Voluntarily. No badge, no threats."

"So she read your mind and just walked over to open the door?"

"Not exactly." Vail almost missed a step but caught herself on the railing. "I may've said something about leaving my cell in Scott's room—"

"Scott? Like he's your buddy?"

"Yeah, like that. Now stop slowing me down, Adam. If I lose my concentration, I'll trip again and fall."

"From your mouth to God's ears." Russell had his phone out and was trying to dial and descend at the same time. "Jamie, I need all undercover units to the Ala Moana Center . . . . Yeah, reason to believe suspect Scott Meece might be there. We're en route from Ilikai Hotel."

"How far are we from the mall?" Vail asked.

"Two minutes. If we go my way."

"If we don't go your way?"

"Ten."

They hit the first floor and burst through the door into the lobby. "Then let's go your way."

"Thought you'd see it my way."

"Funny."

They ran outside and were in the car, the engine turning over, seconds later.

Russell cut around a car the valet was delivering to a guest and put his light cube on the roof. He waited for a passing van, then turned left and accelerated hard onto the three lane Ala Moana Boulevard.

"Whoa," Vail said, slamming her right shoulder against the door. She grabbed the dashboard and pulled herself up. "This is one-way against us."

"It is," he said, dodging an oncoming vehicle and slowing to allow another to get out of his lane. "There's no fast way to get to the mall. Ten minutes versus two. I told you."

An oncoming car screeched and swerved out of the lane, clearing a path for Russell and Vail.

"I didn't realize that meant you were gonna get us killed."

"First, you didn't ask. Second, I'm not gonna get us killed. But I will get us there before anyone else."

"By the way," Vail said. "Got a call from an attorney. He's gonna take my case."

Russell dodged another vehicle. "That was close. Sorry."

"My eyes are closed. Next time don't tell me."

"And? What'd this attorney say? I mean, he's taking your case, so he's taking your money." He swerved hard right. "But can he help? Those are two different things."

"You know what, Adam? Maybe this isn't a good time to discuss it."

"It's fine. It'll take my mind off what I'm doing."

Vail squinted through tightly closed lids. "That's what I'm worried about."

"Tell me."

"He thinks I'll be okay. But he hasn't seen the case materials yet—I mean, they just started the investigation."

"And?"

"And he's optimistic. Even though it could take a year to get it all squared away."

"Just be on your best behavior going forward."

"Easy for you to say." Vail felt the car pull to a stop. She opened her eyes, noticed they were parked in the Ala Moana parking garage, and sighed relief. "Thank God."

"I've been called many things," Russell said as he got out of the vehicle. "But never God."

"Should we call SWAT?" Vail asked. "This place is huge."

"Seventh largest shopping mall in the country and the largest open-air shopping center in the world." Russell said as they jogged to the center's entrance.

Of course it is. Why should this be easy?

"I think we should have some kind of confirmation he's here before we call out the cavalry. I'd hate to divert the team here if it's a wrong guess. If they're deployed here for nothing, they might not be able to respond to another call."

"Was that an insult?"

"Not at all. You saw a location circled on a map. He could've been here last week. He could come here next week. I'd rather have some confirmation he's on site."

They slowed to a brisk walk as Russell pulled out his phone and tapped the screen. A few seconds later, he said, "Bill, I need you to patch me through to the security command at Ala Moana Center. ASAP."

Vail kept swinging her head left and right searching for a man in a wheelchair as they passed Barnes & Noble.

"Aloha," Russell said into his handset. "This is Detective Russell, HPD. We're looking for a man in a wheelchair. Forties, full beard. See anyone matching that description on your monitors?" He waited a minute as he and Vail continued down the main walkway past a variety of storefronts headed toward Old Navy.

"Two possibles," Russell said, glancing at Vail.

They both stopped.

"Where?" Vail asked. "What levels?"

He relayed the questions to security and listened. "Got it. Either one selling stuff—like bars of soap or chocolate bars?" He blew some nervous air out of his lips. "Yeah—yes, where? . . . Copy."

"Well?"

"Level two," he said, pocketing his phone. "Food court."

"Now it's time to call SWAT."

"Yep." He put in the request and walked briskly to the escalator.

Vail followed, her heart racing faster than mere exercise would cause. It was an adrenaline dump, much like those she had experienced throughout her career, the sense that she was closing in on the offender.

Offender? Too nice a term. Murderer. Killer. Bastard.

They walked up the left side of the moving stairs, then slowed and tried not to look like they were cops searching for a suspect.

Vail took a deep breath as the escalator crested and she stepped off. Her gaze moved left to right, looking for Meece. Russell was back on his phone, alerting HPD they were closing in on their suspect and requesting onsite resources to converge on his position.

It seemed like overkill—where was he going to go?—but he had, after all, murdered several women—that they knew of. The actual death toll could be far higher.

Off to the right, Vail saw an older woman with gray hair carrying a small bag. She reached in, pulled something out and handed it to a friend, who sniffed it.

"Shit!" Vail took off in her direction, concerned that the offender might see her—but not willing to risk a life. "Ma'am," she called as she approached, trying to keep her voice down but authoritative. "Drop that bar of soap!"

Gotta be the first time a cop has ever said that.

She did as instructed, wincing and recoiling in fear. Vail held up her creds and fished around in her pocket for a stray napkin or tissue. She found the former and wrapped it around the still-sealed bar—on which was scrawled the name Mary Hartman in neat red calligraphy.

"Your name's Mary?"

"Yes," the woman said, her shoulders hunched in fear, her gaze moving between Vail's badge and her own—now empty—hand.

Vail shoved the procured evidence into her jacket pocket and turned to see Russell behind her. "Mary, where's the guy you bought this from?"

"I—I don't know," she said. "I mean, he was back there

somewhere. I wasn't paying attention. I'd just finished eating and I—I—came over here to meet my friend."

"Was he in a wheelchair?" Russell asked.

The woman nodded vigorously. "Yeah. Yes."

Without so much as an explanation, Vail walked away from Mary, her gaze roaming the mall, looking for Scott Meece.

"See him?" Russell asked.

"No. But we know he's here somewhere."

They continued another thirty yards, hung a left, and—

Vail elbowed Russell. "There he is."

52

Meece was talking with a woman—too young to be a target—so there was no need to interrupt the sale.

Vail sized up their offender, and damned if Mary Alana's description wasn't spot-on. It did not happen often that a witness provided such an accurate picture of someone based on a casual contact. Then again, such victim or witness accounts suffered because the individual encountered the offender during times of stress—which was not the case here.

Meece wore jeans and tennis shoes. He did not look homeless or destitute, but he certainly had the haggard look of someone in need of pity, with a long beard and baggy shirt.

They came up alongside Meece, Vail on his left and Russell on his right.

"Scott Meece," Vail said, holding up her badge. "We've got some questions for you."

"Yeah," Russell said, placing a firm hand on the man's right shoulder. "Like does the word 'aconite' mean anything to you?"

Meece did not even bother turning to face him. He heaved the box of products at Russell's face, bolted out of his wheelchair and ran—ran—away from them.

As Russell recovered from the flying soap bars, Vail took off after him. Had she been texting, she would've typed, WTF?

For a disabled man without the use of his legs, he was moving quite well.

She heard Russell yelling at nearby patrons not to touch the soap and chocolates, that they had poison in them. She hoped they heeded his warning.

Vail heard footsteps behind her and the sound of tones for numerals being pressed on a smartphone keypad.

Russell . . . no doubt, trailing her. He must have called HPD to report the pursuit because it sounded like he was chattering into the phone. She couldn't quite make it out, but it sounded like, "It's a miracle! I touched his shoulder and he can walk again!"

Or maybe it was law enforcement-speak, providing status and location.

Regardless, Vail was focused on trying to close the gap between herself and their wheelchair-bound-war-veteran-turned-Olympic-track-star.

It's a mall, where can he go?

Into Gucci? Prada?

Nope. He eschewed the ultra-high-end merchants and chose the more approachable high-end Nordstrom.

Then again, have you seen the prices on their women's shoes?

"Anything?" Russell asked.

"Nordstrom. Lost him in the crowd of people."

"Lots of witnesses. Don't worry, we'll get him."

Fuck that. I'm worried.

As they passed through menswear, Vail noticed they were running their half-yearly sale.

I should tell Robby. He needs some slacks.

"Look at all these people," Russell said.

Too easy to grab a shirt off one of the tables and change his appearance.

But a more pressing concern was that Meece could disappear anywhere in the tens of thousands of square feet, the many hidden areas—changing rooms, restrooms, café kitchens . . . and a host of other places obscured by the masses picking through racks and tables piled high with discounted merchandise.

"You think he's still here?"

"No idea," Vail said.

"They're locking down the mall, but it'll take some time. There's a ton of exits and only a handful of guards and HPD officers."

"Control what we can. You go left. Let's try to cover this floor."

Shoulda called SWAT sooner.

As Russell moved off, Vail climbed atop the nearest checkout counter.

"Hey!" The clerk was beside himself, jumping back and holding up his hands. "What are you doing? I'm—I'm gonna call the cops."

"I *am* the cops, buddy." She pulled back her coat, revealing her badge.

That shut him up . . . but it was little consolation since even from this vantage point Vail did not see Meece.

She continued scanning the area, doing a grid-like search. She picked out Russell, who turned to face her. She threw out her hands and shrugged—and he did the same.

Seconds later, her phone vibrated. She leaped off the counter and moved on.

"I'm going down a floor," Russell said. "You go up."

"What about the changing rooms?"

"Dammit, Karen, I don't know! This is impossible."

"What happened to 'don't worry, we'll get him'?"

"I didn't say *when* we'd get him."

Vail's phone vibrated again. "Another call coming in."

"Let me know if you find him," Russell said.

"Oh, you'll know. You'll hear the gunshots. Because when I find him I'm gonna shoot the bastard."

"Karen—"

"I'm kidding."

Maybe.

She clicked off and answered. It was Del Monaco.

"Talk to me, Frank. I need some good news."

"What happened, the UNSUB escape during foot pursuit?"

"Don't insult me." *Even if it is the truth.* "Whaddya got?"

"So your Scott Meece has an interesting background."

"Military veteran?"

"Not even close. His older *brother*, Phillip, was Special Forces—a decorated army Ranger. Died in Somalia, the battle of Mogadishu. You know, *Black Hawk Down*?"

"You're kidding."

"There's more. I did some googling and found a photo of Scott with Brian Layton, a Vietnam War vet who had an army surplus store in Queens. I took a shot and called and guy's still around. He remembered Scott well. Kid worked for him. Didn't talk much but Layton said Scott seemed to have lots of problems with his stepfather. Layton never asked the name, but I see a Nick James residing at their apartment around that time. Layton told Scott to join up, get out of the house and get his degree on the GI bill. But Scott was too afraid of getting killed."

"Interesting."

"That was supposedly a big deal with this Nick guy. He wanted Scott to follow his brother into the army but Scott refused. He demeaned Scott, called him a coward."

"Good find, Frank."

"Last thing. Scott had some emotional problems after Phillip died. Took his brother's death hard. I tried to get more detail out of Layton, but he said he wasn't really sure what was going on. One thing he did remember was Scott experiencing a hallucination."

"Hmm. So maybe he went through a reactive psychosis after Phillip died. A death like that, with everything else going on at home, would be enough to trigger it—as well as a psychotic depression."

"My thinking, too."

Vail knew that if his condition turned chronic, and he wasn't on medication, Scott could be seeing, hearing, or believing things that weren't real.

That might be what's at play here—or it may've only been the start. This has been going on for years.

"When did Phillip die?"

"October 1993."

"Could've been the trigger. Or at least sent him down the serial killer path."

"I also sent a photo over to HPD and TSA. Picture's dated, taken at least ten years ago, but it's better than the phenotype."

"Which wasn't half bad."

"Surprisingly good, actually."

"Look, Frank, about me never saying thank you."

"Yeah?"

"I *do* appreciate this. Losing sleep and all. This is helpful."

"You're being sarcastic."

"No, really. I mean it. You're a shitty profiler and you drive me up a goddam wall most of the time, but I sincerely appreciate all your efforts tonight." She stopped and listened, held the phone away to see if the call was still live. "Crap. I said that out loud, didn't I? Frank? Hello?"

Nope, he hung up. Sometimes the truth hurts.

She had covered a good chunk of the ground floor when Russell called through.

"No gunshots."

"What?"

"Guessing you haven't found him yet."

"No," Vail said, crouching down and looking underneath a line of clothing racks. "But I did find out he's got an interesting background."

"Oh—hey. Getting a call from security. Hang on."

Vail pushed a stack of sweaters aside and climbed atop a table. She scanned the floor into the distance, looking for Meece. No luck.

Russell clicked back. "Got him. CCTV camera picked him up grabbing a child and running."

That doesn't make any sense.

"You sure? Are *they* sure?"

"Why?"

"That's not his MO. It's not consistent with his victimology. It—nothing adds up. Unless he did it to negotiate his way out."

"All I can tell you is what security told me."

"Where is he?"

"Last seen on the third floor, headed east."

"East?" Vail jumped down off the table. "Seriously—you want me to consult a compass? Can you be a little more specific?"

"Hang on. I'll check with security."

Vail headed for the store exit while waiting to hear back, hoping she was moving in the correct direction.

"Forget that," Russell said in her ear. "He's back on the second floor, ran into a restroom opposite the Microsoft Store."

"Heading there now. Status on SWAT?"

"Seven minutes out."

"Ten-four." She hung up and tried pulling up a map of the mall on her phone, then realized it would be quicker if she asked for directions.

Good thing I'm not a guy.

She jogged along the tile, maneuvering around slower-moving people. After passing Banana Republic and Disney Store, she came upon a man at a smartphone repair kiosk. "Hey," Vail said, a bit out of breath. "Which way to the Microsoft Store?"

He must have noticed her chest heaving, trying to suck oxygen. "Why? There some kind of blowout Xbox sale?"

"What? Oh. You're joking." She pulled the badge off her belt and shoved it in his face. "Not so funny now, is it? *Where's* the goddam store?"

He took a step back from her and silently jerked a thumb over his left shoulder.

Vail ran past him and pulled to a stop at a four-way intersection in front of Gucci and Prada. Escalators to her right and left.

"Microsoft?" she asked a well-dressed man coming out of Cartier.

"Um, back behind me. On the left."

She yelled thanks as she jogged on. And sure enough, just past the Omega watch store was Microsoft and its bright, ten-foot-high glass windows.

Whaddya know, the guy was right. Big Xbox sale. I should tell Jonathan.

"Karen!"

Russell was coming off the escalator a bit farther down, near Macy's.

They huddled about fifty yards away in front of LeSportsac. "Last seen going into the bathroom with the boy."

"How old?"

They started walking to the entrance to the bathroom, passing Mahaloha Burger and Ike's Sandwiches.

"Five or six."

"Alone?"

"Just Meece," Russell said. "He had decent control of the kid."

"Kid know him? Or just scared shitless?"

"No idea. I'm getting all this secondhand. Didn't stop to ask questions."

Vail shook her head. "What the hell's up with this guy?"

"Aren't *you* supposed to know?"

"I'm a behavioral analyst, not a voyeur."

"Right," Russell said as they neared the restrooms, where a guard was watching the entrance.

"Did you go in?" Vail asked the man.

"I was told to wait outside, report in if I saw the dude. Detain anyone coming out and prevent anyone from going in."

"So no one came out."

"Correct," he said. "But I only got here a minute before you."

"What do you think?" Russell asked.

Vail moved closer to the men's room and listened. Did not hear anything unusual. She rejoined Russell. "Pretty sure he's not armed. But a knife? Who knows."

"So we just wait for SWAT?"

"Hell no. There's a kid in there. We go in. You take the door in case he gets by me. I'll—"

His phone rang. "Russell." He listened a few seconds, then said, "Got it," and shoved the handset in his back pocket. "Someone called. Kid's in a stall."

They inched closer, pistols in hand, listening as they approached. Vail entered first, followed by Russell—though that's as far as he went, keeping with their plan to safeguard the exit.

She inched through the bright, modern bathroom, past the urinals and up to the stalls. The place looked, and sounded, empty. She knelt to take a ground level perspective. No legs visible.

Vail stepped back a few feet and steadied her pistol in front of her, then kicked in the first door. It shot open and bounced against the right wall. No one inside.

She shimmied right and did the same—and got the same result. As she began to doubt the veracity of the phoned-in tip, the last stall yielded fruit: crudely restrained with a torn-up men's dress shirt, was the boy. The remainder of the cloth not used as restraints was stuffed in his mouth.

"I'm Karen." She holstered her Glock. "Adam," she called toward the entrance. "I've got him."

Russell appeared in the doorway and watched Vail's back—in case Meece was still there somewhere—while Vail worked to untie the knots.

"It's okay now," she said. "You're safe. We're the police."

The boy was wild-eyed and did not speak, even though Vail had removed the saliva-soaked wad.

"See if you can get one of his parents down here."

Russell pulled out his phone as he walked away.

Vail coaxed him off the toilet lid and led him to the exit. A few moments later, mother and child were reunited, the boy remaining subdued even as he threw his arms around her neck and held on tight.

"A diversion," Vail said.

"To escape?"

"Yep. Have security check their video footage of the past ten minutes. All exit cameras."

"You realize how long that'll take? This place is huge, with, like, five department store anchors. Gotta be dozens of cameras."

"Then they'd better get started."

53

It did not take as long as they had feared. With the development of video analytics, facial recognition and AI—artificial intelligence—algorithms, they were able to zero in on specific exits that had captured images of individuals matching Scott Meece's photo and physical description.

As Vail and Russell were making their way to the security office, they were notified that SWAT had arrived and was deploying, along with HPD's Specialized Canine Unit.

Vail pushed through the door into an operations center as impressive as any she had seen in malls and business parks.

"Here's what we grabbed," the geeky guard said, working a mouse and keyboard. "This guy, right here. Wearing the baseball cap." He grabbed a pen and pointed at the screen closest to his left hand.

Vail leaned in close and studied the image. "Can you get me a better view? The hat's casting a shadow over his face."

"Nah, the sun's hitting the cam at a bad angle, so that's about as good as I can do for you. I brightened it up as much as I can. More than that, it'll just be pixel noise and resolution artifacts."

"I absolutely *hate* pixel noise," Vail said.

He turned to her, his expression indicating that he was unsure whether or not Vail actually knew what that was—or if she was mocking him.

"What do you think?" Russell asked. "Is it him?"

Vail blew air out her tight lips. "Yes. I think so. Besides, we've got no other leads. Let's pursue this unless something better sends us in a different direction."

"Keep going through the tape," Russell said to the tech. "Manually if you have to. If Scott Meece is still somewhere on the premises, call Chief Ferraro. He's onsite assisting the SWAT lieutenant in deploying his team." Russell jotted down Ferraro's mobile number and handed it to the man.

Vail was staring at another monitor, a loop playing of the guy resembling Meece as he exited the building and entered the garage.

They walked out and headed briskly through the mall.

"Still think it might be him?"

"Pretty sure. Resolution isn't great. And that pixel noise kept throwing me off."

"You have no idea what that is, do you?"

"Not a clue."

Russell shook his head.

"Sometimes it isn't about technology," Vail said. "It can be a crutch. We're still cops and we need to use our intuitive methods to find the asshole."

"Intuitive methods," Russell repeated. "Okay, I'll bite. Which specific methods are you intuiting right now?"

"The guy's body language kept speaking to me."

"His body language was *talking* to you. You trying to be funny?"

"No. When he walked out, he tried to hide his face from the camera."

"Well that definitely makes him guilty of *something*."

"Maybe I'm reading into it," Vail said, stopping in front of Victoria's Secret. "Seeing what I want to see."

Russell looked up. "Hmm. Well right now *I'm* seeing what I want to see."

Vail glanced over at the object of his attention: a mannequin wearing a skimpy lace bra in front of larger than life photos of bikini-clad models. She brought her gaze back to Russell. "Focus, Adam."

"Right." He turned to Vail. "We have to assume Meece got into a vehicle. Stole one or had one here."

"Or carjacked one."

"That would make it easier." Russell pulled out his phone. "I'll have HPD issue a BOLO. And make sure that any reports of carjacking get reported directly to us."

"Yeah, well . . ." Vail snorted. "Don't hold your breath."

"Now now, Karen. Be positive. Aloha, right?"

She frowned and thought about holding up one particular finger. "You know what you can do with your aloha?"

54

While Russell spoke with Ferraro about the BOLO, Vail noticed he had positioned himself so that he had a view of the Victoria's Secret storefront.

As he finished his call, Vail shook her head in disappointment. "You know those women aren't real."

"What?"

She gestured at the huge posters adorning the window. "Women just don't look like that."

"If you say so."

"When you're able to tear your eyes away from Victoria and her mistresses, we've got some important stuff to discuss."

Russell shifted his body and faced Vail. "Oh, right—you said Meece has an interesting background."

She briefed him on what she learned from Del Monaco.

"This Del Monaco sounds like a good guy to have around."

"Not really. He's a hack. But useful. Well, sometimes."

Russell chuckled. "God knows what you'll say about *me* when you're back in Virginia."

"I can tell you now, but you're not gonna like it. Better that I email you once I get home."

"Can't wait." He shot another look at the Victoria's Secret model, then pulled his gaze back to Vail. "As nice as the scenery is here, I really don't wanna sit around waiting to get a hit on the BOLO. Any thoughts of where Meece is going?"

Vail sat down on a bench and rubbed her temples. A moment later, she said, "What kind of military presence do you have on the island?"

Russell laughed. "That a joke? There's a ton of military here. What are you looking for?"

"I don't know, maybe some kind of . . . memorial."

"Why?"

"Phillip. His older brother. Scott might not only feel the loss of Phillip but also severe guilt over his death. The military wasn't Scott's thing and his stepfather demeaned him and called him a coward. Maybe he thinks that if he'd served, Phillip would still be alive."

"That's not rational."

"The human mind is not rational, Adam."

"True. Look at you."

"Hey."

"You dish it out, you better be able to take it."

"That another thing Lance Burden taught you?"

"Nope. That I figured out on my own." Russell sat down next to her. "Actually, yes. Can't lie. Moral high ground, right? Turns out, his advice was pretty spot-on."

"I'm not that difficult to figure out."

"Right. But it's *Meece* we're trying to figure out. He has this guilt over his brother."

"I think so." Vail nodded slowly. "And maybe he's looking for some place where he can join Phillip."

"How so?"

"People suffering from psychosis, especially depressive psychosis, are at much greater risk of suicide."

"So he's going to kill himself on a military base? Or at a memorial?"

"It's possible. Suicide by cop. Or MP." She dropped her hands and turned to him. "You got a better idea?"

"I don't."

"So . . . memorials."

He shrugged. "Ever hear of Pearl Harbor? In terms of memorials, they don't get much bigger, more iconic, than that. At least in the United States."

She thought for a moment. "Too big. Can't get close enough to anything for it to have meaning. Well, for the offender."

"You sure? Or you making all this up?"

"Don't be insulting."

"Sorry. Just frustrated."

A moment later, Vail said, "Sixty percent."

"What?"

"You asked if I was making it all up. "I'm only fabricating sixty percent."

He leaned back and looked at her. "I don't know what to do with you sometimes."

"See? Moral high ground isn't always a good thing." Her phone vibrated. A text from Carmine Russo:

fbi played nice
let us take the lead
on our way over now

Vail relayed Russo's information.

"Think Meece's New York crib will help us?"

"You want an answer from the sixty percent or the forty?" She got up and started walking in the direction—she thought—that led the way back toward their car. "What about a military cemetery? I assume you've got one of those here?"

"Yeah. We've got one of those. Punchbowl national cemetery."

"Punchbowl? That a joke?"

"Official name is National Cemetery of the Pacific. It's located inside the Punchbowl volcanic crater, so people refer to it as Punchbowl."

Vail sighed, canted her head ceilingward.

What's the right call here?

"How far is the Pearl Harbor memorial?"

"About twenty-five minutes, unless there's traffic."

"Is there usually traffic on the island?"

Russell harrumphed. "It's one of the most traffic-impacted cities in the country. This time of day, we're looking at probably forty-five."

"What about the Punchbowl?"

"Just Punchbowl. Not *the* Punchbowl."

"Whatever."

Russell shrugged. "Ten minutes. Five if we drive my way."

Vail stood up. "Then that's where we're headed." They started jogging back toward Russell's car. "But I've had enough of driving *your way*. Better we get there alive."

55

Carmine Russo and one of his first-year patrol officers, Jason Cobb, sat in their unmarked vehicle as Russo navigated toward the apartment owned by Scott Meece.

"Whaddya think, boss?"

"Don't know. Skel's got no priors. Kept his nose clean in New Yawk. Could be a case where you don't crap in your diaper because you could be wearing it awhile."

"What?"

Russo leaned closer. "He kills women here, could fuck everything up for him. Not worth it. Does his business elsewhere, far from here, doesn't pollute the water where he lives. Safer."

Cobb harrumphed. "Makes sense."

Russo bobbed his head. "Yeah some of these bastards are too smart for my taste. But they're not as smart as us, so it's a matter of bringing our A game. Keeping our eyes open and doing our jobs like I taught yous."

"So how come, boss?"

"How come what? You gotta finish your thoughts, Cobb."

Cobb looked away. "How come you brought me in on this?"

"Did I make the wrong call?"

"No," Cobb said, almost too quickly. "I'm glad. I was, you know, just wondering. Lots of us deserved to go."

"I chose who I thought would be best for the task. We're not playing around here, Cobb. This is real. A real call. A real killer who's taken the lives of a dozen people. Maybe more."

"Jesus." He licked his lips as Russo pulled up to the curb and killed his lights. "We're a block away."

"Don't want anyone to see an *obvious* unmarked cop car parking in front of the building?"

Russo chuckled. "Definitely cleaner this way. Don't need to take chances. We wanna look like we're just a coupla guys out for a walk."

"At three in the morning?" Cobb shook his head. "Shoulda brought my dog."

"Probably be no one home," Russo said, ignoring the comment. "Meece is on Oahu—and if he's no longer there, he can't be here yet. So *he's* not going to be home. But we don't know if he's got any accomplices or if he lives with anyone else. According to my profiler friend, he appears to be workin' alone. Not married. But is that a guarantee of anything?"

"Nope."

"Right."

"The skel uses poison to kill his victims. So don't be stickin' your nose anywhere it shouldn't be. You don't wanna be sucking any of that stuff into your lungs."

"Copy."

They secured their vests with Velcro and slipped on their winter jackets, Russo pulling a 5.11 Tactical wool beanie over his ears and Cobb donning a New York Mets baseball cap. They headed down the block to the apartment, taking care to avoid making any unusual noises that would set off a neighborhood canine with a keen sense of hearing and a muscular set of vocal cords.

They stood outside the apartment house door and took in the area. Everything looked clear. A moment later the building manager showed up. His graying afro was flat on the left side and stuck out excessively on the right. He probably had no time to get ready—just throw on the clothes, jacket and gloves, and run out the door.

"I'm Captain Russo and this is Officer Cobb." Russo held up his badge. "You the building manager?"

"Walter Vandross."

Russo handed him the search warrant and he shoved it in his pocket, not even bothering to look it over. "Anything I should know?" Vandross asked.

"You got an NYPD captain serving a federal warrant to search the premises of the guy who lives in 10D. That's about all I can tell you. Well, that and you're lucky you didn't get the FBI. Not as nice as me. Bottom line is that this ain't a positive development for your homeowner."

"Yeah, no shit. Got me outta bed in the middle of the night."

"In case you didn't notice," Cobb said, "you ain't alone."

Vandross grumbled as he fumbled a ring of keys, searching for the right one.

"Anything you can tell us about Scott Meece?" Russo asked.

"Quiet guy. Didn't know him too well. I mean, a few times we talked about some things but other than that he kept to himself."

"What kind of things did you discuss?" Russo asked.

"Military stuff. I served. His brother did. He'd ask me about it, what it was like."

"Normal conversation?"

"Most part. I mean, I did a lotta the talking. He asked most of the questions."

"What was he interested in?"

"War. What it was like. How people died. What it was like to kill." Vandross shoved the key in the lock and gave the knob a twist, then pushed through the door.

"Didn't that seem strange?" Russo asked. "I mean, most normal people don't wanna hear that gory shit."

"And I don't like talkin' about that gory shit." Vandross shrugged as he limped down the dimly lit hallway. Like many New York City buildings, this was "modern"—when compared to those built in the early 1900s. It had seen a remodel in the form of a new coat of paint and the replacement of a few broken windows and . . . that was about it. The place was old—and smelled it.

"At the time," Vandross said, "I didn't give it no mind. But now that I think about it, maybe. Yeah. That's not the kind of thing people ask about." He stopped and glanced up at the spider cracks in the hallway ceiling, then harrumphed. "He's actually the first to ever want to know about that stuff. My friends, they just leave me be. We don't talk about it. Any of it."

"Anything else seem strange, now that you think about it?"

He blew some air out of his mouth. "I don't know, man. Mostly kept to hisself."

Cobb pulled off his hat and blotted up the band of perspiration on his forehead.

"All right," Russo said, doing the same. "Let's get in there and take a look." He pulled out a pair of blue gloves and started to stretch them over his hands. Cobb took the hint and followed suit.

Vandross produced another key and rapped on the repeatedly-painted wood door. "Building manager! Please open up."

He knocked again, waited a few moments—until Russo lost his patience and cleared his throat. "Open it up, Mr. Vandross."

Vandross complied and unlocked it.

"You gotta wait here," Cobb said. "Read the search warrant if you get bored."

Russo gave that a chuckle, then drew his pistol and led the way into the apartment. "NYPD serving a search warrant! Anyone here?"

They turned on the lights and, unlike in TV shows, they worked.

"Um . . ." Cobb said. "What's all this shit, boss?"

Laid out before them were foot-square boxes stacked atop one another, in six-foot-high piles. They were arranged to form walls—and thus a path—that led Russo and Cobb through the living room.

They stood on opposing sides of the jamb of a closed door. Cobb twisted the knob and pushed it open.

Russo reached in and found the light switch, flicked it up, and was first inside. He skirted the double bed and checked the closet, then under the box spring. "Clear."

Russo joined Cobb at the low dresser that stood in front of the long wall. Modest-size plastic tubs sat atop the furniture. They were largely empty—except for a residual substance in one of them.

"Any idea what this is?"

Russo shined his phone light into one of the containers. "A soap-making assembly line of sorts would be my guess."

Cobb looked inside and then twisted toward Russo. "How do you get that, boss?"

"Karen Vail told me we might find one. And this does kinda look like that's what this stuff is for." Russo brought his face closer, careful not to sniff up any airborne toxins. "Yep. That's what we got here. Pretty sure." He stood up and looked around. "You see any chocolate bars?"

They moved into the bathroom, then back out toward the front door where all the boxes were stacked. Cobb produced a knife and sliced through the corrugated sides—exposing thin, tightly packed treats. "Got 'em." He pulled out a blue-gloved handful and showed them to Russo, who snapped a photo.

Russo opened a few other nearby boxes and found soap bars. He took another picture, then texted both to Vail with the following message:

its fuckin 3am
hope ur happy
all we got to show for it is soap and candy bars
doesnt look like anyone else lives here
oh lots of military photos on wall

Vail typed back:

photos of meece?

Russo's immediate reply:

hard to say
quality sucks
group pictures
no close-ups
could be his brother IDK

"Hey boss. Lots of plants in here. Kitchen."
"Take some photos. Text 'em to me. Don't touch nothin'."
"And, uh, a bottle of Red Number 40."
"Red what?" Russo made his way into the kitchen.
"That's what it says. On the label, Red Number 40."
"What the fuck is that?"

"Red dye. You ever read ingredient labels? Of food?"

"I read the *Daily News*. Sports pages. Sometimes Page Six of the *Post*. Ingredient labels, not so much."

"Red 40 is a dye, a food coloring."

"So?"

"So it's with the soap making stuff. Maybe it means something."

"I'll send it all over to Agent Vail. Let her figure out if it means something." He lifted his phone and took some pictures, then texted them over to Vail. She immediately responded:

jackpot
bullseye
you rock

Russo chuckled. "Apparently you made Vail very happy."

"And if she's happy, we're happy," Cobb said. "Right?"

"Always keep the woman happy, Cobb. Remember that."

"Now what, boss?"

"Now you hoof it back to my car and pull it out front. Get the crime scene tape. We'll rope this place off and you get to stand watch, make sure no one goes in or out, till CSU gets here."

Cobb fought off a yawn.

"Aren't you glad you came?"

"Sure."

Russo grunted. "Then act like it, rook." He dangled his car keys and Cobb snatched them without hesitation. "Hurry up," Russo said, making no attempt to hide his long yawn. "I wanna get back to bed while there's still some sleep to be gotten."

"Oh—forgot my hat. Put it down somewhere."

"Jesus Christ, Cobb."

The rookie swung his head around, then started off down the hall.

Russo yawned again—and then found himself on his ass, ears ringing from the explosive blast that pushed his chest with a ferocity that pinned him against the worn carpeting.

He wriggled himself up onto his elbows and peered out into the fog of dust and detritus and all sorts of crap that hung in the air.

"Cobb," he shouted. He *thought* he shouted it—truth was, his hearing was muffled and the buzzing prevented him from knowing just how loud he had said it.

He felt around his pocket and found his phone. As he fumbled with trembling fingers to work the touchscreen, he got the call connected. Problem was, he could not hear anything. He waited a moment, then started yelling into the handset. "Officer down, officer down. This is Captain Carmine Russo, I need a bus forthwith to my location."

He moved the device away from his face and studied the display. How the hell was he supposed to know if anyone was on the line?

"Listen, there was an explosion. I don't know if you can hear me, but I can't hear anything. Text me back on this cell and confirm. Over."

Seconds later, he received a message from a number he did not recognize:

copy that captain
bus on the way
eta three mins

Russo acknowledged it and used his hands to walk his way up his thighs. He stood up straight and felt sharp pain in his lower back. He groaned—or at least he thought he did—and stumbled forward.

Pushing aside debris—a chair, or what was left of it—he made his way toward the location where he last saw Cobb.

Please let him be alive. My fault he was here.

Russo made it another ten feet, in the direction of the bedroom, kicking away the now-tumbled boxes of soap bars in his path.

Part of him did not want to locate the young man—out of fear of what he might find.

Another few yards and there was Cobb, lying prone, a portion of his right leg missing from the knee down. "Jesus, Mary, and Joseph . . ." Russo crossed himself as he knelt down to feel for a pulse: slow, thready. Fresh red blood was pumping feebly from the stump.

But he was still alive. "Hang on, kid." Russo was certain Cobb was unconscious, but in truth he was saying it to make himself feel better. "Help's on the way. You're gonna be fine."

Russo pulled off his leather belt and fastened it tightly around Cobb's thigh, hoping to stem the flow of blood until the ambulance arrived. As that thought fluttered through his mind, he heard what he took to be a siren, down below, outside the window. "I can hear again! Kind of." He sighed deeply and placed a hand on the rookie's back. "They're here. You're gonna be okay, Cobb."

There was no response, but moments later the paramedics were calling out, trying to locate them.

"In here, near the bedroom."

The two men immediately went to work.

"Find the leg," one of them said to Russo.

Find the leg. You fucking kidding me?

Russo stumbled around, moving aside debris, bars of soap and fragments of furniture and broken glass. He located the limb atop a box twenty feet away.

This was beyond gross. He made his way into the kitchen and found a Hefty bag, unfurled it with a rapid flick of his wrists, and stood in front of the leg. He stuck his hand into the plastic, grabbed the hunk of human tissue, and then tied off the sack.

"Got it," Russo said as he approached the bedroom.

"Good job. Now fill that thing with ice cubes."

"How's he doing?"

One of the medics was securing an IV. Cobb was already fastened to a spine board, his head and neck stabilized. "Best we can tell, out of danger. He'll need a full neuro workup, films of his spine, make sure his neck isn't fractured."

"What about his leg?"

The man shrugged. "Ain't my call. We get it and bring it in, let the trauma surgeon make those decisions. Getting ready to transport. How *you* doin', Captain? You here when the bomb went off?"

"Don't worry 'bout me. I'm an old horse. Hard to put me down."

The man was closing up his kit. "Answer my question, please."

"I was here. My hearing was shit right after, but it's come back a little bit."

"You need to get checked out. Ride with us in the bus."

"This is a crime scene. Can't leave—"

"Yes you can. Go with them."

Russo turned and saw a patrol officer.

"We got it covered, Captain. Give me his leg. I'll take care of the ice. Go get yourself looked at."

Russo groaned. "Fine." He glanced around to see if there was anything else he needed to do before leaving. He kicked a box that was in his way. "This wasn't the kind of night I'd planned on."

"Yeah?" The paramedic grabbed his end of the spine board. "I think Officer Cobb here would agree with you."

56

Russell turned on Wilder Avenue and navigated the residential streets as they neared the crater. There was a noticeable incline as they rose in altitude, climbing toward the top of the mountain.

Vail stole a look at her phone. "Russo's at Meece's place in the city. Lots of equipment and boxes of 'merchandise' in his bedroom and living room. Soap bars and chocolate. Meece is definitely our guy."

"Boxes? Jesus. I wonder how many women this bastard actually killed."

Vail's phone began buzzing. "Hey, Russo. Thanks so much for that info, it—"

"That info came at a price. My rookie officer lost a leg."

"He what? What are you talking about?"

"Looks like Meece rigged an IED," he said, referring to an improvised explosive device. "Trip wire activation. Cobb didn't see it, set it off."

"Oh my god, I'm—I'm so sorry. I had no idea Meece would do such a thing."

What a stupid thing to say.

Russell gestured at her, mouthing, "What happened?"

Vail waved him off. "Is he gonna be okay?"

"Don't know. He's in surgery. And I'm sittin' here feeling very guilty."

"*You're* feeling guilty? I'm the one who asked you to check out his apartment. I feel like jumping off a goddam pier."

"Well don't do that. I couldn't handle two tragedies in one night."

Vail closed her eyes. She did not know what to say to that.

"Don't feel bad, Karen. We're all just doin' our jobs. Shit happens, right? This is what we signed up for."

"Is that how you feel?"

"Hell no. I'm the rook's captain. But one of us feelin' guilty is enough."

"Keep me posted on his condition, okay?"

"Of course. But you focus on finding this Meece son of a bitch. I'd like to personally rip him a new asshole. Do that for me?"

"Rip him a new asshole or find him?"

"You find him. The asshole thing? That's for me."

"Miss you, Russo."

"Back at ya, Karen. Be careful out there."

She could not help but grin at the *Hill Street Blues* reference.

As she ended the call, Russell glanced at her. "So? What the hell happened?"

Vail told him about the IED, the trip wire, and the officer's injuries.

"Crap. If I didn't wanna get this guy in a room before, I sure do now."

"Get in line."

Russell took the next turn a bit too fast for the neighborhood. Vail grabbed onto the dash. "Tell me about this cemetery."

"Calling it a cemetery is not doing it justice. Setting's beautiful, serene. Expansive."

"I could use beautiful and serene about now."

"Just don't let the beauty distract you. Keep your head in the game."

"Deal. You kept your head in your pants at the mall, so I guess it's only fair I keep my head in the game at the cemetery."

"Wow. How very crass of you." Russell's cell rang. He fiddled with it, then cursed. "Bluetooth isn't connecting." He handed it to Vail.

"Detective Russell's phone. Agent Vail speaking."

"This is Sergeant Aldridge at HPD. Got a report of a carjacking a block from Ala Moana Center. By witness description it sounds like your suspect. Scott Meece."

"When was this?"

"Twenty minutes or so ago."

"And we're just getting told now?"

"Sometimes one hand doesn't know what the other's doing. We've got a big department."

"Which way was he headed?"

"Vehicle was caught on a traffic cam a few minutes later on Pensacola, near Nehoa."

Vail turned to Russell. "Meece jacked a car, last seen on Pensacola, near Nehoa."

"Wow."

"Tell me. I don't know where that is."

"Could be headed to the cemetery. Means we may've guessed right."

"We?"

"You. You guessed right."

"Wasn't a guess. It's called criminal investigative analysis."

"Call it what you want. I'm just relieved we're not headed in the opposite direction."

Vail turned back to the call. "Sergeant, you get any further updates, let us know."

"You got a bead on Meece?"

"Just a guess. The Punchbowl."

"Punchbowl. Not *the*."

I'm never gonna get that right.

"I'll see about diverting some officers as backup."

"I did say it's just a guess, right?"

"Fine. I'll send officers to the *area*. You get confirmation, they'll be in closer proximity to assist."

"SWAT was at the huge mall near here. Can you send them too?"

"Roger that."

Vail hung up and handed Russell his phone. "He may be headed this way," she said, "but that doesn't mean he's coming *here*."

"We'll see soon enough. But I think you're right. And he might be looking to off himself."

"We don't really know what we're dealing with. I'm pretty confident in my assessment, but I'm working on the fly here. A lot of intuition. I haven't had much time to think, not that we have a lot to go on."

"It's okay if you're wrong," Russell said as he made another turn and accelerated. "I couldn't have done any better."

"Glad *you* said that. A few years ago, *I* might've been the one to make that comment. And it wouldn't have gone over too well."

"So you're mellowing with age?"

Vail grabbed the dashboard to steady herself around another curve. "My fiancé might not agree with that assessment."

Russell chuckled as he approached the entrance to the cemetery.

"That's the second crack you've made about my age, Adam. How old do you think I am?"

"Nope." Russell shook his head. "Not going near that one."

57

Though the crater was formed approximately one hundred thousand years ago, the National Memorial Cemetery was much younger, dating to 1949.

As they crested the ancient volcano along Puowaina Drive, Vail glanced left and saw a panoramic top-down view of Honolulu, fronted by high-rise resorts and office buildings, and the Diamond Head volcanic mountain in the distance with a glimpse of the beach and ocean beyond.

"Know what the Hawaiian translation of the name Punchbowl is?"

Vail snorted. "Doesn't everyone?"

"Hill of sacrifice."

"Appropriate for a military cemetery."

Russell bobbed his head. "Except that the name came way before the memorial. Third century, the crater was used as an altar where Hawaiians offered human sacrifices to pagan gods."

Vail chuckled as they drove through the iron front entrance gate. "And fifteen hundred years later, politicians offered human sacrifices—in the form of soldiers—to satisfy their need to conquer and rule over others. Not sure it's all that different."

"Wow," Russell said, "a skilled FBI profiler *and* political commentator, all rolled into one."

"I'm full of surprises," she said as they approached another entrance. "People never know what's going to tumble out of my mouth."

"Apparently, neither do you."

Ahead were two concrete pillars with signage and brass plaques—but Vail's attention was snatched by the grandeur of the landscape ahead: a long rectangular immaculately mown grass mall bordered by full, mature medium-size banyan trees. Sitting majestically at the far end was a massive complex: the memorial, built of multiple levels of stairs that narrowed as they neared the top, where a tall sculpture stood against a cream-colored marble wall.

"You were right. Quite the setting."

"We're now inside the crater," Russell said as he curved by the landscaped roundabout that featured a maritime-themed flagpole.

"You'd never know. It's beautiful."

"Any idea where Meece might go?"

"If I knew what was housed here—other than buried bodies—I might be able to answer that."

"Just do some more of your guessing—I mean, what's it called? Criminal investigative . . .?"

"Analysis. And yeah, there's some educated speculation involved. But it's rooted in evidence, the offender's behaviors, and the unit's database of research. You want to call that guessing, have at it. I usually do a pretty decent job of helping to catch these UNSUBs." She pointed ahead. "Let's do a drive-through and let me get a sense of what we're looking at."

"Yes ma'am."

"We can stop and get out if we see anything that intrigues us."

"Like a fugitive serial killer?"

"Like that, yeah."

As they cruised slowly along the right side of the long edge of the rectangle, Vail rolled down her windows. "What the hell's that noise?"

"Birds. Lots of 'em, living in the banyans. They're always here. Kind of amazing. They make music all day, every day for the fallen."

"Nice thought." Vail glanced around. "Looks like all the structures on this site are clustered around the memorial itself, up ahead."

"Correct." He pointed with the index finger of his hand that was resting on the steering wheel. "That central area, there's a terracing of levels and stairs leading to each level. On each side of the stairs is a landscaped planter—those bushes and small trees—and then beyond that, moving laterally, are individual memorials. Courts of the Missing, they're called. Rooms without ceilings. Names of thirty thousand soldiers missing in action or lost at sea are engraved in the stone on the walls."

"So lots of places for Meece to hide."

"If he's trying to hide, yeah. I thought you said he's here to kill himself."

Yep. That is kinda what I said.

"Can't be sure what he's doing here. I might be right, I might not be."

"That's comforting."

"Hey," Vail said, "remember the sixty/forty rule." She gestured with her chin. "Let's check with security."

Coming into view was a silver SUV with a police badge painted on the doors. It sat parked off to the right, in the shade of one of the large banyans.

Russell pulled in front of the Jeep. They got out and walked over to the deeply tinted windows. Vail cupped her hands and leaned in for a look. "Shit." She grabbed the knob and yanked open the door.

A uniformed female security guard was lying across the armrest, her torso slumping in the passenger seat. Vail felt for a pulse. "Dead." She did a quick pat down and cursed again. "Holster's empty. Handgun's gone."

"So," Russell said, rotating his head in each direction, looking up at the steps to the massive monument. "Would you say we've got confirmation?"

"Affirmative."

"And now he's armed. To kill others? Or himself?"

"He kills by poisoning. I see nothing indicating he *needs* to change that. He does it that way for a reason. And it's been success-ful for him." Vail moved back out of the Jeep. "Then again, he killed the security guard. And he didn't use poison. There was a substantial blow to the nose and left eye, but that's not what killed her. He prob-ably incapacitated her with a vicious backhanded punch. But she was suffocated. Choked."

"So asphyxiation—just another method."

"No," Vail said, looking out at the landscape, hoping to see Meece. "This is very different. Remember, women use poison to kill because it neutralizes a male's advantage. But it's also less 'in your face.' It's harder to stab someone repeatedly to kill them, to choke someone, to break someone's neck."

"It's up close and personal."

"Exactly."

"So what gives? Why the switch to physical violence?"

"Necessity. The guard was a threat and he took her out. Had to be something he could do by reaching into the SUV. Beautiful day, she probably had the window open, he surprised her or engaged her in conversation, diverted her attention and then bashed her in the face. There was a softball-size rock on the floorboard."

"That bought him a few seconds to get the door open and grab her by the neck."

"He didn't let go until she bought the farm."

"Very violent for him, no?"

"Yes. And that could be an indication he's going to take his own life. Nothing else matters. Nothing to lose. If she got the upper hand and shot him at close range, problem solved."

Russell nodded to a parking spot about thirty feet to their right, where several stalls were carved out of the grass. "That the car he jacked?"

"Sure looks like it." Vail glanced around, thanking the deity above that there were very few tourists or mourners onsite. "Let's call this in. Sergeant Aldridge is awaiting confirmation. He was sending officers to the area. Let's have them surround the cemetery. Quietly. Cover all avenues of exit—just in case he's not here to kill himself and he plans on trying to leave."

Russell pulled out his phone and hit redial. "I'll see if I can get some plainclothes in unmarked cars posing as tourists to help clear the cemetery."

Vail nodded. "If we're lucky, he won't notice. Don't want to freak him out. Speaking of which, see if SWAT will fall back and let us handle it."

Russell snorted. "SWAT here is no different than it is anywhere else. They'll tell *us* to fall back and let *them* handle it."

"Then don't bring it up. I have no intention of twiddling my thumbs while SWAT goes through their protocols and procedures."

"You dissing SWAT?"

"Not at all. They're the best. But I want a chance to talk with Meece. And if SWAT takes over the scene, and if Meece is here to kill himself, I'll never get that chance."

Russell grunted. "Fine." He made his call and turned to Vail while keeping his gaze moving about the area. "If he *is* going to kill himself, why not just jump off the roof of the building where he was staying? Why come here?"

"Good question. My answer—which is more *guess* now than analysis—the sixty percent part, in case you were wondering—is that this place has special meaning to him. Maybe because of his brother Phillip. We don't know the depth of his relationship with Phillip so right now we can't say. Remember, he may not be thinking clearly. We don't know what's going on inside his head, so what doesn't make sense to us may seem logical to him."

"No offense," Russell said, "but I like my job much better. Find evidence. Look for motive and opportunity. Interview witnesses and suspects. Make an arrest. You? You people are into all sorts of psycho shit that I just don't understand."

"That's why you brought me out here. And right now, we've got a serial murderer somewhere on this property. He's armed and dangerous, possibly delusional and likely depressed, maybe psychotic. We already know he has a working knowledge of explosives, so we can't be sure what we're walking into."

"As if that's not enough," Russell said, "we have to find him and keep him from hurting himself."

"Or anyone else. We don't know what he's doing or what he's got planned. It *looks* like a spontaneous thing, but he could've been planning this for years. We're going in blind."

"And he's armed with a gun. He thinks he sees the devil, or whatever, he doesn't care who he kills. We do this wrong, we could have more bodies."

"No," Vail said. "No more bodies. I've had enough." She looked up at the monument and seven flights of the grand staircase before them. "Too many places to hide. Let's split up and do a grid, meet at the top if we haven't found him before then."

"The Court of Honor," Russell said.

"Come again?"

"The top, where you want to meet. That courtyard's called the Court of Honor. Part of the Honolulu Memorial. At the far end of it is a huge statue."

"I see it. The woman."

"Lady Columbia, yeah. A symbol of justice. She represents all grieving mothers."

Vail looked in its direction, into the sun, and shielded her eyes.

"Strangely ironic," Russell said. "Don't you think? Scott Meece is avenging the evil his mother imparted against him—we think—by killing women. And he's coming here to take his life under the watchful eye of something that represents grieving mothers."

"Ironic?" Vail said. "Sad." She gave one last look around and then faced Russell. "Let's do this."

"Be careful," Russell said as he pulled out his pistol. "If he's suicidal, he's got nothing to lose. He won't hesitate to kill."

Vail held her Glock out in front of her. *Great. Then nothing's changed.*

58

They moved up the fifty-foot-wide grand staircase, Vail taking the right and Russell the left. Vail maintained a quick but cautious pace, watching for trip wires and other potential jerry-rigging. She texted Russell and cautioned him to be aware of improvised booby traps.

After clearing each individual monument, she emerged from the partially enclosed rooms and made eye contact with Russell. They then moved up another flight to the next level and checked the memorials there.

Vail counted five on each side, with a wall at the top before they made it to the Court of Honor on the uppermost floor, where the primary structure was situated.

As they crested the next landing, Vail heard a rumble behind her. She turned and saw a double-decker yellow tour bus stopping in front of the plaza at the base of the stairs, where the road ended.

She attempted to wave the driver off but before she could determine if he had seen her—or understood her frantic hand signals—a plainclothes detective was at the vehicle and directing it to the outer loop roadway that ran along the grassy mall, leading to the exit.

Well, at least there's one cop here. Hopefully we've got more.

As that thought evaporated, she saw the unmistakable SWAT vehicles drive onto the periphery of the property.

Time's running out.

They moved higher, one level to the next, but did not find any signs of Meece.

If we hadn't found the dead guard, I'd wonder if I'd gotten this wrong.

After checking all the memorials—and a handicap elevator on Vail's side—they convened at the top, as planned.

Directly ahead was the Court of Honor, consisting of a couple of large planters in a hardscaped triangular-shaped plaza. At the point stood the thirty-foot-tall sculpted figure of Lady Columbia, mounted on a marble wall.

To the left and right were open-air wings, covered walkways that housed what appeared to be mosaic tributes to different battles that took place in the Pacific.

"I'll go left," Russell said. "You go right. Meet me in the center, in the chapel."

"Chapel?"

"It's not that big, maybe four or five rows of pews on each side of the center aisle, if I remember right. Fifty people max. Why?"

"That could be where he's going to do it."

"In a place of worship?"

"Symbolic."

Russell noticeably tightened the grip on his handgun. "That would really suck."

"I hope you realize I'm flying by the seat of my pants here a little bit."

"I didn't really buy that sixty/forty bullshit. I figure you've been making it all up since you got here."

Vail had a comeback ready, but instead winked at him and moved off, headed to the rightmost portion of the open-air atrium.

59

Scott Meece looked at the handgun. It reminded him of Phillip, of the day he returned home from his first tour and went out and bought a forty caliber Glock-23. He told Scott that he really enjoyed target shooting and he wanted to stay sharp while away from his unit.

He asked Scott to come along a few days later to the range with him, but Scott declined. "C'mon. When you're old enough, I'll take you to the gun store and we'll get you one of these. The Glocks are nice and light, easy to handle."

"I'd rather have a watch. Like yours."

"This? Nothing special. It's a G-Shock. Lots of guys are starting to use it in Special Forces. Holds up well, even with all the vibration from shooting."

"Can I put it on?"

Phillip laughed, realized Scott was serious, and he unhooked the strap.

Scott fastened it around his wrist and admired it. "I like it."

"Keep it."

"No. Are they expensive?"

"Not too bad."

Scott handed it back to Phillip. "Okay."

"Okay what?"

"I'll go with you. To the range."

That afternoon, they stood at the line, ammo and magazines laid out in front of them, goggles on and ear protection hanging around their necks. Fortunately, they were the only ones there, which made talking much easier.

Phillip put the unloaded weapon in Scott's hand and taught him the proper stance. He explained to him with the patience of a teacher how to line up the sights, what to expect when he squeezed the trigger, and the dangers of using such a weapon irresponsibly.

He then taught Scott how to load the rounds into the magazine and shove it home into the pistol's handle.

"Think about the power you're now holding in your hands. It's like playing God. When you point that weapon at someone, you control life and death. A steady hand and good aim, and the person in front of you will almost certainly die. If you so choose."

"I get it," Scott said.

Phillip studied his face. "No offense, bro. But I don't think you do. You can't. Until you've seen someone die, you just can't relate. It's . . ." he looked off into the distance. "It's life changing. It's something you don't forget."

Scott looked at him. "Did it change you?"

"Yeah." Phillip bit his lip. "Seeing someone die . . ." He cleared his throat. "You can want them dead in the worst way because they're the enemy. But they're not any different from you. They're fighting for a cause, for their country. For their honor. Killing someone . . ."

"What?"

Phillip shook his head and chuckled. "Snipers have it made. They do it from a distance. A hundred, two hundred, three hundred yards away. Yeah, they're looking through a scope, but it's so fucking far away. It's different. It's . . . I don't know, I think it's easier. A sniper may feel the kill, I guess. I've never asked one. I mean, yeah, your target's dead, but you're removed from the dirty part of it. All you have to do is lower the scope and there's no body there. But up close and personal . . . the blood . . . the brain matter . . . " He swallowed. "It's hard."

"Did you have to do that? Up close and personal?"

Phillip nodded. They stared at each other a long moment, a silence that spoke volumes.

"I don't think I could do that."

"That's okay, Scotty. You don't have to do anything you're not comfortable doing."

"That may be true *after* I leave home."

They both laughed.

"All right," Phillip said. "Enough talk. Take the stance I taught you."

Phillip made sure the grip was right. He made several corrections, reminded Scott to lean forward and sight down the barrel to line up his shot.

"I'm ready."

"Okay," Phillip said. "Go ahead. Remember—slow, even pull on the trigger. And don't close your eyes."

Scott did as Phillip instructed, and the round exploded from the chamber with a rapid recoil of speed and power, the likes of which Scott had never before experienced.

Scott looked down range at the bottle target. His jaw dropped open and his hands went limp.

"Wow, brother. You completely missed the target. How'd you do that? And—Jesus, watch where you point that thing, remember?" Phillip grabbed the barrel of the Glock and directed it down range.

"Sorry. Sorry." Scott swallowed hard, his Adam's apple bobbing up and down. "I–uh . . . Wow. That was, that was really awesome." He looked over at his brother. "You were right. I had no idea."

Phillip grinned knowingly. "It's the kind of thing you can't prepare for until you do it. And once you do it, you *know*. You understand. So don't forget. Life or death. That's what you hold in your hands. Don't take it lightly. Be responsible with that weapon. It can save your life or take a life."

Scott refocused his eyes, the memory of that day with Phillip fading into the air. He tightened his grip on the pistol's handle.

"Life or death . . ." he whispered into the moist air. "Today, death."

60

Vail walked down the marble-floored corridor, the Court of Honor plaza to her left. No sign of SWAT officers yet—but she did see a tour group of a dozen Asians, with headphones covering their ears as they listened to their guide's narration. They were staring at ocean blue and earth-toned mosaic maps covering the wall to Vail's right.

She waved at the guide and held up her badge. His eyes, however, went directly to Vail's Glock, which she was holding at her side, by her thigh, to avoid frightening the visitors.

"I need you to get these people to safety."

"What's going on?"

"Down there," she said, gesturing toward the stairs and the grassy mall beyond. "Police are waiting to tell you where to go."

"But—"

"Do it. Now."

Or I'll tell you where to go.

The man turned back to his group and spoke to them through his headset, motioning them back the way they came. Through the open left wall, broken up by square columns, Vail saw another tour bus pulling up to the front and two cops rushing toward it.

Her phone vibrated. *Really? Now?* With the people in the plaza and moving quickly at their guide's urging, she brought her Glock back up to a ready position and answered the call. It was Del Monaco.

"Got some more info on Scott Meece."

"Summarize. I may be engaging him any minute."

"I did some digging and cross-referencing. Meece has ties to each of the cities where bodies were found. Family's got a long tradition of military service."

That certainly makes sense.

"He had family members stationed at bases in each of the cities where he's killed. I mean, we don't know for sure, but it definitely—"

"Go on."

"So he had a grandfather, Emanuel, who served in World War II. He's buried in Oahu, at the National—"

"That's where I am right now."

"That could be signific—"

"I know, Frank. What else?"

"His uncle Ronny was stationed at Fort Hood outside Dallas before getting killed there in a training exercise. Pretty much the same story with the other cities and other relatives. So there's obviously a connection between—"

"Got it, Frank. Thank you. Great work. This helps a lot. Anything else I need to know before I engage him?"

"I'll text you if something jumps out at me."

Hopefully Scott Meece *doesn't jump out at* me.

She hung up and continued down the corridor, more mosaic maps to her right behind a low wrought-iron fence topped with spikes designed to keep visitors away from the artwork.

She reached the end of the gallery, which doglegged left. She passed a couple of American flags flanking the copper-doored entrance to the memorial chapel's anteroom.

Vail turned right—and saw Russell seated in a pew on the left, front row, in front of a gold wall-mounted Star of David and to its right, above the altar, a large cross.

To Russell's left sat Scott Meece.

Vail took in the room in a quick glance: a large domed window on each side, not filled with glass but with an intricate copper design featuring translucent colored squares imprinted with Lady Liberty's face and crown. There were no other entrances or exits besides the one Vail was blocking.

To get out, Scott Meece was going to have to get through her, be escorted out in handcuffs, or carried out in a body bag.

And he ain't gettin' through me.

She glanced around, checking for trip wires.

"Scott," Vail said authoritatively. It echoed in the small, high-ceilinged room. "My name's Karen. Can we talk?"

She took a step toward them.

"Stay back," Meece said.

She figured he had the guard's pistol shoved into the left side of Russell's ribs.

"Scott," Vail said, her voice softer, exuding calmness. "Is your grandfather buried here, at the Punch—at Punchbowl?"

Meece's head twitched slightly. But he did not turn around. Did not answer.

"I know about Emanuel's service. About your *family's* long history of distinguished military service."

Still no response. Russell turned his head a few degrees in Vail's direction but did not dare move his torso.

Gotta have a gun in Adam's ribs.

Vail inched to her right, toward the opposing rows of pews, but did not want to relinquish her position blocking the exit. She got a better angle, however, on Meece.

Another step—and he swiveled his head to make eye contact with her.

She saw a troubled man. A blank, though tense, expression.

Or am I reading into it?

Vail kept the Glock out in front of her, aimed at Meece. Just like her concerns regarding SWAT, an aggressive stance on her part risked escalating the situation. Unless forced to lower her weapon, however, readiness to fire gave her an advantage if the situation degenerated suddenly and spiraled out of control. She was not going to risk losing Russell at the expense of letting Meece live. There was something morally wrong with such a scenario.

"So what are we doing here, Scott?"

His eyes narrowed. "You're here because I'm here."

No shit.

"And you're here because . . ."

He did not answer for a long moment. Then: "I'm here to right a wrong."

"And what wrong is that?"

Meece did not reply. His gaze moved downward. To the gun?

"Is this about your brother?" Vail asked, trying to refocus him.

Refocus him, indeed: his head swiveled hard toward her, his expression changing, eyebrows bunched together, nose creased into a snarl.

"What do *you* know about my brother?"

"I know Phillip died a hero in Somalia. He was Special Forces. Army Rangers."

His gaze remained steady.

"And I know there was some friction with your stepfather. He wanted you to serve, just like Phillip."

Meece turned away. "I don't want to talk about him."

Him. Phillip or the stepfather?

"Tell me about your mother, Scott."

His head shot back toward Vail.

"Tell me what she did to you. About the abuse."

"I don't want to talk about her either."

"We're gonna have to talk about her. She's why you've been poisoning all those women. With the aconite. And the drop of red dye in the soap."

Meece's eyes narrowed.

"Yeah, we know about the soap. And the chocolate bar wrappers. We just don't know why. Was it because of what your mother did to you?"

He grabbed Russell with his free hand and yanked him up. They both stood. "You don't know what you're talking about."

Vail almost laughed.

Adam seems to agree with you.

"So tell me," she said. "Help me understand what happened."

"It was Nick."

Nick, his stepfather?

"What did Nick do to you?"

Meece bit his bottom lip. "I don't wanna talk about it."

"Abuse. I know that much. Emotional? Physical?"

"Yes."

"Sexual?"

Meece's lips quivered. "Yes."

"Scott, no one should have to endure that. I understand what you've gone through. I've dealt with a lot of people who've been victimized like that. Let me help you. I can set you up with someone to talk about it."

Meece hesitated, as if he was considering her offer. Of course, Vail had not bothered him with all the details . . . the trials for all the murders, the convictions, the lifelong incarceration. Sure, there'd be counseling and psychiatric treatment along the way.

But hey, your care and prescription meds will be fully covered. No copays. No deductibles! Such a deal.

"Too late for that," Meece finally said. "What Nick did . . ." Meece shook his head. "What I did . . ."

Vail had to get him back on task. "Why the women? If it was Nick who abused you, why have you been taking it out on women who look like your mother?"

Meece's head cricked to one side.

"Yes," Vail said. "I get it. I understand what you've been doing, even if you weren't completely aware of why. *Do* you know why?"

He stared at her blankly. His eyes glazed over.

Please don't lose touch with reality here. I don't want to have to shoot you.

"Scott." Vail's voice was soft, almost melodic. "Do you know?"

He blinked and refocused his gaze on her face. He swallowed hard. "Because she let him."

"Your mother? Mary let Nick abuse you?"

Meece nodded almost imperceptibly.

"She knew and didn't do anything about it?"

He laughed, a creepy snarl. "She helped him. And she killed my dad. My dad . . ." He swallowed hard. "My dad loved me."

Vail wanted to know more, but now was not the time to probe deeper. Meece was not stable. At the moment, she needed to disarm him and get Adam away safely. "We'll get help for you. I promise. Right now I'm concerned about Detective Russell. Can you give him the gun? I'll make the rest happen."

Scott stood there, the pistol in his hand. Power, Phil had called it. The power to give life or take it.

Yes.

"Can you give him the gun?"

Scott looked at the weapon, at the tip of the barrel poking into the side of his stepfather. A slow squeeze of the trigger and he would avenge the years of abuse.

He felt a stab of pain in his rectum. Memories of Nick's sick idea of discipline. Most fathers disciplined with a slap of the hand on the rump. Some cracked a whip on the ass. Nick liked to ram glass soda bottles up his bottom. Push them in as far as—

"No. No more. Time for you to pay for what you've done."

"Scott," Vail said firmly. "You need to put that gun down. Now."

"Time for you to pay for what you've done."

At least, that's what Vail thought he said. His speech was suddenly slurred, almost incoherent.

He's having a psychotic episode.

"Scott." Calmer, reassuring. "Look at me, okay?"

But his gaze was boring into Russell's neck. And Russell was standing rock still, his head bowed slightly but his eyes locked on Vail. He knew he dare not speak, that Vail had to fix this.

"Scott. That's Detective Russell next to you. It's *not* Nick. It's not your stepfather." She waited for a reaction. "Is that who you see? Do you think Nick is there?"

"Power," he slurred.

Power? What the hell's that supposed to mean? The gun? He's finally got the upper hand?

"That's not Nick, Scott. Look at me. I want to help. Look at me, Scott."

Vail knew that psychotic episodes could end suddenly or last days, weeks, or months. She had no idea if Meece was on medication, if he had taken it, or if he had not been sleeping well . . . It was nearly impossible to adequately assess him. But one thing was clear: he had a loaded pistol in his hand and he saw Russell as his stepfather, a primary source of his pain and suffering.

"Tell you what," Vail said. "How about I arrest Nick and put him in jail? He won't be able to hurt you again. How does that sound?"

Meece's right eye narrowed. He was still staring at Russell's neck. Vail could not get a read on whether she was on the verge of resolving this or if Meece was about to pull the trigger.

She was running out of time. And her forearms were getting tired. She had been holding the Glock out in front of her for several minutes. Her right hand was cramping but she dare not move.

"Scott, I need you to work with me here. Just . . . just look at me, okay?"

He did not react.

Dammit, he's stuck in some alternate reality. I've gotta reach him.

"Scott," Russell said, "I'm sorry. I'm sorry I hurt you. I realize that was wrong. I'm going to surrender to the police, go to jail."

Meece looked down at the gun.

"Scott, you sum bitch, I did what I did because you were bad. You were a bad kid. And I'm gonna do it again. Ima gonna get the bottle. 'Cause you deserve it."

"No. I was *not* bad! I wasn't. Can't do this anymore!"

Scott felt the metal in his hand, the tension of the spring against his index finger.

Power? Yes.

Life? No.

Death? Yes.

He squeezed the trigger. The noise was deafening. It echoed. Maybe this is what combat sounded like.

A hot pain in the chest. Another. Ow. Oh.

And then, nothing.

61

Vail watched with trepidation as Russell played the part of Nick James. It was a huge gamble. Meece was not in his right mind. He would likely hear what his alternate reality created, not what Russell was actually saying. Russell could be unwittingly playing right into the psychotic episode's narrative.

There was nothing she could do but watch and hope her concerns were unfounded. Meece might buy it. Hell, nothing else was working.

He looked down at his gun.

Is he surrendering?

And then he pulled the trigger.

Shit!

Vail fired as well, two shots to the chest and one to the head. Meece went down first, followed by Russell, who was trying—unsuccessfully—to hold onto the back of the pew. Meece's shot was close range, directly into the detective's side.

Vail was on her phone as she advanced on Russell. She kicked away Meece's pistol, which went skittering across the green marble floor.

"Officer down, officer down! GSW. National Memorial Cemetery chapel. Shooter's also down."

She tossed her phone aside, the line still active, and dropped to both knees beside Russell, gripped his right shoulder.

"Hang on, Adam. Help's on the way."

His cheeks were drawn up into a wince, trying to hold it together. "Oh man . . . this fuckin' hurts."

"Seriously? You're in a military cemetery. Lots of these guys were shot multiple times. Some lost limbs. You think they whined about how much it hurt?"

Russell could not help but smile—at least, he tried to. "You . . . suck . . . Karen."

"So I'm told."

"Meece . . . down?"

"Oh yeah." She glanced over her shoulder. "Two at center mass, one in the head. I wasn't gonna miss at fifteen feet. You think I'm a hack?"

"Thought did occur . . . to me."

"Hey, I'm not the one who nearly got myself killed."

He snorted.

"Admit it, buddy. I broke the case."

"You broke . . . something . . . Got a bullet . . . in my side. Just hocus pocus . . . bullshit. You got lucky." He winced again.

Don't die on me!

"I'd rather be lucky than smart," she said, stroking his forehead.

"You got the luck part . . . down." Another wince. "Need to work on the smart part . . . Hone your hocus . . .pocus skills."

A siren in the distance.

"Can you hear it? Ambulance. They'll be here any second."

"A light. I see a . . . bright light."

Fuck.

Wince. "Just . . . kidding."

"That was not funny."

The sirens were loud. Shouting. Footsteps in the gallery hallways. SWAT officers crowded the back of the chapel, yelling commands.

Vail raised her hands. "Karen Vail. FBI."

"ID?" the commander asked.

Vail carefully extracted her creds and held them up. "Detective Russell's been shot. Perp's dead. Ambulance?"

"Medics are on the way up."

Vail leaned over Russell's face. "Stay with me, Adam."

His eyes clamped closed. "Was going to . . . tell you the . . . same thing."

"They'll have to tear me away."

Noises in the corridor. More yelling. A couple of officers pointed their assault rifles in the direction of the approaching footsteps.

"You're gonna be fine," Vail said.

Russell grimaced. "You sure?"

"How should I know? I'm making this shit up as I go."

Russell forced a contorted grin. "That's . . . what I . . . thought."

She bit her bottom lip and looked up as two medics appeared with a gurney.

62

Vail stood on her balcony looking out at the ocean. The sun had risen an hour earlier, spreading oranges and pinks across the horizon. As the sky brightened, she saw the breaking waves rolling in and receding.

So serene. Hard to believe it was the setting of such violence only a day prior.

She thought of Scott Meece, of his family's longtime service to its country, making the ultimate sacrifice to secure freedom and liberty for its citizens. And now, the family name soiled by an outsider— and an errant gene in the mother who apparently did not get the DNA that instills in most parents the innate, overwhelming desire to protect their young children at all costs.

The knock at the door roused her from her fugue.

She turned and walked past her suitcase, then let Harry Bachler in. "Ready?"

"You really didn't have to do this. I could've taken an Uber or a Lyft."

"We appreciate all your help. I guess the chief wanted me to see you off properly."

"*Properly,*" Vail said, pursing her lips. "Very nice. I usually get kicked in the ass out of town. This is a pleasant change."

Bachler was not sure what to do with that comment, so he stepped forward to grab her suitcase.

"Just kidding. You know that, right? Ferraro just wants to make sure I leave his island. That's really what this is about."

"If you must know . . . yep, that's true."

She snorted. "So how's Adam?"

"Still in recovery. Doc says he'll be okay. The liver is a very fungible organ."

"I was thinking the same thing."

Bachler laughed. "Fungible means one part can cover for another. And it's got an abundant blood supply, so it's pretty decent at self-healing if it's not hit in the wrong place. And Adam got lucky."

Vail laughed. "He said the same about me."

"Maybe we all did. I'm not sure Scott Meece would've stopped killing if it weren't for you."

"I had a lot of help." Vail pulled the door closed behind her as they headed down the hallway. "Honestly, it's hard to know. This might've been his plan all along. End up here, at Fishbowl, and—"

"Punchbowl."

"Yeah. Sorry. Weird name, I just gotta say that."

"It's named after a—"

"I know, I know. Anyway, Meece wasn't in a healthy state of mind. Well, I guess that kind of goes without saying. He was a serial murderer. And he was subject to violent psychotic episodes, any one of which could've been a trigger for him to take his life."

"You ever get tired of what you do?"

"Hell no. Every offender's different. Each presents his own challenges. Just when I think I've seen every kind of depraved crime a human can commit against another, a new case hits my desk."

"And hey, you get free trips. Like this one to Hawaii."

Vail harrumphed. "You don't want to hear what my 'free trips' have been like."

Bachler laughed. "I think I have a good idea."

Trust me, you don't.

As they exited the building, Bachler's phone buzzed. He held it up and consulted the screen. "Text from Adam. He's awake. He wanted to say good-bye."

Vail started to open her mouth when Bachler's handset rang.

He raised his brow, then handed the device to Vail. "It's Adam."

She put it to her ear.

"On Skype."

"Oh." She pulled the phone away from her face. "There you are. Miss me already?"

"Hey."

His voice was weak and raspy.

"Hey. You look like shit. You doin' okay?"

"Doc said they ran a blood test when they brought me in and found I had too much lead in my body. Go figure."

Vail chuckled.

"Oh." Russell grimaced. "Don't make me laugh."

"So you called to say good-bye?"

"Not exactly. Got a surprise for you."

"Oh yeah? What?"

A small truck pulled to a stop behind them.

"Harry, did they arrive yet?"

"Who?" Bachler asked. "Oh—the surprise." He swiveled, looked over his right shoulder, and said, "Yep. Just got here."

Vail stole a look and saw a blue van but could not read the writing on the side.

"They didn't find any relatives of Mary Wingate, and none of her friends wanted another dog, so they were going to take Oscar to the pound."

"The pound?" Vail's jaw dropped open. "Adam, you can't let th—"

"But I convinced them to meet you there."

Vail turned back to the truck, where a woman was leading Oscar toward her. The miniature greyhound saw her—and started pulling in her direction.

Vail knelt down. "For me?"

"Oscar," the handler said, "meet your new mommy."

"Let me see," Russell said.

Vail handed Bachler the phone. He swiveled it so the camera was facing Vail.

Oscar was licking her face and wagging his tail so hard his rear end swung in unison.

"May Oscar give you as much shit as you've given me," Russell said.

Vail lifted the dog into her arms and stood up, facing the phone. "Adam, I don't know what to say."

"Thanks for thinking of me is a good start."

"Thanks for thinking of me." She leaned back and with her free right hand, stroked Oscar's fine-featured face. "But I need a crate for the plane."

"Took care of it yesterday," Russell said. "Good thing I didn't die. I wouldn't have gotten the pleasure of seeing this moment."

Vail planted a kiss on Oscar's forehead and left a red lipstick stain between his eyes. "This is one of the sweetest things anyone has ever done for me."

"Hey. I did it for Oscar."

"Yeah. Sure. Anyway, gotta go. You're gonna make me late for my flight."

"Wow," Russell said, shaking his head. "I just survived a major gunshot wound—and I gave you a new dog. And you're worried about missing your flight?"

"I miss this one, I'm stuck here another day."

"Another day in paradise. Where's my violin? Poor Karen."

She leaned closer to the camera. "If this is what paradise is like . . ." She grinned.

"Seriously. I didn't want you to leave before I had a chance to thank you."

"No, no, no," Vail said. "It was a team effort."

"Damn straight it was. But that aconite. That zeroed us in. And you probably saved some lives in pointing us to the memorial. I wouldn't have thought of that. Your criminal investigative bullshit."

"Analysis."

"Whatever. We make a good team."

Bachler pulled out his key and hit the remote button, then hefted Vail's suitcase into the back seat. The crate he set in the trunk.

"I was thinking the same thing."

"You'll keep me posted as to what happens with that inspector general investigation?"

"Don't think I can. Probably shouldn't talk about it anymore than we have already. But I have a feeling you'll be hearing from them before I do."

"Good luck with it."

"I'll be fine. I've got friends in high places."

"You mean, like, God?"

Not sure I'd call Douglas Knox "God," but some on the OPSIG team might feel that way.

"Not exactly what I had in mind."

"Hey. Next time we have a serial killer on Oahu, I'm going to call the BAU and request . . . Frank Del Monaco."

"Go right ahead."

"Oh yeah?"

"Yeah. And two days later you'll be calling back and begging my boss to send *me*."

Russell winked at her. "Let's hope the next serial killer on Oahu will be twenty years from now."

"Twenty years? I'll be enjoying my retirement by then."

"On a beach in Oahu?"

Vail thought about that. "Who knows, Adam. Life is strange. You never know where you're gonna find yourself." She planted another kiss on Oscar's head, then set him on the ground. "Or what curves life is gonna toss your way."

"Hmm. FBI profiler. Political commentator. And now philosopher."

"Didn't you look at my business card? It says, 'Renaissance Woman.'"

"Must've missed that. And I'm gonna miss working with *you*."

"Hey," Vail said, giving Oscar's leash a tug toward the car. "You know what they say. Life's a bitch."

Russell laughed. "This is Hawaii, remember? We prefer 'Life's a *beach*.'"

ACKNOWLEDGMENTS

For me, writing a novel often takes a village. In the case of *Red Death*, it was more like a hamlet. I'd like to thank several people who put their imprints on the manuscript in important ways:

Mark Safarik, supervisory special agent and senior FBI profiler with the FBI's Behavioral Analysis Unit (ret.) and principal of Forensic Behavioral Services International, for reading the manuscript and correcting my FBI and law enforcement procedural errors. He also helped me navigate the male versus female offender issue.

Jeffrey Jacobson, Esq., former assistant US Attorney, for assistance with the attorney general's investigation of Vail.

John Sylvester, Lt. Col., US Army, for assistance with Phillip Meece's rank and army career timeline. **Mark Spicer,** British SAS sniper (ret.), security consultant, military and law enforcement trainer, and CEO of Osprey Group USA, for his assistance with understanding the mind-set of a sniper and the detached feeling that comes over someone staring through a scope. I met Mark several years ago and remain very impressed with his breadth of knowledge and experience. His courage and training are the ingredients of a patriot.

Jane Willoughby, Ph.D., biochemist, for assistance with chemistry—never one of my favorite subjects. Once I realized what I was getting into with homemade soaps and dyes, I knew who to call. Jane made sure my chemical names—and in particular the nature of FD&C Red 40—were properly expressed. Unfortunately, there are no shortcuts in science.

Harvey and Ronnie Hartenstein, cousins, for acting as professional tour guides of their home island and for pointing out places of interest to visit—including Joe's, which is real—*really* beautiful, featuring *really* delicious food.

Success in most industries is a team effort. My team includes my agents, **Joel Gotler** and **Frank Curtis,** who ensure that the royalties, rights, administrative matters, contracts, and foreign sales are executed properly; my editor **Kevin Smith,** the senior member of my crew—having worked on every Karen Vail and OPSIG Team Black novel (sans *The Hunted*)—who helps make sure my characters are consistent from book to book, that the story and characters are well-drawn; and finally my copyeditor, **Chrisona Schmidt,** who corrects my grammatical failings and ensures that everything flows properly and conforms to *CMS* guidelines, the bible of standardized style manuals.

My team is rounded out by my editor, **Philip Rappaport,** and the tireless group at **Open Road Integrated Media**. Publishing a book not only requires tremendous time and effort by many talented individuals, but passion and professionalism. I'm fortunate to be surrounded by all of that at Open Road.

My readers and fans, some of whom read my novels more than once, for the support, review love, and Facebook camaraderie they afford me. Does it matter? Absolutely! I love hearing from you and I appreciate all you do to let friends, family, and neighbors know of my work.

My wife Jill always comes last in my acknowledgments—but first in my thoughts. Aside from reading (and editing and rereading), she makes sure I have the time I need to put the necessary (and seemingly endless) work into the novel. That's no small ask. Remember that village (or hamlet) I mentioned earlier? At the end of the day, all that responsibility falls on my shoulders. My name is on the cover and my sole focus is on giving you, my reader, the best possible experience. I couldn't do that without my wife's ongoing, steadfast support.

ABOUT THE AUTHOR

Alan Jacobson is the national bestselling author of fourteen critically acclaimed novels. In order to take readers behind the scenes to places they might never go, Jacobson has embedded himself in many federal agencies, including spending several years working with two senior profilers at the Federal Bureau of Investigation's vaunted Behavioral Analysis Unit in Quantico. During that time, Jacobson edited four published FBI research papers on serial offenders, attended numerous FBI training courses, worked with the head firearms instructor at the academy, and received ongoing personalized instruction on serial killers—which continues to this day. He has also worked with high-ranking members of the Drug Enforcement Administration, the US Marshals Service, the New York Police Department, SWAT teams, local bomb squads, branches of the US military, chief superintendents and detective sergeants at Scotland Yard, criminals, armorers, helicopter pilots, chief executive officers, historians, and Special Forces operators. These experiences have helped him to create gripping, realistic stories and characters. His series protagonist, FBI profiler Karen Vail, resonates with both female and male readers, and writers such as Nelson DeMille, James Patterson, and Michael Connelly have called Vail one of the most compelling heroes in suspense fiction.

Contact Jacobson via his website, www.AlanJacobson.com, Facebook (facebook.com/alanjacobsonfans), Twitter (@JacobsonAlan), or Instagram (alan.jacobson).

THE WORKS OF
ALAN JACOBSON

Alan Jacobson has established a reputation as one of the most insightful suspense/thriller writers of our time. His exhaustive research, coupled with years of unprecedented access to law enforcement agencies, including the FBI's Behavioral Analysis Unit, bring realism and unique characters to his pages. Following are his current, and forthcoming, releases.

STAND-ALONE NOVELS

False Accusations > Dr. Phillip Madison has everything: wealth, power, and an impeccable reputation. But in the predawn hours of a quiet suburb, the revered orthopedic surgeon is charged with double homicide—a cold-blooded hit-and-run that leaves an innocent couple dead. Blood evidence has brought the police to his door. An eyewitness has placed him at the crime scene, and Madison has no alibi. With his family torn apart, his career forever damaged, no way to prove his innocence and facing life in prison, Madison must find the person who has engineered the case against him. Years after reading it, people still talk about his shocking ending. *False Accusations* launched Jacobson's career and became a national bestseller, prompting CNN to call him, "One of the brightest stars in the publishing industry."

FBI PROFILER KAREN VAIL SERIES

The 7th Victim (Karen Vail #1) > Literary giants Nelson DeMille and James Patterson describe Karen Vail, the first female FBI profiler, as "tough, smart, funny, very believable," and "compelling." In *The 7th Victim*, Vail—with a dry sense of humor and a closet full of skeletons—heads up a task force to find the Dead Eyes Killer, who is murdering young women in Virginia . . . the backyard of the famed FBI Behavioral Analysis Unit. The twists and turns that Karen Vail endures in this tense psychological suspense thriller build to a powerful ending no reader will see coming. Named one of the Top 5 Best Books of the Year (*Library Journal*).

Crush (Karen Vail #2) > In light of the traumatic events of *The 7th Victim*, FBI Profiler Karen Vail is sent to the Napa Valley for a mandatory vacation—but the Crush Killer has other plans. Vail partners with Inspector Roxxann Dixon to track down the architect of death who crushes his victims' windpipes and leaves their bodies in wine caves. However, the killer is unlike anything the profiling unit has ever encountered, and Vail's miscalculations have dire consequences for those she holds dear. Publishers Weekly describes *Crush* as "addicting" and New York Times bestselling author Steve Martini calls it a thriller that's "Crisply written and meticulously researched," and "rocks from the opening page to the jarring conclusion." (Note: the *Crush* storyline continues in *Velocity*.)

Velocity (Karen Vail #3) > A missing detective. A bold serial killer. And evidence that makes FBI profiler Karen Vail question the loyalty of those she has entrusted her life to. In the shocking conclusion to *Crush*, Karen Vail squares off against foes more dangerous than any she has yet encountered. In the process, shocking personal and professional truths emerge—truths that may be more than Vail can handle. *Velocity* was named to *The Strand Magazine*'s Top 10 Best Books for 2010, *Suspense Magazine*'s Top 4 Best Thrillers of 2010, Library Journal's Top 5 Best Books of the Year, and the Los Angeles Times' top picks of the year. Michael Connelly said *Velocity* is "As relentless as a bullet. Karen Vail is my kind of hero and Alan Jacobson is my kind of writer!"

Inmate 1577 (Karen Vail #4) > When an elderly woman is found raped and murdered, Karen Vail heads west to team up with Inspector Lance Burden and Detective Roxxann Dixon. As they follow the killer's trail in and around San Francisco, the offender leaves behind clues that ultimately lead them to the most unlikely of places, a mysterious island ripped from city lore whose long-buried, decades-old secrets hold the key to their case: Alcatraz. The Rock. It's a case that has more twists and turns than the famed Lombard Street. The legendary Clive Cussler calls *Inmate 1577* "a powerful thriller, brilliantly conceived and written." Named one of *The Strand Magazine*'s Top 10 Best Books of the Year.

No Way Out (Karen Vail #5) > Renowned FBI profiler Karen Vail returns in *No Way Out*, a high-stakes thriller set in London. When a high profile art gallery is bombed, Vail is dispatched to England to assist with Scotland Yard's investigation. But what she finds there—a plot to destroy a controversial, recently unearthed 440-year-old manuscript— turns into something much larger, and a whole lot more dangerous, for the UK, the US—and herself. With his trademark spirited dialogue, page-turning scenes, and well drawn characters, National Bestselling author Alan Jacobson ("My kind of writer," per Michael Connelly) has crafted the thriller of the year. Named a top ten "Best thriller of 2013" by both *Suspense Magazine* and *The Strand Magazine.*

Spectrum (Karen Vail #6) > It's 1995 and the NYPD has just graduated a promising new patrol officer named Karen Vail. During the rookie's first day on the job, she finds herself at the crime scene of a woman murdered in an unusual manner. As the years pass and more victims are discovered, Vail's career takes unexpected twists and turns—as does the case that's come to be known as "Hades." Now a skilled FBI profiler, will Vail be in a better position to catch the offender? Or will Hades prove to be Karen Vail's hell on earth? #1 *New York Times* bestseller Richard North Patterson called *Spectrum*, "Compelling and crisp . . . A pleasure to read."

The Darkness of Evil (Karen Vail #7) > Roscoe Lee Marcks, one of history's most notorious serial killers, sits in a maximum security prison serving a life sentence—until he stages a brutal and well-executed escape. Although the US Marshals Service's fugitive task force enlists the help of FBI profiler Karen Vail to launch a no holds barred manhunt, the bright and law enforcement-wise Marcks has other plans—which include killing his daughter. But a retired profiling legend, who was responsible for Marcks's original capture, may just hold the key to stopping him. Perennial #1 *New York Times* bestselling author John Sandford compared *The Darkness of Evil* to *The Girl with the Dragon Tattoo*, calling it "smoothly written, intricately plotted," and "impressive," while fellow *New York Times* bestseller Phillip Margolin said *The Darkness of Evil* is "slick" and "full of very clever twists. Karen Vail is one tough heroine!"

Red Death (Karen Vail #8) > There's trouble in paradise when middle-aged women begin dying suspicious deaths. Upon arriving in Hawaii, Karen Vail encounters a killer who not only employs unusual methods of murdering his victims, but he's been at it a very long time. Can Vail figure out what's going on, and who the offender is, while helping Honolulu Police Detective Adam Russell find the killer before he eludes their grasp and resumes his prolific violence on the mainland?

OPSIG TEAM BLACK SERIES

The Hunted (OPSIG Team Black Novel #1) > How well do you know the one you love? How far would you go to find out? When Lauren Chambers' husband Michael disappears, her search reveals his hidden past involving the FBI, international assassins—and government secrets that some will go to great lengths to keep hidden. As *The Hunted* hurtles toward a conclusion mined with turn-on-a-dime twists, no one is who he appears to be and nothing is as it seems. *The Hunted* introduces the dynamic Department of Defense covert operative Hector DeSantos and FBI Director Douglas Knox, characters who return in future OPSIG Team Black novels, as well as the Karen Vail series (*Velocity, No Way Out,* and *Spectrum*).

Hard Target (OPSIG Team Black Novel #2) > An explosion pulverizes the president-elect's helicopter on Election Night. The group behind the assassination attempt possesses far greater reach than anything the FBI has yet encountered—and a plot so deeply interwoven in the country's fabric that it threatens to upend America's political system. But as covert operative Hector DeSantos and FBI Agent Aaron "Uzi" Uziel sort out who is behind the bombings, Uzi's personal demons not only jeopardize the investigation but may sit at the heart of a tangle of lies that threaten to trigger an international terrorist attack. Lee Child called *Hard Target*, "Fast, hard, intelligent. A terrific thriller." Note: FBI Profiler Karen Vail plays a key role in the story.

The Lost Codex (OPSIG Team Black Novel #3) > In a novel Jeffery Deaver called "brilliant," two ancient biblical documents stand at the heart of a geopolitical battle between foreign governments and radical extremists, threatening the lives of millions. With the American homeland under siege, the president turns to a team of uniquely trained covert operatives that includes FBI profiler Karen Vail, Special Forces veteran Hector DeSantos, and FBI terrorism expert Aaron Uziel. Their mission: find the stolen documents and capture—or kill—those responsible for unleashing a coordinated and unprecedented attack on US soil. Set in Washington, DC, New York, Paris, England, and Israel, *The Lost Codex* is international historical intrigue at its heart-stopping best.

Dark Side of the Moon (OPSIG Team Black Novel #4) > In 1972, Apollo 17 returned to Earth with 200 pounds of rock—including something more dangerous than they could have imagined. For decades, the military concealed the crew's discovery—until a NASA employee discloses to foreign powers the existence of a material that would disrupt the global balance of power by providing them with the most powerful weapon of mass destruction yet created. While FBI profiler Karen Vail and OPSIG Team Black colleague Alexandra Rusakov go in search of the rogue employee, covert operatives Hector DeSantos and Aaron Uzi find themselves strapped into an Orion spacecraft, rocketing alongside astronauts toward the Moon to avert a war. But what can go wrong does, jeopardizing the mission and threatening to trigger the very conflict they were charged with preventing. *New York Times* bestselling author Gayle Lynds said *Dark Side of the Moon* is "the thriller ride of a lifetime . . . a non-stop tale of high adventure that Tom Clancy's most ardent fans will absolutely love!"

SHORT STORIES

"Fatal Twist" > The Park Rapist has murdered his first victim—and FBI profiler Karen Vail is on the case. As Vail races through the streets of Washington, DC to chase down a promising lead that may help her catch the killer, a military-trained sniper takes aim at his target, a wealthy businessman's son. But what brings these two unrelated offenders together is something the nation's capital has never before experienced. "Fatal Twist" provides a taste of Karen Vail that will whet your appetite.

"Double Take" > NYPD detective Ben Dyer awakens from cancer surgery to find his life turned upside down. His fiancée has disappeared and Dyer, determined to find her, embarks on a journey mined with potholes and startling revelations—revelations that have the potential to forever change his life. "Double Take" introduces NYPD Lieutenant Carmine Russo and Detective Ben Dyer, who return to play significant roles in *Spectrum* (Karen Vail #6).

"12:01 AM" > A kidnapped woman. A serial killer on death row—about to be executed. Karen Vail has mere hours to pull the pieces together to find the missing woman and her abductor—before it's too late. In a short story that reads like a novel straight out of the award-winning Karen Vail series, *USA Today* bestselling author Alan Jacobson sets a new standard for short form fiction.

More to come > For a peek at recently released Alan Jacobson novels, interviews, reading group guides, videos, and more, please visit www.AlanJacobson.com.

THE KAREN VAIL NOVELS

FROM OPEN ROAD MEDIA

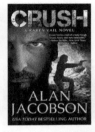
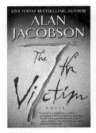
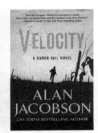

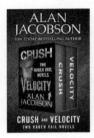
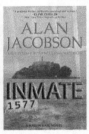
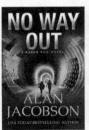

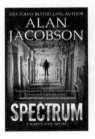
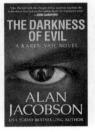
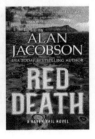

THE OPSIG TEAM BLACK SERIES

FROM OPEN ROAD MEDIA

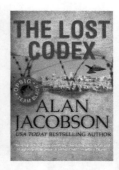

OPEN ROAD

INTEGRATED MEDIA

Find a full list of our authors and
titles at www.openroadmedia.com

FOLLOW US
@OpenRoadMedia

9 781504 063579